All's Fair in Love and Theatre

A Novel

L.V. OAKS

ALL'S FAIR IN LOVE AND THEATRE

Cover design: Gia Uncareful from RuzEstudio

To my grandmother, who lives on in every succulent and beautiful flower I see,

and to any person whose creative dreams were ever belittled: I promise the world needs your (he)art.

Playlist

"The Chain" by Fleetwood Mac

"Forever" by CHVRCHES

"Animals" by Neon Trees

"Anything Could Happen" by Ellie Goulding

"Beige" by Yoke Lore

"Romeo and Juliet" by Peter McPoland

"Skip the Charades" by Cold War Kids

"Third Eye" by Florence + The Machine

"Songbird" by Fleetwood Mac

"Mess Is Mine" by Vance Joy

"Bleed to Love Her" by Fleetwood Mac

"Go Your Own Way" by Fleetwood Mac

"May I Have This Dance" by Meadowlark

"I Melt With You" by Modern English

Chapter 1

Dafne

It's my time.

I have waited for this moment for so long. Well, not waited, exactly. Worked so hard there was no time for anything else, spent endless nights wide awake running lines with my best friends and a crew of unaware stuffed animals as an audience, and anticipated it with every fiber of my being.

I'm looking at the cast list, and my name is at the *top*. I press my hands to my cheeks to keep myself from squealing in the middle of the hall.

Dafne Wright - - - - - - - - - - - - - - - - - - -Juliet Capulet

I immediately search for my phone in my tote bag, not taking my eyes away from my name.

I frantically send a full-of-typos text and my screen lights up with an incoming call in the span of a few seconds.

"*You did that you actually did that I told you you'd*

smashed that audition oh my gosh Juliet bloody Capulet Daf this is–" my roommate Phoebe yells into the phone, and I need to cover the receiver with one hand to keep my right eardrum from bursting. "Hold up. Wait, wait, wait," she continues, never taking a breath, and I still haven't had the time to say anything back. Her voice drops low on the other end of the phone, as if not to be heard by potential eavesdroppers.

"Dafne … who is playing Romeo?" she asks, and as if on cue, someone clears their throat somewhere on my left.

"Call you back in a minute," I mumble to Phoebe. I hang up the phone and brace myself for the worst.

"Well … that's a surprise," a honeyed, unfortunately well-known voice sighs next to me, and I have never wished for teleportation more. "Not me, I was clearly going to get Romeo, but I guess you don't strike me as a Juliet," he adds, ever the gentleman. Not.

Theodore Price. Six feet-something of entitled, self-centered prick. His preferred activity whenever we find ourselves in the same room seems to be disagreeing with my every opinion and just overall annoying me until I want to crawl out of my skin just to escape him but, alas, I can't.

He's handsome, too, although not in an obvious way–which makes everything that much worse. It'd be easier to ignore his jabs if his whole appearance wasn't so … striking. It pains me to admit it, but that's the most appropriate word to describe him.

He's always impeccably dressed, which you'd think is weird for a twenty-one-year-old. I'm quite sure he owns the same exact cotton sweater in every colour available. His nose is on the bigger side, but so straight and regal, that really, it looks perfect on him. His hair is all chestnut waves, and there's a tiny scar on his chin that most probably wouldn't notice, but I like to pay attention when I talk to people.

Or argue, in our case.

He's definitely not brawny, but I know for a fact he works out regularly because the afore-mentioned sweaters never fail to highlight his muscular arms. Also, my best friend Ollie always sees him at the gym.

Logic says he's hiding even more, great, lean muscles under the layers of clothes. How unnecessary of him.

If you ask anyone here at APDAS, The Actor's Path Dramatic Arts School, they'll tell you how Theodore is *so* polite or *oh so* charming; it's all show, of course. Unless, by polite and charming, they mean cocky and unpleasant. I haven't even looked at him yet, but I just know he's sporting his signature smug expression, and I'm extremely tempted by the idea of smacking it off with a rolled-up script. I subtly stand straighter and turn around in the most confident motion I can work with.

I plaster on a smile I've tailored to look genuine; I don't want my annoyance to be as blatant as it usually is, because if I show myself unaffected, then I win.

"Price, congratulations," I say, and the thing is, some

twisted part of me means that. Despite the fact that he's basically just told me I shouldn't have gotten the part. He's a good actor–great, actually, and I can't deny that; or rather, I will deny it until my dying day if anyone asks, but I was never good at lying to myself. Most people assume a good actor equals a proficient liar, and I clearly lack in the latter department. He narrows his eyes, his expression falling imperceptibly for a second, then the corners of his mouth curve back to the usual self-satisfied smile.

"Why, thank you, Wright," he says, sarcasm so thick in his voice my eyes automatically roll into my sockets, my good resolutions to be stoic quickly slipping away. I start in the opposite direction without another word. You know how the saying goes, if you can't say anything nice, don't say anything at all–Theodore clearly never got the memo. Before I can make my well-deserved dramatic exit, he reaches me in a few long strides thanks to his ridiculously long legs and plants himself in front of me, hands coming to a prayer position and pointing at me. "Not so fast, love," he says, which makes the urge to smack him resurface with a vengeance. "We have several things to discuss. After tomorrow's table read, we will need to plan a strict extra rehearsals schedule, because if you think whatever amount of hours Ms. Patterson puts together will be enough, I can guarantee you–"

Propelled by some mysterious force, I place a finger a scarce inch from his lips to shut him up, and much to my surprise, it works. Nobel Peace prizes should be awarded to whoever can make Theodore Price close his mouth for over five seconds; I'll expect a letter from Oslo's town hall. His lips are parted, and he looks somewhere between offended and dumbfounded, as if nobody had ever dared to interrupt him before.

"Listen, Theodore," I start as I remove my finger from its hovering place, already over his soon-to-be condescending speech, "allow me to clear a few things up. Number one, I don't remember giving you permission to give me nicknames, and better yet, you could save precious breath and not refer to me at all.

Two, the fact that *you* think I don't deserve this role doesn't change the fact it is *mine*. I've earned it. I promise you, even if I shatter several bones before opening night, I *will* be on that stage. And three …" I pause for the suspense because apparently, I'm an actor first and a person second, and step closer to him, smoothing the slightly crumpled collar of the shirt he's wearing under his brown sweater.

"...Did you get dressed in the dark today?" I whisper.

His eyes grow wide with horror, and yep, I've got him. It's so easy when you know your enemy's weaknesses, among which his fragile ego. I step around him and quickly make my way out of the hallway as I push on the cold glass door, a winning smile tugging at my lips, feet taking me to the dorm room for my half-hour break.

"I would've gladly skipped lunch to witness such a historical moment," Phoebe says, a stray blonde curl bouncing on her forehead, my favorite mug–the one with the *Shakespeare loved a good Hamlet for breakfast* pun that she got me last Christmas–warming her hands.

APDAS' dormitories, which are located in West London, can get quite chilly when it rains, which means they reach unbearably low temperatures every other day. But as Ms. Patterson, our Classical Acting teacher and Assistant Director for our play loves to belt, "Actors thrive in adversities!" which is a small consolation when no amount of fuzzy socks can warm your feet at night.

"I guess it was quite epic," I say, drowning a digestive biscuit in my tea. "I can't believe he had the audacity to practically tell me I'm *unqualified* to play Juliet," I say as my dismembered biscuit floats around the cup, sinking to the bottom of it, much like my respect for Theodore.

When I auditioned for APDAS after graduating college, I was granted a full scholarship. It sounds commendable, in theory, but some people tend to think there has to be some obscure reason behind it and judge you for it. Luckily, I've never cared much about what people who don't even know me think of me. As for Theodore, when I first met him, he didn't seem like the warmest person on earth, and I'd first attributed it to the nerves of auditioning. When classes started and we had our first one together, he resorted to downright hostility, loathing even, and now–

"Hello?" Phoebe singsongs in her beautiful soprano voice, wiggling her fingers in my face as if she were casting a spell.

"I'm here," I say, my eyebrows shooting to my hairline in affectionate annoyance.

"I know working with Price is going to be a bloody feat babes," she ponders, "just don't let him get to you, alright? You've worked too hard for this to let anyone, let alone Mr. *green backdrops make my eyes pop* ruin this for you," she raises one shoulder, and although Phoebe's never met Theodore face to face, I've perfected his impression in her presence so many times, the resemblance in the simple gesture is uncanny. I snort and place my mug on the small oak nightstand between our beds so that I don't accidentally spill its contents and drench the floor.

Phoebe Nilsen is the funniest person I've ever met. Not only she's sunshine in human form with her cascade of light-blonde curls, but she's the kind of person that makes you believe there's still hope for humanity. She's a Musical Theatre student at APDAS, so we don't share any classes, but we're each other's fans through and through. Bless the day her parents decided to move from Norway to Oxford – even though she was barely five then, and I know she misses it a lot.

"He did say that once, didn't you tell me so?" Phoebe adds as I shake my head in silent laughter, while her own laugh makes her nearly topple off the bed.

"He did, and you're right. I can't afford to let him mess with my head and ruin the one thing I've craved since coming here. In fact, I won't." I vow, and Phoebe nods enthusiastically before letting herself drop on the bed like a dead weight, her hair bouncing on the pillow as she hits it with her head. "Let's get this bread, Juliet," she sighs happily, and I catch my heart making a happy little leap at the reminder of what I've accomplished.

Chapter 2

Dafne

As we take our seats around what students call 'The Round Table' –not for its actual shape, but because you know that if you get a seat at it, you qualify as acting royalty in this school–I take my stationery set out and glance around the room with casual indifference. The whole cast is here on time, as no one would dare be late at Mr. Hackle's table reads. He's the most feared teacher in the entire faculty, both by students and other teachers. According to the legend, a student that was playing Titania's monologue from *A Midsummer Night's Dream* used the word *lies* instead of *forgeries;* he shouted at her with such sheer force, the very core of the school shook, and the massive portrait of the Bard that hangs in the middle of the main hall fell and cracked in half. It's a myth, of course, but he is still the one professor you don't want to upset. You know, just in case. As our play's director, though, he chose me among twenty-one candidates, and that has to count for something. Despite what people say about him, he's an incredible teacher, and as much as I have never been the kind of person with a burning need for everyone to like them, his opinion matters to me. Much to my dismay, the seat to my right is lifted from the floor as its soon-to-be occupant sits next to me without sparing a look in my direction. I said I wouldn't let him bother me, and I suppose that if we're going to be Romeo and Juliet, we can't be at each other's throats all the time, so I say nothing. Mr. Hackle enters the room with his spotless script in hand, a bottle of sparkling water in the other, and everyone scrambles to the nearest chairs. It's its own type of funny, really, how a single plaid-clad man can be so intimidating, even when all he does is walk into a room. I steal a look at Theodore, who has schooled his features into perfect student mode; he's already annotated his script in that illegible calligraphy of his, which is perhaps the only not so perfect thing about him. While I can't read what words he used, I know for a fact he's filled the pages with personal notes on the character, because I have done the same.

"Right, before we begin, allow me to set some ground rules, which you should already be familiar with–but just in case. In my plays, nobody slacks off, nobody ever misses a rehearsal, and nobody *ever* comes unprepared," Mr. Hackle says, not bothering to meet anyone's gaze, which is somehow ten times more threatening. "Fail to appease these simple rules, and I will have no trouble replacing you. In fact, your understudies will be glad to do

so." Someone's swallow in the silence echoes as if they'd just yodeled on top of a mountain, but if Mr. Hackle notices, he doesn't let it show.
"Let's begin," he huffs, and the familiar flipping the script open to the first page expands across the room.

Fun fact about Juliet: she doesn't have the most lines in the play, yet it's every actor's dream to tackle her role. To me, it was never about having a lot of lines, but having the lines everyone is anticipating, even those who are not familiar with the play; when Juliet declares her love on that balcony, you just can't take your eyes away.

The table read starts, and Romeo's first words are uttered at my side. My eyes dart to Theodore, my ears attuned to the clear but deep timbre of his voice, and just for a second, my mind wanders to an alternative reality in which things might've been different.

After our very first class together nearly three years ago, I'd been so impressed with his skills. We'd never gotten the chance to act together in any of the school plays because, upon admission, APDAS splits new students into two groups to train separately for the three years of courses. We only shared certain classes, and always worked on separate shows with our respective groups. Until now, the third and last year, when we were allowed to audition for either play if we wished to. No offense to *As You Like It*, but who wouldn't want to at least give R and J a try? Being cast as the leads, *the* Romeo and Juliet, in our final year's showcase–it's a big de-

-al. But Theodore and I being civil, if not friends, is just wishful thinking. If only I knew what put those ill feelings towards me where they have taken roots, perhaps I could also eradicate it. But why would I even want that, when he's done nothing but antagonise me? He has determined he can't stand me and made it very easy for me to reciprocate the feeling.

I force my gaze back to my own script, pretending to annotate something, and stare at the pages as I wait for my turn to read in Scene Three of Act One, when Juliet is getting ready for the family ball. Isabel and Margaret, who respectively play the Nurse and Lady Capulet are reading too, and I'm glad both got cast along with me. It's not long after that that the Garden Scene comes, after the young lovers have met at Juliet's family ball, and it's so romantic it simultaneously makes me want to sigh and be sick. I have a complicated relationship with romance in real life, which is why I try not to entertain the idea of developing romantic feelings again anytime soon. So it's clear how playing a girl whose greatest wish is simply to *get* to be in love is no small feat to me. That's part of the reason I wanted this role so much though; I've never shied away from a challenge. We get through the dialogue unscathed, and from the corner of my eye, I see Theodore stealing a glance at me. I refuse to look back, to acknowledge whatever resentment is surely simmering in his hazel eyes. Maybe he's not above making a scene, however subtle, in front of our colleagues–but I am.

Theodore

Once out of the table read, I pause for a few minutes just outside the door. I like observing people and stealing mannerisms, expressions, the way someone will furrow their brows in thought, or tip their head when laughing at their friend's joke. It's not as creepy as it sounds, I promise. It's one of the first things we were ever taught: steal what you can from any person you meet and reapply to your characters. Dafne Wright passes me, eyeing me for a fraction of a second, so I eye her right back. She has this power to get under my skin just by looking at me, and I don't like it. It's as unsettling now as it was when I first met her. It wasn't my intention to come here and have petty fights with my supposed colleagues. I came here to be the best. But it seems that she had different plans for me and started messing with my head with that disarming honesty of hers. I'd never met anyone who speaks their mind all the time; what kind of sociopath does that? I wasn't raised to be rude, but she manages to push my buttons with little effort. It doesn't help that she is wildly talented, though I would rather let a herd of chimpanzees walk over me than ever say out loud. I'm about to put an earbud in my ear when an arm abruptly wraps around my shoulders and steers me towards the hall.

"So," my roommate and best mate Devon starts, "that was intense, huh?" I narrow my eyes at him. "If you're referring to Mr. Hackle's terrible aftershave, then sure, could be smelled fr–" he interrupts me by lightly hitting my nape.

"No," he rolls his eyes, "the read. You and Dafne looking like you either wanted to stab each other or make out on the table."

I choke on my saliva. "What on earth are you talking about?" I whisper, my eyes flickering around us, dreading someone might hear Devon's nonsense.

"Oh, alright mate, you want to pretend that never happened, then it never happened."

I love Devon, I really do, but he's a gossip. He watches too much Netflix, that's his main problem; sees dramatics and romantic ploys where there are none. Certainly not between Dafne and me–she's insufferable, that one. I'm convinced she thinks having the shiniest hair you'll ever see is a personality trait. "You should spend more time working on your downward blow now that you got Tybalt, rather than making up scenarios for your own entertainment," I say with a sigh.

"I assure you my blow is just fine," he teases as he winks and begins walking backwards ahead of me. I shoot him a dry look, and he does finger guns at me, which in Devon Language means see you later. I have five minutes before I need to head to my next class, so I rummage through my jeans' pocket again for my earbuds, pluck them in, and grant myself four minutes and thirty seconds of blissful peace as I allow *The Chain* by Fleetwood Mac to fill my ears.

Chapter 3

Dafne

After a brief stare down with Theodore outside the table read, I'm walking down the corridor to my History of Theatre class that starts in twenty minutes, taking my phone out to type in my notes some thoughts I didn't have time to annotate during the table read, when I feel a pair of hands on my eyes.

"Guess who–" I hear, and before they can say anything else I turn around and launch myself at the person in question. "Ollie, you absolute dick," I squeal in the crook of his neck. "You should have told us you were coming back today, you just missed the table read." I'm sure it comes out very muffled, but it doesn't matter because one of my favourite people in the world is here.

Ollie and I are platonic soulmates. Our mothers have been friends for most of their lives, and so have we. I'm an only child, but he's never made me miss a sibling.

"I told you I would be making an entrance," I feel rather

than see him smirk as he squeezes me for a few short seconds before I detangle my arms.

"I also couldn't smack my taxi driver into going faster, but I wasn't even supposed to get here until tomorrow, so," he shrugs.

"Oh, wait," he adds as his smile drops and my stomach immediately churns with worry.

"Do I need to book an appointment to speak to you now, Miss Capulet? I hear you're very busy these days, between making out with your boyfriend and chugging poison vials," he mock inquires, and my shoulders immediately release the tension they'd gathered at the mere possibility of bad news.

I flick him lightly on the chest and he scowls.

"Says you, *Mercutio.*" He makes a noncommittal sound, as if it were nothing.

"It seems it's our year," Ollie gestures for me to go ahead and we resume the walk down the busy corridor. "All that talking you and Phoebe did about–main character energy, was it? It seems to be paying off," he says, and maybe she and I did spend too much time on Pinterest for our own good last summer, but if that helped in the slightest to make the Universe pay attention, I'll scroll through endless more aesthetic posts.

"So," Ollie drawls, shoving his hands in his pockets, "I know about Price. That I have to play his best friend is bad enough, but … is he going to be a problem?"

He's not looking at me, and I can tell there's a tinge of

worry in his tone. When Theodore decided he didn't like me, with no explanation as to why, Ollie swore he would confront him about being a jackarse, but I begged him to let it go. That doesn't mean it never stung.

"Aside from the snarky comments nobody asked for, you mean? He hasn't pushed me down the stairs yet, so that's comforting." I joke, trying to keep any bitterness I might feel out of my voice. Before Ollie can comment on that, I take a sharp turn to the left, nearly making us both topple on the marbled floors. "Daf–" he starts, but I'm quick to interrupt him.

"Don't think you can pretend you haven't been away for two whole weeks, sir, I want to know everything about the–" I look around, making sure no one's being a busybody and listening to our conversation, "clinic," I whisper. "In fact, why are you even here instead of being in your room, *resting,* as I'm sure your doctor has recommended several times–"

Ollie pins me with *the* look. The look that says, 'I see right through you, Dafne' and 'You are avoiding the topic, Dafne.' I can't really blame him, as we have been video chatting every other day while he was away, and I likely know more about his medical records than his own doctor does.

"Right. I suppose we can talk about *that* later," I mumble, and as we come to a stop, I realise we've reached my class.

"I'll go find Mr. Hackle since I'm already excused for the

day, then I'll stop by your dorm before dinner so I can catch up with Phoebe too. Sounds good?" Ollie offers with a small smile, and I feel something tugging at my heart.

Under the blinding yellow light that hangs next to every classroom's door, the bags under his eyes are more evident than I'd ever seen them, his tawny skin not as clear as it usually is, and I wish I could wrap him in a blanket and protect him from all evil. No matter that he's almost six-foot-two and I would need an unthinkable amount of fabric to cover even half of his massive body. Ever since his epilepsy was diagnosed in our senior year in college, I have always made sure he was dutiful with taking his medication before he was allowed to stop taking it at some point last year. A few weeks ago, his ridiculously rich–but amazing–parents managed to get him a spot in one of Europe's best (or most expensive) neurology clinics in Zurich; not being able to go to class and perform, in addition to the incessant tests they'd run on him for two weeks, has clearly taken a toll. But I know he can take care of himself.

"Okay," I concede, and step inside my next class.

Chapter 4

Dafne

"I am overjoyed to be tackling this dance with you, everyone," Ms. Eisner says the next day at our first dance rehearsal, her hands resting above her heart. "I believe it will truly set the tone for the show, which is why it needs to be unforgettable," she continues, passing her piercing blue gaze over us, her hair slicked back in a bun so tight I've always been worried her brain was going to come out of her ears at some point. One of the very first things we will be working on is the dance where Romeo and Juliet meet, neither aware of who the other is behind their masks. It's a crucial point in the story, as upon seeing Juliet for the first time, Romeo completely forgets about the girl he thought he was in love with.

Only Juliet exists now.

Mr. Hackle decided he wanted to put emphasis on their dance as a metaphor for their relationship. I'm excited, really; I love dancing, but if Theodore steps on my feet, I will never let him live it down. It's a win-win.

She makes us pair up; the choreography will revolve around Theodore and me at centre stage. I fix my ponytail once before meeting him halfway, his stare impassible as Ms. Eisner begins to explain the moves, the first being a curtsy for me and a bow in his case. "I could get used to you doing this every time you see me," Theodore whispers.

"Only if it involved throwing up on your shiny loafers, Price," I whisper back, rising with a too-sweet smile on my lips. That seems to shut him up.

"Now, meet your partner's right hand first, then the second, like so," our teacher demonstrates with her assistant, and we repeat. I try not to be self-conscious about the fact that my hands are freezing, while his are pleasantly warm. They're also… big. My fingertips-barely-reach-his-middle-joints kind of big.

"I thought this was Romeo and Juliet, not Dracula," he quietly drawls.

"You want to blame me for genetically poor blood circulation, go ahead," I hiss, focusing on our joined hands rather than his face.

And then he chuckles. It's brief and quiet, but he was definitely amused, and now he's scrambling to hide it. I don't have recollection of another time he's laughed at something I said–in a non-mocking way, that is.

"Everyone is bound to cave at my irresistible humour sooner or later," I smirk as we start turning in a slow circle.

"I didn't think you had a single funny bone in your body, Wright," he stops at the same time as Ms. Eisner's assistant, then comes closer and places both hands on my waist for the next step.

You can't stand this bloke, Dafne, remember? Don't you *dare* blush. I position my hands on his shoulders, and he lifts me up in a half twirl with a stupid grin. "You're enjoying this too much," I mutter as he puts me down, one hand brushing on my waist a second longer than necessary before he joins it with mine midair, one, two, three steps forward; one, two, three steps back.

"While I'm sure this is *torture* for you," he says, the usual amount of sarcasm seeping through the words. Ms. Eisner claps once, then walks up to her computer.

"Alright everyone, from the top with music, then we'll continue."

We don't speak anymore for the next hour, but the air is heavy with the unmistakable charge of competitiveness, pressing closer with each new step. I know it's not right, and it probably does my blood pressure no good, but sometimes it's almost an ache–how badly I want to excel. It must be the same for Theodore, so in some twisted way, I understand why he is the way he is. Not enough to justify his attitude towards me, though.

At the end of the lesson, we've learned most of the choreography, and Ms. Eisner asks that we kindly keep practicing so we don't forget anything, mostly because it will be vital to help build chemistry between our characters. I glance sideways at Theodore only to notice a muscle ticking in his jaw. I think I might have underestimated how deeply he hates being stuck with me in this.

Ollie comes up to me with the bag I carried to dance class already on his shoulder.

"My brain is threatening to shut down. Coffee?"

"Don't make jokes about your brain shutting down, please," I raise one eyebrow as I zip my bag open to grab my water canteen.

Ollie snorts and looks behind my shoulder. "So? Is Price ready for *Dancing with the Stars*?" he whispers.

"Not if I'm his partner, he's not," I huff. "Look at his face. It's like he'd rather hold hands with a cactus than dance with me for five minutes."

"Maybe he's just constipated."

"Ollie!" I laugh, unable to keep my voice down as I push him towards the exit. I pick up my APDAS sweat-shirt from where I'd tossed it before class, just inside the door, and when I look up, Theodore not-so-subtly drags his gaze away from me. Alright, creep.

"I used to be constipated, don't discriminate," I add to Ollie with a quiet laugh, and glance at Theodore one last time before we leave.

Theodore

How we are going to get through months of this is absolutely beyond me. It's not even that working together is hard–that's not it. I think we are both aware of how important these roles could be for us moving forward. I made the mistake of looking at her as she was leaving, and of course she noticed.

I wasn't even thinking, I just–

"Theo," Devon says before taking a swig of his water bottle, "Are we still on for that extra stage combat workout?"

"Uh, sure," I mutter, stuffing my belongings in my rucksack.

My friend clears his throat, and I look at him with a raised eyebrow. "Are you going to lose your mind after every rehearsal with her? Because at this rate you're going to need aromatherapy ev–"

"Remind me why we're friends again?" I purse my lips, mostly because I don't want to laugh.

"Because I'm wise beyond my years and you need me to be the shining light that guides you," he says matter-of-factly.

As we make our way to the showers, I am immensely grateful for the fully packed day of lessons ahead. I need to keep my head and body occupied and focused. I need to be prepared for tomorrow.

Chapter 5

Dafne

The next day, at two in the afternoon sharp–which in theatre lingo means *at least* half an hour before whatever time the call sheet states–our very first rehearsal begins. I've done my stretching and vocal warming, taken a nice sip of water, and am confident I know my lines; I had no trouble learning them up to Act One and Two, as they're not that many, really. That being said, this whole play will still take longer to tackle than it would if there was any other director in Mr. Hackle's place. I don't blame him for being thorough, but we also don't have much time, as APDAS' prerogative for last-year students is not to grant the usual six months a play of this magnitude would require, because '*Time is not a luxury actors can afford in the real world.*'

As Devon and Jack–respectively playing Tybalt and Benvolio–take in Mr. Hackle's stage directions, I see Theodore lowering himself on the seat beside mine, and I slowly turn my head towards him. Is this a new habit of his now? "There's plenty of other empty seats," I hiss.

Theodore leans in and whispers, "The world doesn't revolve around you, love. Besides, it'll be my turn soon and this is the closest seat to the stage." I pointedly ignore his perfectly plausible explanation for sitting here and scoff at the endearing term. I need to remind myself he does this all the time with the sole purpose of taunting me.

In my defense, I'm a romantic at heart; despite having sworn off romance as a general rule after what happened last time, it somehow bothers me that he'd say that to mock me. I don't want to be called *love* for nothing. That's a big word and it shouldn't be thrown around like that.

I briefly consider elbowing him in the ribs or *accidentally* dropping a cup of boiling tea on his freshly pressed shirt, but I'd rather not get exiled for injuring the star of the show. I tilt my head, considering my options, then decide to hit right where it hurts: the lad's fragile ego.

"Is that so? Because I distinctly remember you checking me out after dance rehearsal yesterday," I turn to him in the dimness of the stalls and grin. He purses his lips, and he looks like he's about to give me a compendium of reasons why I'm wrong, but Mr. Hackle nods in my and Theodore's direction and calls our names. "You two, I'd rather go over Romeo and Juliet's first conversation before we continue with Act One. "On stage," he commands. We clearly weren't expecting to go straight to that scene since we both have a couple of others before, but we wordlessly rise and quickly make our way up the few steps that lead to the stage.

"Let's consider this your chemistry test, hmm?"

I glance at Theodore and have a double take, because he's taking a deep breath and wait–is he sweating? Theodore 'I know the entire Inferno from the Divine Comedy by heart' Price?

Nah, it can't be. Except that's precisely what it looks like. But as he reminded me mere minutes ago, it's not because of what we're about to do, since the world doesn't revolve around me. He also wasn't checking me out yesterday–*uh huh.*

He turns towards me, his face is completely transformed into a focused expression, so different from the smile he usually wears like a medal, and despite everything, I can't help but be a little in awe of it. It's the first thing I'd told him, after that first class together, how incredible he was at disappearing completely from his own face, his own posture. He didn't take the compliment too well, which you'd find weird for someone who seems to feed on praise the way Tinkerbell does on people believing she exists.

We stare in each other's eyes for a few seconds, and I let myself pretend that there is no mutual dislike threatening to crumble completely between us–or at least use the negative charge in my favour. I'm a professional and can handle whatever curveball is thrown my way. As he steps forward, I take in the fierce look in his eyes; he's close enough that I can see how the green swirls in the brown. I am distantly aware of Mr. Hackle reminding us of the circumstances, what happened just before this scene, even though he knows we're prepared. He wouldn't have chosen us otherwise.

"*If I profane with my unworthiest hand,*" Theodore abruptly says, his voice deeper than usual, "*this holy shrine, the gentle sin is this*." His eyes flicker from my own to my lips. Great actor indeed.

"*My lips, two blushing pilgrims, ready stand to smooth that rough touch with a tender kiss,*" he continues as his hand brushes mine. So that's how it's going to be. Lovely.

"*Good pilgrim, you do wrong your hand too much, which mannerly devotion shows in this,*" I reply as my pointer finger traces his palm. "*For saints have hands that pilgrims' hands do touch, and palm to palm is holy palmer's kiss*."

A small smile tugs at his lips. "*Have not saints lips, and holy palmers too*?"

"*Ay, pilgrim,*" I start, letting go of his hand abruptly and turning, facing away from him. Thankfully, Juliet is supposed to be thirteen–I'm fairly sure I'm blushing like a teenager. "*Lips that they must use in prayer*."

"*O then, dear saint, let lips do what hands do*!" he pleads, "*They pray: grant thou, lest faith turn to despair*." I turn my head so that he can see my profile.

"*Saints do not move, though grant for prayer's sake.*" He pauses, and just before I'm about to glance at him to see if he's still breathing, he's turned me around by my waist, and we're nearly chest to chest. "*Then move not while my prayer's effect I take,*" he says, and now he's leaning in and he's actually going to kiss me right *now–*

"Stop," Mr. Hackle says, a few fingers raised in midair.

Both Theodore's and my heads snap towards our director at the same time.

I barely register him stepping away from me quietly a few seconds later, and I mostly notice because there's a loss in the warmth I felt where his hands were.

"I don't know how often the two of you enjoy yourselves outside of here," Mr. Hackle says, and I press my lips together tightly to stop myself from laughing in his face while Theodore clears his throat to my right. We both know what kind of enjoyment he's referring to.

"I know we don't usually work on intentions first, but I do want to make something clear. You need to understand that Romeo and Juliet are two kids who fall for each other instantly; there's no logic involved. They're listening to what their hearts are telling them and that is 'this person belongs with you.'" I release a breath I was very much aware I was holding and turn to Theodore, who's already looking at me. He nods, and I nod back. Message received: we're going to have to step it up.

"Make me believe these two would die for each other. Because they will. No overthinking on my stage."

I know it sounds preposterous, considering this is the very first time we've rehearsed any of our scenes together, but if what Mr. Hackle just saw wasn't honest enough from the get-go, then we need to attune to each other as soon as possible. It's going to take time and patience–lord knows Theodore is going to test my already fragile threshold of tolerance whenever he's within three feet of me–but I'm willing to do the work. And I hope that even if it doesn't thrill him, he is too. We start the scene from the top, and this time … we get to the kiss.

Theodore

Once again, we break apart from the kiss. Is this the fifth or sixth time? I'm not sure. It's hard to keep track. Mr. Hackle was always very clear that there's little space for modesty on stage, which means we need to be prepared to do this. You know, kissing over and over again. From this close, I can't help but notice certain things about Dafne I'd never lingered long enough to take in before. Why I didn't is very clear to me now. I think I was subconsciously shielding myself.

For one, she smells nice. Like peaches and–patchouli, I think. There's always a patchouli soap at my grandparents' house, that's why I know. Her lips are soft, too, and rosier than before, for obvious reasons. Some chunks of her hair are almost curly, the ones by her ears. Her eyebrows are perfectly symmetrical, which either means she's lucky or spends a long time on them. There's a single small mole on the slightly upturned tip of her nose, and her lashes might just be the longest I've ever seen–not that I'm in the habit of staring at people's lashes specifically.

Given different circumstances, I'd probably compliment her on each of those things.

Naturally, I'm extremely bothered by the information about her I've just catalogued in my brain, despite the fact that kissing someone I've been incessantly bickering with for years turns out to be surprisingly easy. Maybe what irks me is that I haven't kissed a girl in a while, and now it has to be her. We've been over the scene for a while now, so if anything, we're getting the hang of it.

Mr. Hackle's directions were clear, but he also leaves us space to try new things, and perhaps fail, which is the only way to understand what works on stage and what doesn't. What's believable and what feels fake.

I notice the sensation of having my stomach in knots that had been plaguing me all morning is mostly gone. Now, if my eyes stopped dropping to her mouth, that'd be really great.

Two years, four months ago

We're not allowed to attend other candidates' auditions, so we're expected to wait in the hall just outside the theatre. I keep taking deep breaths, because I have the faint worry I might pass out before I even get in the room. I'm on exhalation number eight when the main door that leads to the theatre slams opens. The girl that steps out of it looks like she's just run a marathon. Her cheeks are flushed, pupils dilated, her dark hair looks like she's been blow-drying it. Maybe I'm not the one about to faint, after all. She sits next to me without realising I'm there, because her brown eyes are fixated on something on the wall when she lowers herself on one of the chairs anchored to the walls. There's a beat of complete silence, and it's incredibly awkward, so I ask, "How'd it go?"

She turns towards me slowly and huffs a surprised, "Oh, didn't see you there." She breaks into a soft laugh then, one that sounds as if she'd been holding it in for hours. "I think it went … really well," she says, a little out of breath. I don't know her, obviously, but I have the feeling she's saying *I think* when what she means is *I'm sure*. Despite the obvious adrenaline from the audition, there's a confident quality to the way she rolls her shoulders and raises her hand to tuck a strand of hair behind one ear, adjusting herself on the chair and looking at me with more intent than I'm comfortable with.

"Grand," I mumble, my stomach churning with tension, and I suddenly don't feel like prolonging the conversation more than necessary. After all, if she gets in, that means one less chance for me to get accepted. I get up and start pacing in small circles, hoping that gets the message through, but she rises in one swift motion as well, surety and the unmistakable stage-induced energy high still clinging to her every movement. I would find it fascinating, if I wasn't in the process of quietly losing it.

"Don't let the nerves get the best of you ..." she starts, offering her hand to me. I stare at it for a few seconds, before shaking it lightly. It's soft but bloody cold, and I briefly wonder if it bothers her.

"Thanks," I say, my mouth pressed into a tight line, and her expression falls a little, like she heard what I was thinking. I'm not actively trying to be an arsehole, but I'm one step away from running for dear life and forgetting about the audition altogether–manners aren't exactly my top priority right now.

She nods, shaking back more firmly than I did and says "I'm Dafne. With an *F*, not *Ph,*" she chuckles, seemingly recovered from the second before. "Good luck then, fellow actor."

She turns around, gathers her bag from where it lays on the floor, and leaves on stealthy feet without looking back. This two-minute interaction leaves me both irritated and yearning for more information on the doe-eyed girl, but before I can dwell on it too much, I am called in

for my own audition.
When I see her at our first lesson together barely a month later and hear she got in with the only full scholarship available, it rubs me the wrong way. My roommate, Devon, says it's unfair of me; after all, I know little to nothing about her, except for the spelling of her name–*and the fact that she wasn't above giving unwanted advice to a stranger*, I add in my mind. When she stands in front of the class and does Lady Macbeth's monologue though ... I feel like I've been hit with a club. Ran over by a truck.
She is good.

More than good. Better than me, which I hate, because if it's obvious to me, it won't take long before it becomes obvious to everyone else. And I've made a promise–that I would be the best. Actors often get told perfection doesn't exist in what we do; there's only studying, and refining, and trying until it works, over and over. But in my eyes, what she did couldn't possibly be more, and I hate that the same can't be said about me.

After the seemingly never-ending ball scene, Mr. Hackle has us go back to the previous scenes until eight in the evening. When he dismisses us for the day, I get off stage and start gathering my things, and I just can't wait to shower and stuff my face with a warm pie and mash. As I daydream about delicious gravy, Devon nudges me with his elbow.

"You lucky bastard," he says, nodding–in what I'm sure *he* thinks is a subtle way–to my left. A few feet from me, Isabel and Dafne are chatting about something, the former's expression growing increasingly… upset, I'd say, about whatever Isabel is showing her from her phone screen.

"What about them?" I ask, my tone apathetic, more out of exhaustion than anything else.

"You got to kiss her something like twenty times in the span of a few hours, and every single guy in here except for me and David never wished they got cast as Romeo more," he whispers, and I'm not sure whether I want to roll my eyes at the implication in his voice or congratulate him for managing not to shout that for the whole theatre to hear. I can definitely feel the annoyance prevail, and before I can think twice I snap.

"Yes, Devon, *so* lucky," and now he's shaking his head vehemently, but I can't stop the words from coming. "Not all of us have the privilege to spend their days basking in the *oh so great* Dafne Wright's pres–" I start turning, but am interrupted by Dafne holding up a phone, her eyes so bright as they burn into me that I'd have no trouble believing looks could kill. As I take in the Instagram page on the screen, I realise I have massively mucked up.

Chapter 6

Dafne

I'd consider myself a patient woman. Understanding, too, even when people make it hard for me to be. But if there's something I don't tolerate, it's disrespect. And this is too bloody much, even for Theodore Price.

"Look, Wright," he starts but I raise my free hand to shut him up, and I'm more than satisfied to see it works.

"No," I say simply. "You don't get to do this. 'Talent means little if you can't back it up with passion,'" I recite. "'Let's just say I'm not sure passion is Dafne's most shining quality'–did I get it right?"

"You know how these things are, they caught me off guard with that question–" he looks around us, surely terrified Mr. Hackle will overhear. Lucky for him, I'm not that kind of person, and made sure our director left before confronting him about what Isabel showed me: a video interview on APDAS' Instagram page where he talks about his recently obtained role as Romeo, as well as, ap-

-parently, answers questions about me. His shoulders slump, and perhaps for the first time since I've known him, he looks unprepared.

"The difference between you and me is that I have the guts to say things to your face," I add before turning around, placing Isabel's phone back in her hands, and grabbing my bag as I walk out of the theatre.

I'm trying very hard to keep my composure, but it's like I can feel my brain heating up, processing Theodore's words. But I promised myself I wouldn't do that a long time ago.

It's not worth it.

It was stupid of me to believe he could be nice, if only for the sake of peace during what is an insanely stressful time for all of us, but of course not. I fish for my phone in my tote bag as I rush down the hallway, hoping nobody will notice the frustrated tears welling up in my eyes. I like to think I'm tough enough, but I'm also an easy crier, which proves useful when you're an actor, much less when you're supposed to be a functioning human being in society. I'm about to call Phoebe so I can distract myself and calm down, when a voice stops me in my tracks.

"Oy," Ollie says. "Where are you running, Forrest?" I look over at him as he closes the men's bathroom door behind him, and I can't stop an angry tear from slipping out.

"Daf, what is it?" he says, his thick brows knitting

together.
"It's nothing, that's the point. I let *stupid* things *stupid* people say get me worked up and–" I take a deep breath. "Can we go get hot chocolate?" I sniff. He pats my shoulder twice and chuckles lightly. "Sure. Let me grab my stuff and then we'll get some serotonin in your system."

As soon as I'm cradling a steaming cup of coconut-flavored chocolate between my hands, I figure it'll be easier to put things into perspective.
"It's not groundbreaking news that Price is a dickhead," Ollie says simply, munching on his sugar-free muffin. We love having breakfast food in the evening–it was always our thing before APDAS, and Ollie is determined to keep the tradition until we're old and grey. "He's all smiles and charm as long as he doesn't feel threatened, that's what his problem is."

I scrunch up my nose as I listen. "Threatened? By me?" I ask. I suppose there *has* been an unspoken challenge between us, but we're Romeo and Juliet now, for crying out loud.

We should have the same goal, just this once. Ollie eyes me, eyebrows raised. "Don't tell me you never noticed," he continues, trying to take some of my chocolate with his spoon. I bat his hand away playfully, then rotate mine as to say *do go on.* "It's been that way ever since our first class here. Your Lady Macbeth obliterated his

Edmund," he says matter-of-factly, making a cut-throat gesture. "Add that to the fact that you got in with a full scholarship with the fact that you could fill an Olympic-sized swimming pool with the guy's ego … two plus two equals four."

I grab an abandoned blueberry from Ollie's muffin and roll it between a thumb and forefinger.

"It's not like I stole his place or something," I say thoughtfully. "I've earned it, same as anyone else. And that interview is a whole other beast, Ollie. That's public humiliation."

Ollie shrugs in agreement. "There's always the other option," he adds quietly.

"Which is…?"

"He was born an arsehole and he'll die as one," he says simply as he props his head on a fist.

"That's a possibility," I smile, "except for the fact that he doesn't seem like such an arsehole around other people. He's always been decent to *you*. It's like I'm a red cape and he's the bull." I rub the tip of my finger on the border of my cup, when something else occurs to me. "He also probably hates kissing me, so that's just–" Ollie interrupts my self-deprecating moment by clapping his hands.

"Do *not* finish that sentence. I know for a fact you're a great kisser," he says with a smirk, and I roll my eyes.

"We were *twelve*. And if I recall correctly, you started dating Maisie Anders a few days later," I remind him as rest my chin in my hands.

"The two things were not correlated at all," he says, trying to stifle a yawn.

"Still haven't caught up with sleep hours, huh?"

"Don't even get me started," he groans. "What kind of monsters wake you up at five in the morning every single day for two weeks? Not to mention Tam has been pestering me with messages all the while."

Tam is Ollie's ex-girlfriend. They'd been together for four years all through college.

I liked her; she was fun and sensible and really smart, but when she and Ollie had to part ways–he at APDAS and her at the University of Limerick, Ireland–she told him long-distance wasn't good enough for her, and broke things off. It's been literal years, but every so often she starts to text and call him and beg him to give her another chance. Ollie was inclined to do so at first, but then he realised she was unreliable, and he didn't want to risk getting hurt again if he could help it. That's just one of the many things he and I have in common: we were let down, and don't feel like playing spin the wheel for another try. On the bright side, APDAS keeps its students busy, so thinking about a relationship is the least of my worries (and no, the occasional one-night stand doesn't count, a girl has needs).

"Is she going to call me in tears again? I'm out of excuses as to why you won' t pick up the phone, Ollie."

"She could have gotten on a plane if she was so

desperate," he retorts.
I nod in agreement, and while I support him all the way, I can't help but feel sorry for her. I've been in her position, after all. As if he heard my thoughts, Ollie says, "Speaking of arseholes … Have you heard about Noah?"

I look up at him, my brows furrowing at the mention of the biggest sod that has ever lived, also known as my ex.

"Heard what? I've blocked him on social media and never bother to answer his stupid birthday wishes, you know that."

Ollie grimaces and says, "I know, it's just … he's engaged."

I tilt my head, not even sure I've heard him right.

"Engaged as in–"

"To be married," he confirms softly. He's looking at me like he's afraid I'm going to crumble to the floor at any second. I feel a smile creeping on my lips, and the news should probably make me want to throw up, but I feel the weirdest mix of relief and disgust. I really am through it, but the memories still sting. His last gift before we parted ways forever was a packet of trust issues tied with a pretty bow. "Well then, I hope they're terribly happy," I say as I raise my mug for a toast. "Cheers to one less idiot roaming the market," I add as Ollie clinks his mug with mine and laughs.

Theodore

After a night of staring at Tom Hiddleston's life-size cardboard cutout creeping in a corner of our dorm room–that I never would have allowed Devon to get if not for a lost bet–my alarm goes off, and I practically fall off my bed out of sheer exhaustion.
Guilt is a strange thing. It starts as a kernel of flame, fed by increasingly bigger chunks of wood, and the next thing you know, it's a whole bloody bonfire. I hate it. My alarm keeps ringing obscenely loud, but Devon doesn't budge; I'm not sure a herd of elephants playing the trumpet would be enough to wake him up when he's snoring like this.

I wash my face in a poor attempt to look like I've had more than ten minutes of sleep, brush my teeth, and force my brain to focus on picking out an outfit. I throw a slipper at Devon's head, who suddenly sits up on his bed mumbling a "I want a real sword this time!"

"You want a real sword, I'm afraid you've chosen the wrong career path," I say, and he groans a *Shut up*. "We're not allowed to skip class so we can get more sleep," I remind him, picking my rucksack up. "Get ready, and for the love of Tom," I point at the cutout with my thumb, "do not be late." As I'm closing the door behind me, I hear the muffled thump of the slipper being thrown at the door and laugh. Perhaps today won't be as bad as I thought. Maybe Dafne will have forgotten all about it. Right?

I'm going through my usual stretching routine, keeping my eyes as wide as possible in a desperate attempt not to fall asleep on stage. Isabel and Oliver are chatting while stretching a few feet from me, and I, unwillingly, pick up on their conversation.

"It was awful," Isabel says, the grimace on her tan face evident in her voice. "I should have said something, but I didn't want to interfere."

Bollocks. She's talking about last night, isn't she?

I have my back to them, so I don't see what Oliver does in the next few seconds of silence, and I hold my breath.

"Dafne's not mad at you, don't worry. She can handle arses like him," he says.

Yeah, the arse is me. My stomach drops. I really need to apologise–I'll do that as soon as she gets here.

I didn't realise how harmful my words could be when I did that stupid interview, and when I was asked about Dafne … I panicked. What was I supposed to say? That she's likely the best student this school has ever seen?

Maybe. It wouldn't be a lie.

My thoughts are interrupted by Dafne's presence, as Isa-

-bel calls her name to greet her. I release a breath, then turn to them. She's smiling to her friends, her bag

smoothly slipping off her shoulder, and then she shoots me a look. It's not angry, it's not sad; I would never able to tell if she's imagining strangling me or doesn't care enough to have murderous thoughts about me. Either way, I need to patch things up and not allow this thing to hover over us for the rest of the year.

I take a few steps towards her, and she raises an eyebrow, her arms crossed against her chest. I reach her, Oliver and Isabel, who are standing in a semicircle, and clear my throat. Her friends don't even bother to look at me, and Dafne scoffs lightly.

"Can I talk to you for a second?" I ask, shoving my hands into the pockets of my track pants. Dafne considers me for a moment, eyes narrowing as if she was reading something written on my forehead in too-small handwriting. Oliver eyes me then, displeasure clear in his gaze, and I try my best to ignore it.

"Sure," Dafne says, and walks to the proscenium. When we're out of the others' hearing range, she cocks her head in silent question, a bored look on her face. Her cheeks are lightly flushed.

"Look," I start, licking my lips. Suddenly my salivary glands have bid me farewell. "What I said was… distasteful."

Her eyebrows shoot to her hairline. "That's one way

to put it," she smiles, but it doesn't reach her eyes. I'm about to apologise properly, because I know anything else won't do, but she interrupts me.

"You know what, Theodore?" she resumes, that weird smile still on her lips. "I don't know what your problem is. I don't know if you're so unsatisfied with your life, you feel the need to take it out on me." She ponders, her calm tone not matching her words, and I can feel the color draining from my cheeks. "But from now on, I demand *respect*. You'd rather share the stage with a different Juliet because of some petty disliking you took to me for no apparent reason or just because you'd rather be kissing someone else–*I don't care.* Own up and do your job and I'll do mine, and we never have to breathe the same air again once this is over," she snaps before walking away, her ponytail swishing.
My throat is completely dry, my stomach has plummeted to unfathomable depths, and I know all I can do is exactly what she's asked of me.

Chapter 7

Dafne

The next days of rehearsals pass by relatively quick, and most importantly, with no more incidents on the Theodore front. Our usual back and forth jabs have drastically slowed down too. For the first few days I thought it was nice not to have to be ready to snap back, but I have to admit, I'd been almost missing the comfort of our relationship, however strained it is. I was glad to see things hadn't really changed today when Taylor, our yoga teacher, paired us up during our collective lesson as a cast; neither of us failed to point out whatever was wrong with our crow poses. It also didn't help how distracting his arms were, since I had them right in front of me before every bloody downward dog position. Once I saw the thin veins that line his arms, I mentally kicked myself for thinking that they made him look ten times hotter; what can I say, they're my kryptonite. Not Theodore's specifically, to be clear. I could swear I saw a hint of a blush when he, regrettably, caught me staring, but a glare took centre stage on his face in no time to compensate.

We're starting to work on Act Three, and Mr. Hackle has been tougher on us, which means he's yelling for a misplaced prop on a good day and throwing said prop without looking where it lands on a bad one. We're used to it by now though–theatre kids have thick skin by necessity. You can't let your fragilities overwhelm you on stage or on a set. You have to tame them and exploit them when you need to, learn to tuck them away where they can't get in the way the rest of time. It doesn't mean emotions should be repressed, but they shouldn't rule you either. Mr. Hackle is about to dismiss us, when Ms. Patterson clears her throat politely to his left. He eyes her for a second, then presses his thumb above his eye socket.

"Right, we're going to see a production of Romeo and Juliet at the Globe on Saturday," he grunts, which gains him a round of quietly enthusiastic sounds from the cast. "I want to remind you lot of what a serious show looks like."

Ms. Patterson nods vehemently and hands Isabel, who is nearest to her, a red clipboard with a single lined paper sheet on it. "Sign your name and pass it on, will you Isabel?" she asks with her too-polite smile. Sometimes I think her composure is all for show and she secretly imagines strangling us every time someone snickers at Shakespeare-born words like *bawcock.*

"Off you go," Mr. Hackle says once we've all signed the sheet, already halfway down the stage's stepladder. "You look like hell," Ollie grimaces at me, and I raise one eyebrow at his assessment. Because I am very mature, I also stick out my tongue at him. "It's not like I've-been in here like the rest of you since eight in the morning, have I?"

He laughs at that and waves a hand at me. "The shower awaits," he bows, and I smile in goodbye. I start collecting my things from the front row of chairs, but I'm interrupted by Ms. Patterson, who approaches me and says my name in that this-means-trouble tone.

"I know you're over for the day, but I need you to do something for me. Well, mostly for you." I internally sigh and nod, the promising idea of filling my grumbling stomach sooner rather than later disappearing just out of reach.

I've been tasked with sorting through some boxes filled to the brim with various pieces of fabric in the props room; I need to look for a specific handkerchief Ms. Patterson *swears* is vital Juliet carries with her at all times. I don't see why it couldn't wait until morning, but I'm not in the position to refuse such a simple demand. It occurs to me that Mr. Hackle never says a word about these requests of hers–not that she doesn't know what she's doing, but I wonder if there's a reason for that other than the fact that he'd rather keep the tiniest possibility of discussion at arm's length.

"These all look the same to me," I mutter, before hearing the door creak open and footsteps shuffling in. I freeze for a second, because nobody else is supposed to be here. I drop the box in a haste and rush towards the door–

"No...*No, no, no,*" I groan, slamming my hands on the door that just groaned shut.

"Why are you here?" Theodore asks, scratching his forehead.

"Why did you let the door close, damn it?" I yell, not bothering to answer his question. "Did you think someone put that bucket in front of it to make an architectural statement?" I gesture frantically behind us. "Didn't you hear what the caretaker said this morning, the lock's *defective*, oh my *God*–"

Theodore steps towards me and looks like he's about to touch me, but the expression on my face is enough to make him retreat.

"Calm down, Wright," he says, and I really wish I could, but isn't it common knowledge telling someone to calm down doesn't ever work?

"We are stuck in here, Theodore." I articulate for him, my pulse thrumming. Apparently, the point is not getting through.

"I'll call Devon, he'll go to the caretaker's st–" he closes his eyes in resignation as he extracts his phone from his pocket and the screen lights up. He curses under his breath.

"Yeah. No reception, Sherlock." The only silver lining, I think to myself, is that I texted Phoebe I'd be in the heatre for longer than expected, and not to wait up for me–at least she'll likely be asleep by nine and won't start printing missing person's posters.

"You should have been more careful," he says then, pinching the bridge of his nose, and I turn towards him as slowly as humanly possible, my heart beating furiously in my chest.

"You're joking," I say, my hands itching to grab the first pointy object available and engage in a duel. "*You* had no business being here. *You* let the door close." I fume, poking at his chest with a finger instead of a saber. Why do we keep finding ourselves at barely two inches from each other? He furrows his brows, slowly lowering my hand from where it's digging a hole in his shirt by cupping his own over it. It's only for a second, but I'm painfully aware of the moment we're not touching anymore, and it's probably the fact that it's freezing in here and so is my entire body, while his is definitely not. It's still annoying.

Without taking his gaze off mine, something like indecisiveness flashes in his expression.
"You're impossible," he declares, and storms towards the small sofa in the corner of the room, which is also the only proper sitting space in sight. Fine. I take a deep breath and decide on going back to my handkerchief quest instead, if only not to give him the satisfaction of forcing me to lie down in defeat like Julius Caesar after getting stabbed. It hasn't been more than ten minutes of bitterly rummaging through endless squares of fabric,

when I see Theodore approaching from the corner of my eye. I tell myself I will *not* be starting another argument, when an extended hand lands in front of my face. I raise an eyebrow and look up at him, only to find a soft expression on his mouth, and it's such an appalling contrast to the usual tightness of features he displays in front of me that I blink rapidly a few times to make sure it's really there. Apparently, this small change alone is enough to suppress the ever-present instinct to fight him back.

"Look, if we're going to be here for the rest of the night, we might as well acknowledge each other's presence, call it a truce if you want," he sighs. I eye his hand, then him, and before I can convince myself this is some sort of trap, I curl my fingers around his. His palm is still warm, just like the other times I've held it–for acting purposes, that is–and he lifts me from my crouching place with no strain. "What do you propose?" I ask as I lift an invisible piece of lint from my cream-coloured sweater.

"We could eat something, for starters," he says, a corner of his mouth kicking up. "I've some mixed berries in my bag. It's not a roast, but at least–" He doesn't manage to finish the sentence, because I've snorted so loudly the caretaker might have heard and come rescue us after all. I slap my hand over my mouth, my eyes wide with amusement.

"Is something funny?" he asks, genuine surprise in his tone.

"I'm sorry–" my lips twitch, trying my hardest not to

burst out laughing. "Sorry. Nothing funny at all about you carrying around *mixed berries,"* I say, my tone thick with mirth, to which Theodore glares.

"They're packed with Vitamin A. They're good for your cardiovascular system and–" he stops his perfectly plausible explanation short, because I'm nodding with exaggerated interest and can't help but mouth a *tell me more* as I quickly cross the room and land on the sofa. I fold my legs under me, and pretend to annotate with a pen and notebook made of air. My improv teacher would be so proud of me.

"Never mind, more for me." He huffs as he plops next to me, and I can tell he's reigning in a smile.

He slowly extracts a small food container from his abandoned rucksack, and when the lid pops off, my eye catches on the glistening black and rich red of the berries. It occurs to me this is the only dinner I might get.

"Alright, you win, I'll taste one," I say, reaching out to grab the closest piece of fruit, when he catches my hand in his.

"I thought mixed berries were hilarious," he drawls, and my mouth opens and closes like a damn goldfish. He licks his lips, and of their own bloody accord, my eyes fall to the gesture. I'm not sure how long we stay like that, because the next thing I know, Theodore is turning my palm and pushing lightly on my knuckles so that it cups, and he pours a bunch of berries in my hand.

"Is it really genetics?" he asks pensively, his gaze cast

down at my hands.

"Oh," I breathe when I realise what he's referring to. "Yep. From my dad's side, apparently–thank you," I mumble as he drops the last berry in my palm, and I lean back into my side of the sofa cradling the fruit as if it were made of crystal. I can practically hear Phoebe's voice in my head shouting *Snap out of it, babes*. This is a truce, not the end of the war.

We munch quietly for a minute, until Theodore clears his throat and begins to say something I don't catch as I open my mouth to voice the question I should've asked when he came into the prop room earlier. Our eyes meet, and he moves his hand as if to say *you first*.

"Why did come in here past rehearsal time? I thought you'd left with everyone else," I ask, popping another juicy blueberry in my mouth.

"I was told there was a spare sword in here and I wanted to practice my sword work," he says, looking at his lap. "I've never had this many fight sequences before and they need to be, well, perfect."

I nod, and a few minutes of silence pass. I'm shocked to notice it's not uncomfortable.

"My grandmother grows these," he adds then, surprising me for the second–third?–time tonight. There's a mellow quality to his voice now, which I assume can only be attributed to the mention of his grandmother. I've never known anything about his family though, so I'm a bit startled by the information he's freely giving me.

"Her garden is lovely. Not big, but the care she puts into it…" he looks over at me, and I allow a small smile to show.

He nods once and looks away, that flicker of emotion already gone from his eyes. It's too bad–I thought it made him look more human, and less perfect robot-actor. I wonder if he's aware of being a walking contradiction. I consider whether I should share something in return, but I don't want to break this careful balance we've now wordlessly established.

I could just be glad we're not bickering and leave it alone; but being who I am and craving closure, the itch I've been wanting to scratch for quite literally years now is possibly within reach to be scratched, and I doubt we'll ever be locked in a room with no possibility of escape again anytime soon.

"Are you ever going to tell me what I ever did for you to hate me so much?" I ask in a single breath, staring straight ahead. Theodore is quiet for a long moment, and from the corner of my eye, I can see his hands have stilled where they were drumming softly on the plastic container balanced on his knees.

I wonder if he's going to say anything at all or get up and pretend like he didn't hear me or change the subject altogether–

"It's not–I don't hate you," he sighs, and my lips thin into a humourless smile.

"See, that's hard to believe when I'm the only person in our entire course you ever treated the way you do," I say, my words laced with bitterness.

He could just admit whatever the reason for starting this stupid feud with me was, and I'd accept it. I don't believe in judging people on instinct alone, and I can't recall a single time he said or did something that didn't scream *I don't like you.*

"You think you've got all the facts straight, but you don't," he says, his jaw clenched.

I hold onto the curve of his elbow as he gets up, and he looks down at me, a pleading look in his eyes.

"Then tell me." I say slowly, letting go. He looks almost angry, but at who, I'm not sure.

"Why does it matter *now*?" he sounds genuinely confused. I search for the right words in my brain.

"It matters to me. Because I'd like to know if we've spent three years making each other's lives that much more difficult for a valid reason or not."

He swallows hard, shakes his head lightly, and just as he's started walking away, I say, "I thought you were a lot of things, Price, but not a coward."

He stops then, his expression one of disbelief.

"Is this an attempt on … revenge, for that interview? I've tried to apologise. I've left you alone. You don't get to judge me, Dafne."

I immediately know I'm in the wrong, but my stubbornness prevents me from doing anything about it. So I let him walk to the other side of the room without another word.

I'm tired, the full day of rehearsal suddenly weighs on me like a boulder, and I turn around with my back to him, curling up on the sofa to rest for a few minutes.

The distinct feeling of falling wakes me with a jolt, making me sit up straight in the pitch darkness.

I pass a hand over my face, and when I try to stand, I feel a jeans jacket slip off me.

"Price?" I croak, lowering myself to the floor instead and groping around for my bag.

Nothing. I wouldn't put it past him to somehow have forced the door open and left me here. I get up, my sense of direction completely twisted, until my forehead painfully collides with something.

"Can you watch where you're going?" Theodore groans, and his face is lit up by the torch on his phone. "In case you haven't noticed, I'm not an owl," I snap, rubbing the point where my forehead collided with his stupidly toned chest. "I can't see in the bloody dark." I snatch his phone from him so I can light up my surroundings until I see my bag. Right next to where I was sitting. Of course. When I turn around to give him the phone back, my eyes fall to the lock screen; it's a photo of what I assume is a baby Theodore and a middle-aged couple, holding him in their arms, smiling from ear to ear. "Are

these your parents?" I ask as the single lightbulb on the ceiling lights up, and Theodore rushes toward me from the wall where he'd just turned the switch on.
"Grandparents," he says apathetically, snatching the phone from my hand.

Before I can wonder what *that* was or how warm the hug in that picture looked, or how cute baby Theodore was in his navy jumper, he tells me that it's nearly seven and the caretaker should be here any minute. I nod absently, the clinging haze of sleep making it hard to process the bits of information I've just been handed, and the ones I'm missing. Did he get any sleep? If yes, did he sleep on the floor? At what point did he blanket me in his jacket, which by the way, smelled amaz–

The door opens as a whistling Mr. Davies, the caretaker, gasps in surprise at finding the room occupied.
"What are you two doing in here?"

Theodore

Dafne starts explaining what happened to Mr. Davies, and I gratefully accept the opportunity to flee.
"I'll see you at rehearsals," I say gruffly as I grab my jacket and slip my rucksack on my shoulder, stiff from sleeping in a sitting position, and make my way past the

both of them before either can stop me.

I know that the image of her face when she asked me why I hate her is going to haunt me. I thought she didn't care, that she was fine with it, even. Because that's the way it's always been between us, that's how it bloody works. And what the hell was I thinking, telling her anything about Grandma? I need ten hours of sleep. Or Two days.

Once I get to my room, much to my shock, I find that Devon is wide awake and reading on his bed. The second I close the door behind me, he drops his book and launches himself to his feet. "Where were you?" he yells. "I was about to call the police, you goddamn idi–"

I raise both hands in a placating gesture. "Turn the volume down, would you? My eardrums are begging for mercy."

Devon's jaw goes slack. "Did you spend the night getting drunk without me? I swear, Theo–"

I throw my rucksack into his hands and that startles him enough to stop talking. "Believe me, I would have loved the sweet oblivion of alcohol," I say before launching myself stomach-down on my bed, "but alas, the only available company was Dafne's."

To which I almost opened up about personal things I don't ever speak about, I don't say. My voice is muffled by the pillow, but Devon hears anyway, because the next thing I know is I'm being rolled onto my back and my head thuds against the wall. "Ouch," I groan, but he's al-

-ready asking too many questions. Why is it the one time I–unwillingly–spend the night out, when I come back he's not snoring like a harvester, but looks like he's had a triple espresso at barely eight in the morning? The interrogation leaves no time for me to articulate proper answers, so I let him go through it on his own.
"You mean *our* Dafne? Juliet-Dafne? The same girl I've been trying to get through that thick skull of yours to notice the mad chemistry you have?! You actually ended up sleeping with her, I–"

I abruptly sit straight.

"No, no, no, get your mind out of the gutter, man. We got locked in the prop room. There was no reception and breaking the door open wasn't really an option, so…" I sigh and glance at him. He's still hanging onto my rucksack as if it were a stuffed animal, his mouth trying to work out words that aren't coming. I think I've broken him. After a minute, he finally manages a, "Your luck is almost as frustrating as your stubbornness," and lets himself fall on his bed with a grunt.

"In what world is being stuck in a room with Dafne with no possibility to escape, called luck?" I ask.

I think I've got a massive headache coming.

"In the oblivious world, of which you are the supreme leader," he laughs, and I scrunch up my nose. "Have you ever considered, and I know this is a wild thought, that sometimes people just don't get along, and that's that?"

"I'm sure you believe that, but hey," he turns his head towards me slowly. "Why don't we bet on it?" he asks, already sounding too self-satisfied with whatever idea's popped up in his head.

"The last bet cost me a man made of paper taking permanent residence in our room," I say, pointing at the smiling Tom in his usual corner. "I'm not betting with you ever again."

"Just this once, and I promise–no paper hotties involved this time," he pleads.

I roll my eyes. I'm going to regret this, but last night's awful sleep on the freezing floor of the prop room doesn't grant me the strength to fight him. I gesture vaguely as to give him permission to speak, and he rises from the bed impressively quick.

"Grand," he wrings his hands, my rucksack long forgotten, the excitement in his voice meaning trouble. "I'll make it a double. I bet that I can pair Dafne up with someone," he says, and the awful-night-induced mist in my brain dissipates instantly. I snap my head towards him as he raises a hand. "I *also* bet you'll get jealous and kiss her out of rehearsals before opening night. Because deep down you like her, but you're too fixated on the whole tormented actor thing to ever admit it." He smirks, crossing his arms with a pleased nod.

You'd think he's the one who got barely any sleep, coming up with these insane ideas.

"First of all, there *is* no tormented actor thing," I say,

quite offended. "Second, and most importantly, how do we determine that? If you find someone who'll go out with her, and in the nonexistent scenario in which I'll care and kiss her, I would never tell you. How would you know?"

"Despite your best intentions, you're not that hard to read, Montague. You're also *the* most upright person I know."

"I doubt an upright person would make bets at all," I scoff.

"Come on, now. What do you have to lose if you're so sure you're right?" He offers his hand for me to shake, and I eye it, unconvinced. He wants to make Dafne like someone else to prove the point that I allegedly like her? "Sorry, I don't get it," I say, propping myself on one elbow. "If you think I secretly like her–which, again, I don't–what's the point in putting this farce together? If you have someone lead her on she'll end up heartbroken and that could jeopardise the play," I explain.

Devon's smirk falls immediately. "Is that your concern? That she won't *perform* as well if she goes on a few dates? For all you know she could have a string of suitors waiting for her to accept their invitations."

"She doesn't," I retort, stifling a yawn.

"How do you know?"

"I just do." I do not.

Devon snorts. "Maybe you're right," he adds a moment later. "If you really liked her, you'd give her more credit."

He drops his hand and starts walking towards the bathroom. Something unpleasant stirs in me, because I know accepting this is a potential recipe for disaster, but I also know that I just lied, because any fool could take one look at Dafne Wright and know she cannot be stopped.

I guess that, on top of the fact I'm still mad at her for calling me a coward, is what possesses me to blurt out my next words.

"Alright, you've got it. The bet is on."

Chapter 8

Dafne

Phoebe and I are having breakfast, and I'm finishing my round of calls to my relatives–which my friend apparently thought wise to alert of my absence as soon as she woke up and didn't find me in my bed, nor answering my phone–to reassure them I'm safe and sound. She's munching on her digestive biscuits when I put my phone down and looks up at me with her best puppy eyes.

"I should have waited up for you, but I was *so* exhausted," she sighs, and I feel terrible for making her worry so much, but it's not like I could have prevented it. If only a certain someone had been more careful.

"Stop thinking about it, Phoebs. If there's anyone to blame it's Price." Phoebe suddenly turns quiet, and I shoot her a suspicious look.

"What is it, Nilsen? Breakfast is your most chatty meal of the day, isn't it?" I say, repeating one of the first things she'd ever told me when we met. "Spill it."

She shrugs, feigning innocence. "I just wonder if anything happened last night that you wanted to talk about. You know, roomie to roomie." She smiles sweetly, and I don't believe the act for a second. I snatch the biscuit she's about to dunk in her tea, which has her pout make an appearance.

"Nothing you need to concern yourself with, I assure you. I'm not that desperate, despite what you think," I joke as I break the biscuit in half.

It's true–there is no Universe in which he and I could be a thing, unless that thing was a detonator. Even if we'd become best buds when we first met, we're too similar. We want the same things, and that always leads to ugly feelings like jealousy and resentment. If it wasn't clear before, it is now, even though he apologised. Or he would have, if I'd let him. But either way, last night was the tipping point. Phoebe looks thoroughly unconvinced, of course.

"I know you're not *desperate*, don't paint me as a bad friend," she says, holding her hand out for one half of the biscuit, which I obediently place in her palm. "I'm just saying–if something did happen, I wouldn't be shocked. I certainly wouldn't frown upon it. I mean, I know you've got this whole nemesis thing going on, and I've only seen him from afar, but if his social media photos are unedited, even for all the …" she makes a vague gesture with her biscuit-free hand, "... *arseholeness*, he's still something to look at."

I snort and back out of my chair, starting to clear my mug and spoon from the small table, trying to avoid this conversation in the least obvious way possible. I have seen him up close, and I know for a fact he is much more than just something to look at.

Hell, I've *kissed* him multiple times. One would have to be oblivious or simply lying to themselves if they didn't find him attractive, with his stupidly long fingers and his soft, chestnut hair. Well, I assume it's soft, it's not like I've ever run my hand thr–

White-painted nails are prying the mug out of my hands and any thought about Theodore's hair texture is forcibly pushed out of my mind.

"Can I get a ticket?" Phoebe asks, her mouth twitching.

"A ticket?"

She snorts. "Yeah, babes, a ticket to wherever *you,*" she taps my forehead twice, "just went." She winks at me, and I can't bring myself to be annoyed at the ever-present implications in her words.

"Don't you have a meeting with your study group you're late to?" I muse, folding the top of the biscuit packet and securing it with a heart-shaped peg. Phoebe glances at her phone and launches herself towards the door, nearly tripping on her own bag in the process. "I do, but this conversation isn't over! Later babes!" she yells, and I'm left alone with many irritating questions I shouldn't be asking myself at all.

Chapter 9

Theodore

I couldn't care less. Truly. It doesn't bother me that Ethan offered Dafne his hand to help her stand after lunch–mostly because she looked at him like she thought he was on drugs–nor how he told her how good she looked in her red turtleneck. I'm sure she's aware of the fact, just like I'm sure she won't fall for cheap compliments. She probably won't even realise he's flirting with her, and when I win this bet I'll make Devon shove paper-Tom under his bed for good. Ethan's one of the many American students at APDAS, who came here for the school's renowned stage photography program; Devon hooked up with his brother once, that's how he had the brilliant idea of nudging him in Dafne's direction. He thought he'd be the perfect choice, because he's not exactly bright, and he wouldn't ask unwanted questions once Devon suggested he asked Dafne out.

He was right–he simply started talking to her. Not that any of it should matter at all, since the night in the prop room established once and for all Dafne and I are on completely different wavelengths.

I chug half my water down after a particularly intense workout in the school gym, where me and the other lads took the habit of going on Saturday mornings. Devon doesn't tag along often, just because he'd rather get those extra hours of sleep in, but by the time I was ready to leave this morning, so was he, and–conveniently, but not uncommonly–we met Ethan in the locker room.

"So you waited until our last few months here to try and date her?" David, one of my castmates, asks him, which regrettably catches my attention. I turn around as nonchalantly as possible, and see Ethan shrug.

"I mean, she's cool, isn't she?" he says, and my roommate gives me a pointed look. I notice Oliver by his locker, clearly interested in the conversation, but trying not to make it obvious. I glare at Devon, and gesture for him to come closer. When I'm positive the others are out of hearing range, I cross my arms over my chest. "What in the ever-loving fuck are you doing?" I whisper.

"I'm not telling anyone about the bet, that'd be cruel. But I figured if the opportunity arised for Ethan to actually tell people he's into Dafne, she might get word of it, and there won't be any suspicion," he explains, as if there was any logic to this whole plan.

"But he's *not*," I hiss.

"He fancies her enough," he beams. What is there to beam about?

"All I had to do was tell him she was single and that they had a lot in common."

I roll my eyes so hard I'm afraid they might get stuck in my head. What could Dafne possibly have in common with a guy that looks straight out of an energising drink commercial?

"You do know Oliver's right there and can hear everything you lot are saying?" I remind him. "He's basically a tower compared to you, so I'd be more careful what kind of things Ethan says about his intentions with Dafne when he's around." Devon turns slowly and looks Oliver over in what I'm sure he thinks is a subtle move, but is very clearly not.

"Ethan's saying nice things, isn't he?" he considers distractedly, "And it's good that her best friend is listening, the more witnesses the better. I should actually go talk to him directly, it'll make me win sooner." He winks, starting towards Oliver, and I barely have time to grab his arm and halt him.

"If anyone gets hurt, I'm going to be pissed, Dev." I try sounding as stern as Mr. Hackle when he critiques a performance in class, but some part of me knows it won't get through. Most importantly, whatever happens will be on me just as much as him for accepting the blasted bet in the first place. It's like I can hear my grandmother telling me not to make decisions in the heat of the moment, but it's too late to ignore the piece of advice.

Devon clicks his tongue and braces himself on my

shoulders. “You need to relax! When was the last time you checked your blood pressure?” He jokes, and I swat his hands away.

“Now if you’ll excuse me, I’ve got someone to charm.” He walks over to a shirtless Oliver who, despite the conversation about his best friend that was happening mere seconds ago, greets Devon with a casual smile. I thought he’d be pissed, but maybe he’s just being polite. Then again, I don’t know him at all.

I can’t help but think to myself how different, and much easier, things would have been if I’d been less proud. Less demanding of myself. Less everything. I huff out a breath and reach for my shirt on the nearest bench. When I’m ready to leave I say goodbye to my friends still lounging in the locker room, and shoot Devon and Oliver one last look, only to find out the latter is already looking at me while Devon is talking to him. I nod in his direction and he nods back; I notice one corner of his mouth going up, and I’m fairly sure it’s the first time in three years he’s ever looked anything less than tolerant at me. Not that I blame him–I wouldn’t be mates with someone who had the kind of relationship Dafne and I have if it were Devon in her place either. I need to stop overthinking this whole ridiculous situation, so I hurry out as I sling my gym bag over my shoulder. On the way out, I run into a girl from my History of Theatre class, who starts talking about how this year’s textbooks are heavier than the ones we previously used and how it’s affecting her posture. Not the most entertaining chat, but a wel--come distraction nonetheless. When we part ways, I walk straight to the nearest coffee shop, and while I'm in line my phone beeps from my backpack's side pocket. I take it out and see a message from my grandfather, asking me how to stop '*strangely excited e-mails about how I've won a million pounds*' from swamping his inbox. I smile, and before I can answer another notification glows on my phone screen, the reminder I've set telling me it's almost time to go make sure I know my lines better than I know my own name.

Chapter 10

Dafne

It is finally Friday afternoon, and even third year acting students get some time off, even though they're playing the main character in their final showcase. And they also have rehearsals first thing in the morning. I've been consciously delaying thinking about when all of this is going to end, though, to be honest. As excited as I am when I think of the day of the play, when casting directors from talent agencies are going to be there, taking notes on our every move and inflection, it will also mean time is up. If I imagine what life is going to be like when I don't have Phoebe and Ollie by my side every day … I'd just rather not. Thankfully, my phone buzzes and interrupts the intrusive thoughts. There's a message from an unknown number, but it doesn't take a master's degree in physics to realise who the sender is. Suddenly, intrusive thoughts don't sound like such a bad way to entertain myself with.

Come in an hour earlier tomorrow, so
we can work on Act Two.
Sent: 14:43 p.m.

Not a please or thank you in sight. As lovely as a drill on a cavity. I assume he's still mad over the other night, and although I'd realistically be pissed too in his place, I can't bring myself to brush over the curtness.

And by the way, how did he get my number? I ponder my answer for a minute, then I decide to go for sarcasm. That's at the core of all our interactions anyway.

Yes, Master. Your wish is my command.
If you wanted my number so badly,
you could have asked me rather than coerce one of
our castmates to hand it over.
Was it Isabel? Or Margaret? :)
Sent: 14:45 p.m.

How highly you must think of yourself.
I found it in the Group Chat.
Sent: 14:47 p.m.

...Of course. Enjoy your stay at Arsehole Town.
Population: Theodore Price.

After a sleepless night, mostly due to nightmares of me toppling down the balcony during opening night and slicing my forehead open or worse, like letting Theodore take all the glory, I make my way to the theatre, stifling a yawn as I push with a little too much force on the heavy stage door and let out a hiss when it doesn't budge. Yep, it's locked. Why not add a dislocated shoulder on top of only twenty minutes of sleep? I release a huff of the freezing February air, typing aggressively at Theodore to get his arse over here before I do something impulsive, like cut holes through his script as soon as I get my hands on it.

A thought strikes me then. What if he's pulled this elaborate joke by making me wake up at the crack of dawn just so he can shove it in my face that I came as soon as he called?

When a few minutes pass, and he's not replying to the damn texts, I remind myself I can't let him get to me any more than I already have. Never mind late-night, soft-spoken tales about his grandmother.

He wants to play? He'll have to find a different toy–

"You actually showed up," Theodore huffs as the stage door creaks open from the inside. "Pigs are going to start flying above us any second now," he considers, squinting his eyes as he pops his head out the door and looks up.

"Ever thought about doing stand-up instead of acting?" I ask, the utmost serious expression on my face, as he purses his lips unimpressed.

"Why weren't you answering your phone?" I shrug my coat off as he pulls the door closed behind me.

"I wasn't texting my side piece if that's why you're asking," he replies drily, and I try to ignore how the poor choice of words affects me. It's not like he could know. Without saying another word, I turn and walk towards the stage.

"We can use the balcony," Theodore says after I stretch and do some vocal warming, his eyes roaming over his script. "Mr. Hackle said it was fine." I give him a mock salute and head to the few stairs that lead to the small platform where the makeshift balcony has been built, even though this self-proclaimed Assistant Director vibe I'm getting from him is already annoying me beyond repair. Once in position, I secure my hair in a high ponytail and wince a little at how stiff my neck and shoulders feel. Theodore clears his throat and mumbles, "You alright?"

It's almost as if being nice to me brings him physical pain. Which I'm sure is true enough. I also hadn't realised he was watching me.

"Yeah, I've just been having trouble sleeping, is all. Let's just get on with this, we're wasting precious time," I say impatiently.

He simply nods and takes a few steps back to re-enter for the scene, and I do the same.

"*But soft! What light through yonder window breaks*?" he starts. I step on the small balcony and lightly place my hands on the styrofoam cornice when he adds,

"*It is the East, and Juliet is the sun!*"

I internally smile, because poison business aside, I get why Juliet would fall for this guy. He knew how to talk to *and* about a woman. He gets through his monologue, and listening to him like this is so pleasant, for a moment I let myself pretend he's actually a teenager who speaks in verse, rather than a bloke who enjoys the sound of his own voice too much.

"O Romeo, Romeo–wherefore art thou, Romeo? Deny thy father and refuse thy name. Or, if thou wilt not, be but sworn my love. And I'll no longer be a Capulet," I say as a stray thread from on my jumper's sleeve snags my attention and makes me wonder how that happened. Didn't I buy this barely a month ago?

I assume he's trying something new by not saying his next line back, but the silence stretches for too long, so I look down at him. He's staring at me with an unreadable expression, and my skin prickles with unease.

"What?" I snap, crossing my arms over my chest.

"You're not doing what you and Mr. Hackle agreed on," he says, a displeased edge to his voice that I don't like one bit. "How would you know what Mr. Hackle and I *agreed* on?" I huff, making my way down the steep staircase that leads back to the stage.

"You left your script next to mine the other day," he

explains once I'm standing in front of him.
"I read the new directions he gave you. You're supposed to think about something you really wanted, but never had when you say this line."

I bat my eyes rapidly at him. "Who gave you the right to read through my personal notes?" He's about to answer, but I'm not done. "And how on earth would you know what I'm thinking? Are you a mind reader now, too?" I know I'm losing my temper over something that might not be that big of a deal, but the fact that he would be so presumptuous to think he knows me–as an actor, or at all–rubs me the wrong way. He made sure he wouldn't get to know me, so that's on him and him only.

He looks at the ground with his hands on his hips, seemingly pondering his next words. Wise choice, because I'm running on far too little sleep, a tiny paper cup of watered-down coffee, and a good amount of slightly irrational anger.

"I want this performance to be perfect. I *need* it, us, to be perfect. Look, Dafne, I'm going to tell you something now, and you probably won't like it. I know–I know you can do more. So much more. All I ask is that you do it. All of it, no matter if we're rehearsing or if it's opening night. Don't hold back."
My shoulders sag, and my eyes roam all over his face, as if in doing so I could figure out whatever he meant by *that*–and for some reason, I can't bring myself to be mad anymore. I'd just never heard him be so …

honest. When he's not acting, that is; I always thought him nothing but irrevocably real on stage. The idea that each time he teased me or put up a fight could be any less than true had never crossed my mind before. But now? I'm not so sure. Which is the real Theodore? The one that acts like he owns the theatre and could singlehandedly take on the world, or the one that looks almost afraid that the result will be any less than outstanding? If the sorrow that laced his words means anything, is that he cares about this show going well more than I could imagine. The reason for that, though–besides the normalcy of wanting a play you've worked on for months to succeed–is rooted somewhere deeper, I think. I suddenly feel guilty.

The lights are unforgiving in their brightness, and now that I'm closer I notice the white speckles reflected in his eyes, honey brown amongst the green bursting from the pupil. His hair is, for the first time, slightly tousled, and for a split second I wonder what he looks like in the morning–guard down and all.

"I told you, I'm just tired, is all," I say simply.

"We can try again in a few minutes," he adds quietly. He's about to turn around, but I shake my head firmly. "No, I don't need a few minutes. I've got it." He searches my face and nods, but before he can walk back to his mark, I call his name. "I'm sorry, by the way. For what I said about you. I don't think you're a coward. And … I should have let you apologise. For the interview. I think you really were sorry."

He looks positively stunned and he blinks a few times, like I've told him he's just grown horns.

"Thank you," he says with a furrowed brow.

When he turns again I release a breath, slap myself lightly in the face, and jog up the staircase to the balcony. We repeat the scene, and this time I really think about it. Something I wanted but never had? I have something close enough. So close that I've been gingerly *avoiding* thinking about it, if you can believe that, and the fact that Theodore somehow figured that out is disturbing.

So I think of how Peter, Phoebe's boyfriend, kisses her hand in greeting, how it makes her giggle every time; how he never fails to support her dreams. How his thumb brushes over her knuckles whenever they're sitting together, a silent reminder that he's got her back, always.

That's something I want, or at least I used to. And I had it, for a while, until it got lost. I suppose that'll have to do.

Theodore

"I gave thee mine before thou didst request it," she says, a hand to her heart. *"And yet I would it were to give again."*

I take another small step back. "*Wouldst thou withdraw it? For what purpose, love?*" She smiles softly. I'm suddenly and uncomfortably really grateful for changing my monthly contact lenses this morning–I can see everything so clearly, even from afar. Provided, the balcony is really not that high, but still. She leans slightly on the parapet. *"Sweet Montague, be true. Stay but a little, I will come again."*

The scene continues, but this is as far as we worked on it during rehearsals. I'm trying really hard to ignore the part of my brain that wants to go on and see what we can do with it, but I refrain from voicing that; in hindsight, I've probably dashed out enough unsolicited advice for today, and I'd better not push my luck.

"That was good!" Dafne says.

"Yeah, better," I concede, because apparently I'm not mature enough to admit the past three times were *very* good and I thought she was great. Just like I knew she could be–and is, usually. I also cannot believe she apologised, nor that some part of me is relieved to know that's not what she really thinks of me.

"Do you want to go through the ball scene once? Just to

make sure we're still on track?" I ask.

She looks at me intently, and it seems she's having a conversation with herself, but eventually settles on a quiet, "Sure." She comes down from the stairs, and we settle into the familiar rhythm of Act One, Scene Five. Considering the number of times we've already kissed, it should be best known as the Thirty Kisses Scene. I must be low on sleep too, especially because it takes more than a few seconds to register she's skipped right to the lines that precede the actual kiss. I try not to show my surprise at how abrupt this is, and I go along with it; hell, I'm even pleased that she's taking the lead. She says her line. *"Then move not while my prayer's effect I take."* I reply. We gaze at each other for a moment, then she leans in that much more, bringing us dangerously close. Her left hand grips my elbow to bring me even closer. This is definitely *not* what we rehearsed before.

"What about you, Price? Are *you* holding back?" she says then, her voice unwavering, her gaze fierce, and I find myself completely, wholly, *unquestionably* turned on.

For fuck's sake.

I open my mouth to say something, *anything*–

The lights in the audience turn on, a door slams, and Dafne lets go of her hold on me so suddenly I would think it was all just a fever dream.

"Lookie, lookie," Devon shouts across the theatre, hopping down the velvet corridor that leads to the stage, immediately followed by Margaret, Jack, and other figures in the distance whose names I can't be bothered to remember right now. "I didn't know we were doing Method Acting," he beams, lifting himself on stage and winking in my direction. "Sneaking around just like a proper Romeo and Juliet," he nods approvingly. I make my way towards the proscenium and shake my head once at him in warning. When I look over at Dafne, her cheeks are pinker than they were before, but other than that looks like everything is perfectly fine. She reaches us and leans a hand on my friend's shoulder, uttering Devon's name in greeting before moving to his left, her hand lingering for a second longer than necessary. I cannot for the life of me see why it should bother me–but it does. Whether it's because I'm quite sure we were on the verge of making out or if it's just because centuries of patriarchal society have instilled in me some latent, awful to God possessive instincts, that remains to be seen. Possessive of what, exactly? I'd slap myself if I were alone. Now I need to decide whether I'm more bothered by that, by whatever the hell just happened, or the fact that I'm even bothered at all. My brain is really not a fun place to be sometimes.

I watch her retrieve her script from the proscenium where she'd left it, then place it over a trunk the others are trying to lift onto the stage as she picks one side of it up herself.

"Was that you hitting on Ethan's girl?" Devon jokes, and

a choking sound escapes me and I fake a cough to hide it.

"You refer to any girl as *Ethan's girl* ever again I will report you to the local authorities," I say, trying to keep my tone light.

"You could end your suffering by admitting defeat," he drawls, coming to stand casually next to me.

I know he's right; calling the bet off would be so easy and spare me unnecessary stress and confusion. If I had any amount of self-preservation, I would tell him he's right and we could just move on. Just because now that I've been close to her–quite literally–I keep thinking about the next time it'll happen, it doesn't mean I like her that way. Or at all, if the past three years are of any indication. I can find her attractive *and* intolerable–the two things aren't mutually exclusive–even now that we've shared unthinkable amounts of saliva. It doesn't mean I want to move in a studio flat with her and adopt a couple of Dalmatians. Devon eyes me like he can hear the monologue unraveling inside my head, his face breaking into a pitying smile. He starts toward Dafne to help with the trunk, whistling like he just won the lottery. I am miserably aware of how thoroughly unequipped I am to handle each part of this mess, and especially–her.

Chapter 11

Dafne

I tell Ollie I have a headache, which I do, and not to wait for me for lunch, because there's no chance in hell I'm telling him or Phoebe anything of what happened earlier–what I almost did, rather–until I sort it out with me, myself and I. Wrapping myself in my black wool coat and putting on sunglasses, I walk to my favorite tea shop down the street from APDAS. As I'm about to push the door open, someone shouts a *Yo Dafne* at my back.

Uh, well.

I turn around with my hand still on the handle, my eyebrows bunching when I notice a blond bloke looking left and right before crossing the street although not a single car is passing.

"Ethan, yeah?" I ask when he's closer, and I'm fairly sure he was the one who helped me set the projector up when I took my two-week intensive stage photography course for extra credits last year; it looked very expensive, and I didn't want to fry it inside out by pushing the wrong button.

"It me," he grins. "How's it going?" he rests one hand on his hip as the other pushes a lock of pale blond hair behind an ear. I should ask what conditioner he uses.

"I'm good," I smile, pushing my sunglasses on top of my head. I'm not about to dash my problems to a half-stranger. "Hope everything's fine for you too."

"Yeah, all is chill," he says, dragging out the word.

There's a beat of awkward silence, and I decide I'm just really hungry, so I say, "Well, I was about to…" I move my thumb towards the door.

"No, totally, I was just gonna ask if you wanted to grab a bite sometime."

I tilt my head, slightly confused. Is he asking me out?

"Alone?" I ask for clarification.

"Well, I think there might be other people if it's a place where they make food," he says pensively, as if he were actually weighing the possibility.

"Right," I drawl, my attention caught by someone huffing impatiently next to me because I'm blocking the entrance. Ever heard of speaking? Is anyone not passive-aggressive anymore?

As for the invitation, I'm not sure what to make of it, and as I move from the door I say, "Ethan I'm flattered, truly, but I'm not really looking for a relationship right now." Unless he randomly decided he wants a new friend, in which case I've just made a fool of myself by assuming anything.

"There's no harm in getting something to eat, right? I promise not to ask you to marry me," he grins.

I guess he's right. And when was the last time I socialised with someone who wasn't Ollie or Phoebe or one of my classmates?

"If you promise," I concede then with a smile, and when I ask if he wants to save my number, he tells me he already has it. Odd, because I don't remember giving it to him. He winks at me in goodbye, and I'm left to wonder whether I've just made a mistake.

Chapter 12

Dafne

We're meeting everyone in front of the Globe Theatre at five forty-five pm, so of course it's six and there's two people missing. Two people as in Theodore and Devon. Ollie nudges my shoulder with his and shoots me a *you okay?* look. I quickly nod. I've briefly mentioned to him about Ethan but didn't mention almost making out with Price because I all of a sudden felt this bloody stupid pull towards him–and Ollie looked surprised, if not a little skeptical. I *have* been saying I don't want or need a boyfriend for the longest time, but I reckon it wouldn't kill me to appreciate some unexpected attention. From … Ethan, that is.

Mr. Hackle eyes his watch, huffs impatiently, and gestures for us to follow him inside. Theodore and Devon have been here plenty of times, as have we all; I'm sure they'll manage to find their way to us. It hasn't been more than five minutes in line to get our tickets checked, when a voice shouts, "We're here!" It's Devon, being ob-

-noxiously loud. Ollie chuckles and I look at him in question. "Theodore just smacked Devon in the head," he smirks. The benefits of being as tall as my best friend is it's like getting front row seats to everything, not just plays. Never mind we don't have actual seats at the Globe since we always get the yard tickets. Not only they're much cheaper, but there's also nothing quite like being this close to the stage. It's well worth the two hours of standing.

"It's not like Price, being late," I consider, turning back towards the slowly advancing crowd.

"My guess is he got lost in his wardrobe–like Narnia, you know?" Ollie says, and I snort at the serious expression on his face. "Or he was busy making moon-eyes at that girl," he adds, looking straight ahead. Moon eyes?

"What girl?" The words are out before I can stop them. Ollie's expression is somewhere between amused and innocent.

"I saw him and some girl talking outside the gym. I'd never seen her before," he shrugs.

I lick my lips, thinking of something that will translate as casual and disinterested to say. It's ridiculous, because Ollie doesn't even know about this morning, but still, I come up with the next best thing. "There must be something profoundly wrong with the lot of you if you're going to the gym on Saturday mornings. New girl included."

Way to sound disinterested, girl. I suddenly find my

ankle-cut boots very intriguing.
"Dafne," Ollie says, turning to face me fully, "Do I detect *jealousy*?" he presses his pointer fingers to his temples in mock imitation of a fortune teller.

"Ha!" I laugh, my voice sounding more pitched than intended. "The only time I've ever been jealous is when you asked Susan Porter to the school dance instead of me." Ollie rolls his eyes.

"You had the stomach flu, was I supposed to miss the very rare chance for free booze?" I ignore that and take another step forward; it's almost our turn before we can get in. The ticket lady is Ginny, who knows me and Ollie by name by now; this must be out thirtieth-something time here in the past three years. She greets us warmly and tells us to enjoy the show. We thank her and make our way behind Mr. Hackle and Ms. Patterson, who are quietly chatting amongst themselves. Like there are not dozens of people squishing them from left and right. Isn't that something?

"Either way," Ollie unexpectedly resumes, "I wasn't familiar with this jealous *and* delusional side of you, Daf," and I slowly cock my head to face him.

"I couldn't possibly know what you're talking about, Oliver," I say, a sickly-sweet smile on my lips. I am not falling for his bait. He shakes his head lightly, and when he speaks again, his tone is devoid of all previous sarcasm. "It's not a big deal, you know," he considers, "if it bothers you to think of Price dating someone. He is *your*

Romeo, after all."
I huff a humourless laugh.

"Ollie, he is *my* nothing–" I'm interrupted by someone tapping my shoulder. "Who's nothing?" Devon asks with a lazy smile, one eyebrow raised. I press my lips tightly together, and wave my hand dismissively. "No one," I make a half-laugh, half-choking sound. "No one is ... nothing." Ollie clears his throat to my right, and I elbow him in the ribs while looking straight ahead. To Devon's left, Theodore is looking intently over at the play about to start, not bothered in the slightest by whatever's happening right next to him.

Once the play is over, we wait for most of the audience to start leaving before we do the same, and I send one last longing glance at the stage. If you asked me what one thing I'd want engraved in my mind forever, it's this. A stage after a play, seemingly the same, but inevitably transformed. The lingering music, the thundering applause, the final bow. Those are the only butterflies I should crave.

As we walk, Ollie steps at Devon's side with Theodore. "Sounds like there's going to be a storm tonight," Ollie says, nudging Devon's arm, who doesn't seem particularly shocked by the gesture.

I shoot my friend a questioning look, taken aback that he's actually touching someone who isn't me or

Phoebe, and keep a tight smile plastered on my face. I notice Theodore's eyes are glued in front of him. It's almost like he doesn't know us and just happens to be walking by.

Guess he didn't enjoy my little stunt at rehearsal. This is not going to be embarrassing at all moving forward, huh?

There's quite the crowd as we make our way out, and the passage is narrow enough that Ollie and Devon need to pass as a pair. Theodore's friend clasps Ollie's elbow gently so that they stand closer.

Suddenly, I find my right shoulder pressed to Theodore's. He finally looks at me, and I'm really starting to think he didn't realise I was there at all, because he looks at our joined shoulders like there's a third head sprouting where the fabric of our coats meet. It all happens in a matter of seconds, but I can tell–he doesn't like this. Doesn't like this proximity, however brief, because he's already forced to spend an upsetting amount of time with me. Not to mention the little number I pulled this morning when I had clearly been possessed by horny Dafne. The more I think about it, the more I want to shove my face in the sand like a flamingo and never come back up. Ollie and Devon chatting like long-standing friends isn't helping, either. I'd be willing to bet Price is a Leo–always striving to be the one in control. His natal chart must be an astrologist's nightmare.

For his sake as much as mine, I dive to the left as

soon as there's enough space for me to make my way through, and we're finally reunited with the rest of our group. The air smells heavily of rain, and everyone is already extracting their small umbrellas from their bags, me included. You can't in good conscience call yourself a Londoner if you're not carrying one with you at all times, rain or shine. "Alright, everyone," Mr. Hackle says, struggling to open the biggest tartan umbrella I've ever seen. "We'll discuss on Monday. I want you to think long and hard about what you saw, take notes if you must, but I expect you to have learned something useful tonight." Ms. Patterson is rummaging through her leather purse for her umbrella, nodding enthusiastically, as she always does. "We'll see you bright and sharp next week, then! Please do not forget you are required to attend Mr. Boyus' seminar after rehearsal on Monday." The reminder elicits more than a few grumbles among the group. Attending a seminar about the history of Spanish Theatre in the 18th century after an exhausting day of class and rehearsal should be fun *indeed.*

As Mr. Hackle and her turn and leave, the rain makes itself known with fat drops, and we all start towards the train station to get back to the school, Theodore's pace slightly faster than everyone else's.

Theodore

For the whole albeit short time we spend on the train, Devon incessantly babbles to Oliver. That leaves me to do small talk with David, who is raving about some action movie I truly could not be less interested in. Dafne sits across from me, and not once does she raise her eyes to mine. So this morning we were about to make out and now we're back to ignoring each other's existence? I'm just trying to wrap my head around it. She probably just wanted to intimidate me. The speaker calls our stop, and we start storming out of the train, the rain unrelenting. Once we jog up the stairs and out of the station, barely a few seconds pass before a car speeding way too close to the pavement all but soaks in puddle water Dafne's white corduroy pants up to the knees, along with most of her coat. "Bloody hell," she groans, her tiny umbrella long forgotten on the ground next to her in favour of furiously rummaging through her tote bag, I assume for anything that could dry the mess up. Her dark hair is plastering itself on her face, and my legs are moving before I can put too much thought into it. I lead her by the elbow under the nearest portico before the next passing car drowns her completely. She looks at me dumbfounded, and I raise an eyebrow. "Where's Ollie?" she asks then, going back to her task.

"You're very welcome," I reply dryly, closing my umbrella.

"I don't know where Oliver is, he was behind me with Devon and–" I'm interrupted by my phone's vibration in my jeans' back pocket. "Seriously?" I say under my breath as I read the incoming message, and Dafne rises on her toes to look over my shoulder at the lit-up screen.

> I'm walking back with Ollie,
> he was telling me the most
> interesting story and I couldn't wait
> to hear the rest of it!
> He says to tell Dafne he's sorry and to remember
> the countless favors he's done her
> throughout their lives :D
> *Sent: 20:43 p.m.*

"I'm going to put a spider in his bed," Dafne declares, more to herself than to me. She tiptoes to retrieve her now half-broken pale pink umbrella, holding it by the handle and muttering a string of interesting curses as she gets back under the porch.

"So unladylike of you," I muse, hoping to break the tension, but possibly making it worse.

"Never said I was a lady," she sighs. We're quiet for a minute, standing next to each other but not doing much else to acknowledge the other's presence–except I'm all too aware of hers. Without warning, Dafne starts walking into the pouring rain again, clutching the handles of her tote bag for dear life.

"What are you doing?" I yell over the cacophony of cars bustling the streets at this time of the evening.

"What does it look like I'm doing, Price? Going home," she says over her shoulder. I should let her go, since it looks like asking me to share an umbrella didn't even cross her mind–but if it's even just to prove that I'm completely unaffected by what happened this morning, I won't. I close the short distance she's walked on her own and place my umbrella higher over both of our heads. She glares at me, but before she can tell me to piss off, I raise my free hand. "You're already likely to catch a cold as it is," I say, pointedly looking at her soaked clothes, "and we can't afford to skip any rehearsals because of your pride."

She scoffs, but at least it looks like she's not about to use my umbrella as a weapon against me.

"And here I was, thinking you were being decent just for the sake of it," she eventually retorts, her hands rubbing her shoulders to get warm.

"I am always decent," and I'm not sure if I'm saying that to convince myself or Dafne. After a few minutes of walking in silence, she flinches, an involuntary response to the sharp cold. We've still got a ten-minute walk before we get to the dormitories, so I think I need to figure something out, since the rain doesn't seem likely to stop pouring anytime soon. It seems we're in luck, as I can see the dimly lit neon sign of an all-nighter coffee shop about fourty feet from us. "Come on, I'd rather you didn't freeze over and have to explain to your roommate why I'm leaving a Dafne-sized ice cube on the doorstep," I say as I redirect her towards the red lacquered door.

She stops a few feet from the door, her gaze falling to the hand I'm still holding onto her forearm. I hastily remove it.

"What's your endgame? You need something from me, is that it?" she asks then, her eyes boring back into mine, suspicion and bitter cold scrunching her features. I'm sure I look as appalled as I feel.

"My *endgame,*" I start, turning her around and lightly pushing her forward, "is that you get a fill of something hot and stop being so difficult."

Oh God. That was a poor choice of words.

Chapter 13

Dafne

Theodore gestures for us to sit at the booth closest to the door, which makes me wonder if it's a strategic position for escape should the necessity arise. Which is silly, because he's the one who practically forced me in here in the first place. Both of us take off our damp coats; he folds his own neatly next to him, fixing the collar, and I unceremoniously roll mine up and abandon it somewhere at my right. Two kinds of people, I guess.

"I don't suppose you have a change of clothes in that bag of yours?" he asks, making one of the two menus on the table slide across to me and unfolding the other.

"I do not," I reply, my eye immediately falling on the hot chocolate section on the front page. "How foolish of me not to think about the possibility of someone mistaking me for a house fire." He looks over at me, eyes bright with hesitant humour, and I try my best not to share the sentiment. Although I suppose it is sort of funny, in a way. I take some of the napkins from the napkin holder placed at the centre of the table, and try drying the top of my thighs, rather unsuccessfully. It's like London rain is thicker than rain anywhere else. I eventually give up, and turn my attention to Theodore, who is going through his menu like he's trying to decipher a coded message.

A waitress approaches us without taking her eyes off her notebook. "What can I get you?" she seems bored out of her mind, which I find quite amusing, until she finally looks up and takes Theodore in. I hadn't paid attention before, distracted by the whole I-am-freezing-business, but he's wearing a forest green polo neck sweater that hugs his arms very … nicely. I instantly remember Phoebe and I making fun of him for saying green made his eyes pop and, well, I'm taking it back. He was *right*.

The waitress–Madeleine, her tag says–seems to be having my same exact thoughts, which is why I feel the completely irrational urge to redirect her attention elsewhere. I open my mouth to order, but Theodore speaks before I can. "She'll have the coconut hot chocolate, and I'll have the–" he throws another glance at the menu, "cinnamon one. Thank you," he says, a polite smile gracing his lips, and I can tell my eyes are wide in genuine shock. There is more than one thing to be shocked about, really. His knowledge of my hot chocolate order, the fact he's a cinnamon kind of guy, or that he's never been this nice to me and I have good reason to believe he's fallen and hit his head *hard.* He could have left me in the rain, or could have told me to get on a bus, but decided to walk with me and make sure I wouldn't die of hypother-

mia.
Alright, that might be a tad dramatic, but the point still stands. I see Madeleine smile pleasantly at him from the corner of my eye.

"Coming right up," she says with an unnecessary amount of eye batting, and turns slowly towards the kitchens, gaze lingering on Theodore for a second long enough to get on my nerves. It is absolutely preposterous of me, but here we bloody are. Theodore clears his throat, and when his gaze lands on me again, I blink and scratch a spot under my jaw in a poor attempt at concealing the mix of wonder and unease I feel.

"All good?" he nods in my direction.

I don't fail to notice it's the second time he's asked me that in one day, after years of barely civil conversation.

"Yeah," I start, both adamant about showing myself unaffected by what happened, and ever too curious for my own good. "How do you know what my favorite hot chocolate is?" I ask, tucking my damp hair behind both ears. He clicks his tongue, and the realisation that it's not something he should know off the top of his head seems to dawn on him as he presses his lips together.

"You must have mentioned it out loud once," he says after a beat, passing a hand through his hair. "I have terrific memory." I know he probably means it, but there's also a playfulness is his tone I think I'd like to hear more. I snort and nod knowingly, mouthing a *right,* which draws a small smile out of him. It's like being in this other Theodore's company, the same one that shared his food with me and spoke of his grandmother with heartfelt admiration. I wonder if he's playing at it for the sake of circumstance, and if not, how exhausting it must be to hide this part of himself most of the time.

This is so strange. Phoebe is going to lose her head over it. So is Ollie–if he survives my wrath, that is. What could have possibly been so important that he couldn't even let me know he was going ahead? My thoughts are interrupted by the clink of the mug placed in front of me, the sweet scent of coconut filling my nostrils and the promise of chocolate goodness about to fill my stomach and warm me up making me instantly happier.

"Enjoy," Madeleine says to Theodore alone with a wink, and I can't stop an unimpressed eyebrow from raising. I'm fairly sure that winking as a form of flirting is something best suited to nineties rom-com films. After she's left, Theodore huffs a breath, and I look up to find him holding up a tiny piece of paper.

"Seems like you've made quite the impression," I say, cupping my mug with both hands as my shoulders sag in relief at the warmth.

"She's got the wrong impression, then," he replies, folding the scrap of paper with Madeleine's number on it and making sure she's not around before tossing it in the little trash bin behind his loveseat. I internally cringe at myself for the satisfaction I get out of that and proceed to take my first sip. A "She's really pretty," leaves my traitorous mouth then, and if someone handed me a bat right now, I would gladly hit myself with it. According to Ollie, he'd been chatting amiably with some girl earlier today, so he might already have his eye on someone else. *Good for him.* And what do I care?

Theodore stirs his chocolate with the tiny spoon placed on his saucer, entranced with the flurry of the hot liquid swirling in his light blue mug.

"Perhaps." It looks like he's not going to elaborate on that. Which is fine. I take another sip and can't stop the little moan that escapes me. Theodore looks at me like I've just pulled up my sweater and flashed the entire coffee shop my bra.

"What? It's *so* good," I drawl, licking my lips, and I notice Theodore tracking the movement with his eyes.

"What was that, Dafne?" he asks then, a serious expression suddenly hardening his features.

"Oh, for heaven's sake," I start, lowering my mug, "I was just showing appreciation for the–" He waves a hand. "I'm not talking about *that,*" a tinge of annoyance in his voice as well as something I can't quite put a finger on. "I'm talking about this morning. At rehearsal."

Only now do I realise that the real reason for bringing me here was so he could corner me. Well played, Price.

"What about rehearsal?" I ask with as much innocence I can possibly muster, uselessly trying to delay my fate.

"Are you going to make me spell it out?"

I lean back into my seat.

"What do you think it was, Theodore?" I play the nonchalant card.

"I don't bloody know, *Dafne*. I wouldn't be embarrassing myself by asking if I did, now, would I?"

"I suppose you wouldn't."

He closes his eyes. "You're really going to pretend nothing happened, aren't you?"

A corner of my mouth lifts–I was dreading the possibility of this conversation, but now that it's actually happening, I'm thoroughly enjoying how distressed he is over it. Am I a terrible person or just seeking revenge for every time he's said something nasty about me?

"Look," I concede, because I'm not completely heartless, "I guess part of me wanted to get back at you for mansplaining my own directions to me, by sending you into a shock." Theodore opens his eyes, looks down at his mug, his long fingers drumming against the pale ceramic the only sound I can focus on for a whole minute.

"And the other part?" he adds after what seems like a small eternity.

The smugness I felt bubbling up dissipates abruptly at the question. He looks at me like someone waiting to hear their sentence in appeal court, and just like that, the feeling I had this morning resurfaces. I recall the way he said he needed us to be perfect, and my stomach flutters in a way I hoped was dead and buried.

Maybe it's just the chocolate.

I shrug and open my mouth, but no good explanation comes out.

He takes a long sip of his beverage then, looking somewhat defeated, and out of all the things I could be raking my mind over, I can think of nothing except of how I'd like to taste cinnamon hot chocolate.

Preferably his.

Right from his mouth.

Bloody fucking hell.

Theodore

We finish our drinks in silence, and when she assures me she's warmed up enough, I head straight for the register to pay.

"No, no, no, I will not have debts with you, Price," she says, stepping in front of me and snatching the brown leather wallet from my hand and shoving it in her bag. She jogs to the register, pays, and walks back to me, the wallet reappearing in a matter of seconds.

"How is it fair that now *I'm* in your debt then?" I ask as I take it back, careful not to brush my fingers against hers.

"Haven't you heard? Life isn't fair," she says, wrapping

her red scarf around her neck with a dramatic flare. She smirks then, or at least attempts to, the almost-conversation we had barely fifteen minutes ago lingering in the space between us. She readjusts the handles of her bag on her shoulder and makes a gesture that means *after you.* I hadn't even noticed, but it's finally stopped raining, which is both a blessing and a curse; the rain would have provided an excuse to rush and get no talking done, the lack of it makes for the perfect setting to pick up where we left off. Not that she seemed eager to have that conversation in the first place. I don't know why it's so important to me that we talk this through–maybe it's because I don't want there to be things left unsaid nor distractions as opening night approaches. Or maybe I'm just an insufferable idiot. It's a tough call.

"You're not going to use any of this against me, are you?" Dafne asks, her broken umbrella dangling from her fingers. I look at her, and she's not looking back.

"I didn't take a video of the waterworks, so no," I reply, and she wipes her forehead with the back of her hand in mock relief.

"It's going to be so weird, not being here next year," she changes the subject a beat later, something akin to sadness seeping through her words. "I can't even think of moving out of my room."

Cardboard Tom suddenly pops up in my mind, and I snort. "I didn't think my despair was so entertaining," she considers, only this time the words are void of any trace of melancholy.

"I was just thinking I will not miss *my* room much," I chuckle, "Devon is terrible at interior design."
Dafne makes a noncommittal noise and asks, "Speaking of which, what's gotten into him?"

My grandmother always tells me I don't know when to be quiet for my own good–and was she ever right. Why did I bring Devon up? "I've no clue what you're referring to," I say, hoping I sound more relaxed than I feel. There's an uneasy tingling sensation in my back, but I try ignoring it. "He's always been over the top, it's part of his charm." I shove my hands into my coat's pockets to keep myself from fidgeting.

"All of a sudden he spends time with Ollie despite having known him for just as long as you," she adds. I've been wondering the same but had honestly forgotten all about it before the past hour we've spent together, and I just can't seem to focus on what she's talking about.

I try recalling the reasons for finding myself here, with her, which seemed perfectly plausible. But all I come with up is the incessant babbling in my head that centers on a song called '*I Have No Kind of Feelings for the Girl Walking Next to Me*'. Snippets of our constant bickering over the past two and a half years echo in my mind then, and I am painfully reminded of why any of this happened in the first place. Why I allowed my fears to turn into this ugly thing that doesn't belong to who I am–and I now suspect, neither to who she is.

I quicken my pace and heave a sigh of relief when we round the street corner and APDAS' gates finally appear before us. Our rooms are in the same building, which means we will have to walk upstairs together.

That's never happened once before tonight, but then again neither did us having a hot chocolate for dinner together like two old chums.

I'm on the second story, while Dafne's room is on the third. I know that because I've heard Oliver complain about having to walk three flights of stairs several times to give her back a script she left around somewhere.

When we reach my landing, she thanks me, offering a small smile. "You didn't have to do any of that, but I appreciate it," she says as she feels the bottom of her bag to identify where her keys are.

"Romeo and Juliet should have had the chance to get hot chocolate before dying horrible deaths," is the only coherent phrase I manage. She huffs out a laugh as she finds her keys.

"See you tomorrow, then." She turns to leave, and so do I. I'm one step away from inserting my own key in the lock when her voice stops me in my tracks.

"The other part," she starts, and I turn around slowly, her body half to me, her left hand gripping the banister.

"Was wondering what it would be like if we *let go*. Just once."

She disappears up the stairs, and I'm left with the sound of her leaving after dropping that bomb on me.

Chapter 14

Theodore

"Devon, it's me," I shout over the sound of the shower water running, "and I'm going to kill you," I add quietly. I can't say for sure whether this whole thing was a ploy to force me and Dafne to spend time together–after all, there were too many variables, no guarantee it would actually happen. Devon has, however, watched *The Parent Trap* an unhealthy amount of times, so I wouldn't put it past him. I gulp some water from the canteen on my nightstand, drop on my bed, close my eyes, and hope today's events will soon fade into a dusty compartment of my memory, knowing damn well it's not likely to happen.

I really do have a great memory. It's quite useful when learning lines, much more annoying when you're unable to forget a pair of impossibly long lashes. "Theeeeo, my man," Devon singsongs from behind the bathroom door. "I'm going to be awhile but get ready to spill all the delicious tea!" he thrills, steam seeping from under the door. I walk to said door and lean back.

"I don't understand why this is so important to you," I say, both depletion and an odd feeling of hesitant gladness settling within me. I don't let myself think the latter is because of tonight. That's dangerous territory.

"I mean besides the fact that you'll launch yourself off a mountain top before giving in in any capacity," I add after a beat, shaking my head.

"Like you're not the exact same," he replies, and I hear the squeak of the handle turning the water off.

"This could be good for you, mate. *She* could be good for you, whether you see it or not." The water starts running again, and I take that as a suggestion to think about it. And despite myself, I do. I think.

What if, and it's a big if, in the midst of this madness, he's actually right? About the fact that it could be good, somehow. Ignoring this … whatever is going on between us? It feels stupid.

I'd like to think I'm not a complete idiot, most of the time. There's a tension, of sorts, that wasn't there before. Or maybe it was there all along and only now that we've been forced to spend time together on stage–and off, if my best friend has a say in it–is it finally making itself heard.

You know that voice that tells you not to do something because it'll come biting you back in the arse? Mine is either dead or in hibernation.

I grab my keys and start towards the door.

Dafne

If you looked up the definition of *impulsive fool,* you'd probably find a picture of me smiling from ear to ear. Today has been the most bizarre series of events in twenty-one years of walking the earth, next to that day I took a swig of iced tea straight from the fridge, and for a solid five minutes was sure I would pass away on my grandparents' kitchen floor out of thermal shock.

I could lie and say I wouldn't be able to explain what was going through my head when I challenged him with that question this morning just so I could–what? Get a reaction out of him that wasn't one of contempt? I have never cared for his attention, and there are probably not enough good reasons why I should start now.

But I do know. Does it have to do with admittedly perfect hair texture and arm veins? Of course. But also, and most importantly, with how for the first time since I've known him, he's looked me in the eyes without that impenetrable wall of his. I don't know why that affected me so much, but it bloody did.

The fact of the matter is, these glimpses of humanity and warmth I've been getting of him don't magically change how we've been at each other's throats for this long, nor the fact that he's probably got a small army of women already hanging off his words and I refuse to become part of the ranks. I meant what I told him when we were stuck in the prop room–that I wanted to know whether it'd all been for nothing. And maybe it's wishful thinking, but I'd rather we proved we were better than a petty rivalry. I genuinely feel that my brain is at full capacity today, and something will have to get kicked out of it eventually.

Phoebe isn't back yet, so I take my formerly white pants and the rest of my clothes off, and fling myself into the shower, hoping the steaming water will help with the painful knots in my shoulders and scatter my thoughts. Unsurprisingly, only the first comes true. I wrap myself in my softest bath towel, put my wet hair up in a bun, and pad towards the bed to retrieve my phone. There's a missed call from Ollie, a message from Phoebe–letting me know she'll be back in fourty minutes tops and to pretty please wait for her to watch the *Great British Bake Off*–, and one from my mum, who's sent me a blurry photo of what I assume is a new set of hair curlers. My priority seems obvious right now.

I scroll to Ollie's chat and press call. Not a whole ring goes by before his voice picks up, clear and bright. "Daaaafne," he drawls, and I interrupt him immediately. "Do not *Dafne* me," I purposefully draw out. "Care to tell me why you left with Devon without even letting me know?"

Ollie makes a *hmmm* sound on the other side of the line. "What if I told you that you don't need details?" he asks, and we both know that's a rhetorical question because I won't settle for anything less than details.

"Alright, listen, I got caught up in the moment," he starts again at the impatient sound I make in lieu of an answer, "but why don't you look at the silver lining?

I scoff, holding my bath towel in place around my chest as I put on clean knickers.

"Which is?"

"Maybe spending time outside of rehearsals with Price could prove to be a good thing in the end. For the play, of course." Of course my sweet arse.

"What happened to *he was born an arsehole and he'll die as one*? Those were your exact words, and at the Globe you brought up that *it's okay if you don't want him to date other people* nonsense, I mean, where is all this coming from?" I get up from the bed, and crouch to retrieve my pajamas from the pink wicker basket I keep under the nightstand, holding the phone in place between my ear and shoulder. Where the hell are they?

"I know what I said but … sometimes people de--serve second chances, right?" he says quietly, and my brows pinch together at the sudden seriousness in his tone.

"Ollie, is there something else you're not telling me? Are you okay?" I ask as I unknot the towel and shift my gaze around the room to look for at least the top part of my pajamas. Before I can insist he tell me what's wrong, I hear a shuffling sound from outside the door, and I freeze.

I tiptoe towards it and press my ear just below the *Something witty this way comes* banner I won at least year's monologue competition we did in class. It sounds like someone is walking back and forth just outside the room, but I don't hear any voices.

I am naked and someone is about to break in and murder me–is this how I'm going out? That'll make quite the story in my hometown.

"Ollie," I whisper, clutching the top of the towel so that it covers my breasts, as if that would provide any protection from an actual murderer breaking in. "I think there's someone outside my door who isn't supposed to be there." He snorts, all traces of weariness seemingly gone. "It's probably Phoebe turning her bag inside out looking for her keys."

"She would be knocking," I hiss. "Alright, screw it, I'm opening the door," I decide then, because at least they won't call me a coward in my eulogy. I let go of my towel and grab my vintage Fleetwood Mac shirt I've left crumpled on top of the bed, which I hastily put on.

"If I die you can have my Dame Judi DVD collection," I whisper in the phone, clutched so tightly it might just break.

"No one uses DVDs anym–" I place the phone on the nearest shelf, grab the first potentially blunt object I can find, and I take a deep breath before wrenching the door open.

Chapter 15

Theodore

Dafne opens the door abruptly as I'm pacing just before her–or her roommate's, I assume–Broadway-themed doormat and … bollocks. This has to be a joke.
She's wearing a 1968 UK Tour's Fleetwood Mac shirt. And … little else.

Her deep walnut hair is up, and she is clutching what looks like a plastic Academy Award in her raised hand.

"Oh my *God,*" she starts, lowering her arm, her shoulders slumping. "You scared the hell out of me!" Her big brown eyes wide in distress.

"I'm, uh…" I try, but it comes out hoarse, and she raises an eyebrow, surely unimpressed with my poor use of proper syntax.

"You're sorry?" she offers, throwing the fake award on the bed beside her without looking whether it actually lands there. I nod, my mouth parts, and I must look like a dignified fish. Enough, Theo.
"Price," she says, having calmed down just enough, "if

you're here because of what I said earlier–" she doesn't finish, because I've said to hell with second-guessing. I step into her space and kiss her full on the mouth.
It is bloody glorious.

Dafne

Theodore Price's tongue is stroking mine. Good Lord *above*–he's never kissed me like this before. *Why* hasn't he done this before? Why am I liking it so much? There are too many questions and apparently not enough oxygen is reaching my brain for me to focus, so I'm going to leave those for later. All I know in this moment is this kiss feels absolutely incredible and I never want it to end. I let out a soft moan as his lips press against mine again, and that seems to drive him harder against me. I'm not quite sure what my hands are doing but I desperately want him closer. More. I can taste the faintest hint of the cinnamon chocolate he had earlier, and it's just as delicious as I thought. An unclear amount of time passes, and we detach with a soft pop that does nothing to placate the heat pooling in my belly.
"You should probably get dressed," he breathes after a quiet moment, his lips hovering a scarce inch from my

nose.
"Are you wasted?" I ask, barely audible, because I can't find another reason for him to be doing what he just did if that's not the case. His eyebrows rise so quickly they look like small boomerangs.

"No. No, I'm definitely not wasted. Are you?"

I shake my head vehemently, stray drops of water trickling down my nape.

"Good," he adds, rooted in place, the hands that were cradling my face barely a minute ago now resting on my arms. Some part of my brain is aware of being nearly naked standing inches from Theodore in a hallway where anyone could see us. The other part of my brain is unsuccessfully trying to figure out whether I'm dreaming. Or dead.

Come on, Dafne. *Say something smart.*

"This doesn't mean anything, right?"

"I thought you wanted me to let go," he murmurs. "That was me letting go."

I'm about to point out he didn't answer the question, when I'm reached by a familiar humming from the stairs.

"It's my roommate," I push him lightly and he stumbles, caught off guard, but catches himself just in time. "Act natural." I beg him, reaching for the still damp coat I'd hung on the hook closest to the door and hastily putting it on. Why didn't I wear this before opening the door in the first place?
I stand by what I said–impulsive fool. I force my mouth

to curve in a smile as Phoebe hops up the last step only a few feet from us. A teal paper bag is dangling from her left wrist, one I immediately recognise as belonging to our favorite tea shop. Her happy humming abruptly breaks off as she takes us in, her free hand rising to remove one earbud from her ear.

"I didn't know we were expecting a guest, *Daf,*" she chirps, sheer intrigue so thick in her voice I just might pretend to faint to spare me whatever she'll say next.

"I don't believe we've met before," she adds to Theodore as she reaches us. She cuts me a look then, only to notice my hair is wet, I'm barefoot, and wearing a coat.

A lunatic, basically.

He glances at me, then holds out his hand for her to shake. She takes it, her mouth twitching.

"I'm Theodore, I am Dafne's–"

"Theodore plays Romeo, Phoebs," I interject before he can say something we both might potentially regret.

Phoebe smiles widely as she removes her hand from Theodore's grasp and nods knowingly.

"Mr. Hackle asked me to tell Dafne about a … change, in a scene," he explains then, and my eyes flutter closed in silent exasperation. He has no idea who he's talking to, and it shows. Phoebe's bullshite meter must be singing *We Are the Champions* right now.

"*Right.*" She nods once, her lips curving inward to repress the laugh I know is rising like a tidal surge within her. I won't live any part of the past three minutes down until I drop dead.

"Well, thank you, Price," I say, snatching Phoebe's arm and pulling her over the threshold. "I'll see you around."

He opens his mouth, but I slam the door in his face.

I start peeling my coat off as slowly as possible–knowing damn well I am buying myself mere seconds. When I turn around, Phoebe's arms are crossed over her chest and she's looking at me like she's bloody Poirot and I'm the murderer in the interrogation room.

"You are *so* full of shite!" she yells, and I step forward to slap a hand on her mouth.

"Be louder, do you mind?" I hiss before releasing her.

"I knew it–I *knew* there was something going on," she resumes, her blond curls swinging wildly along with her head. "Were you going to tell your best girlfriend, or did you expect me to find out in five years from some gossip magazine?"

I cringe, and if only to stop myself from fidgeting–or having a breakdown, who knows these days–I plop onto the edge of the bed and untie my still-damp hair.

"It wasn't … whatever you think you saw–" I start, and Phoebe braces herself on my knees.

"Dafne Wright. Look me in the eyes and tell me you weren't making out with Theodore Price on top of my embroidered doormat. Go on," she smiles sweetly, "lie to my face."

I groan and bury my face in my hands.

"I need to be wearing more clothes for this conversation. I will also require the strongest tea you have," I mumble through the gaps between my fingers. Phoebe makes a satisfied noise and pats my right knee.
"One *steaming* cuppa tea coming right up."

Chapter 16

Theodore

It's the day after one of the potentially worst ideas I've ever had, and at rehearsal neither of us so much as hints at what happened the night before; whether it's because we're determined to pretend it never actually happened or are waiting for an appropriate moment, I don't know. Thankfully, Mr. Hackle wants to focus on Act Three this week, which means no kissing. That's great–*splendid* in fact. Perhaps this pause from physical contact will make both of us realise how utterly ridiculous the whole thing was. Mostly me.

We're actors. Not bloody trapeze artists. We don't need to *let go* off-stage. Never mind that I felt so sure it was the right thing to do. Or that I don't remember giving–or receiving–a better kiss than last night's. I will not think about it if I can help it. I haven't told Devon what happened, for obvious reasons. Not only he'd never let it go, but he'd call the bet off and proclaim himself the winner, probably by hanging a banner on our door that says something way too literal, like: *Theodore Price likes Dafne Wright. I was right, thank you for believing in me.* I can picture it with striking detail.

"Alright lads," Mr. Hackle says, rubbing his chin as he eyes his script. "Let's go through the duel one more time and then you can go off doing whatever twenty-year-olds do instead of studying your part." Each time we've rehearsed the duel–which Ms. Walker choreographed and later recorded us in action, so we could learn it to perfection by watching it over and over again–I've had the distinct impression Oliver is scrutinising me, as if by piercing me with a stage weapon he could make me spill all my secrets instead of my guts. When I asked Devon what he and Oliver had actually talked about last night on the train or when they'd both left me and Dafne after the play, he'd simply said chatting with him was fun, and the perfect excuse to nudge Dafne in Ethan's direction through them both. Then Devon told me Ethan had officially asked Dafne out–and she said yes. Which is fine, I guess. It happened before I showed up outside her dorm room like a madman, and not only I doubt that changes anything, but we wouldn't be each other's property anyway. If we were–

"*Boy, this shall not excuse the injuries that thou hast done to me,*" Devon booms as he approaches me, "*there fore turn and draw.*" I shake my head free of my stupid thoughts and raise one hand in a placating gesture, stepping to my first mark.

"*I do protest I never injured thee, but love thee better than thou canst devise, till thou shalt know the reason of my love. And so, good Capulet, which name I tender as dearly as mine own, be satisfied.*"
On cue, Oliver steps in front of me, a hand going to the hilt of his sword. "*O calm dishonourable vile submission*!" he draws in the sword and goes into position.

"*Tybalt, you ratcatcher,*" he hisses, and I swear I see that draw a hint of a smile out of Devon. "*Will you walk?*" Oliver raises his chin, and it's just an inch, but he seems infinitely taller.

"*Will you pluck your sword out of his pilcher by the ears? Make haste, lest mine be about your ears ere it be out.*" What a fun way of saying 'I'm about to murder you in cold blood'.

"*I am for you,*" Devon states with much less fury than required. Still the battle begins, as brief as it is.

Romeo–that's me–interrupts the duel because the Prince of Verona forbids violence in the streets; in the chaos of the retreat, however, Tybalt skewers Mercutio fatally. Mercutio and Romeo, life-long comrades and friends, are separated forever–which is as much a tragedy as that of his and Juliet's, if you ask me.

Jack, who plays Benvolio, enters from the left side of backstage. "*O Romeo, Romeo, brave Mercutio is dead! The gallant spirit hath aspired the clouds, which too untimely here did scorn the earth,*" he cries.

I walk to my centre mark. "*This day's black fate on*

more days doth depend; this but begins the woe others must end."

Devon is back, and the second part of the battle begins. This time Romeo lashes out, and murders Tybalt–Juliet's cousin. Weird how both of Dafne and I's real-life best friends perish in the same scene.

Devon falls to his knees after I make my move, and I stare at him in horror.

"Scene," Mr. Hackle says, effectively dragging me out of it. Devon turns his head up and gives him a toothy smile. "Wasn't that decent?"

David and Oliver reach us at centre stage, and Mr. Hackle claps his hands once. "It was more than decent, smart-arse," our director confirms, holding out a hand to help my friend stand up.

"I think you've got the dynamic down. There's one thing I want to ask you though," he adds, nodding towards Devon as he talks to them both. "Do either of you think Tybalt and Mercutio were secretly lovers?"

Oliver tilts his head and squints, like Mr. Hackle just spoke in ancient Greek. Devon, on the other hand, shrugs and says, "I think we can all agree there is plenty of *not-so-straight* tension in this play, Mr. Hackle," a playful smile stretching on his lips, his freckles more visible after the strain of repeating the sequence multiple times having coloured his cheekbones. Oliver goggles at him. I look

between the two of them, and our director seems completely unaware. I presume he's grown a shield to protect himself from the dramatics of theatre kids decades ago.

"I think so too, Devon, so feel free to explore the implications of that. Dismissed!" he turns, Ms. Patterson furiously taking notes in tow. Oliver and Devon exchange an unreadable glance, the former nods to us both in goodbye and reaches the front row of seats, where Dafne has been taking notes for him while he was on stage.

"That was int–" I start, but Devon is walking away, so I follow him backstage. "Hey, mate, you alright?" I try again, placing a hand on his shoulder.

His face is serene, but I know him like the palm of my hand, and something's unraveling in his head.

"I'm alright. Brilliant, actually. Also…" he smacks his lips, his hands splayed on his waist. "I have a big, fat crush on Ollie."

Chapter 17

Dafne

Ollie has been quiet ever since we got out of rehearsal, which is unlike him, but I haven't pushed it. Before parting ways to go shower, he told me he'd meet me and Phoebe in the canteen for dinner. Phoebe and I get back to our dorm room from our respective rehearsals almost simultaneously, so I warn her not to point out if she later notices anything abnormal about his behaviour.

"I hope it doesn't have anything to do with the epilepsy," Phoebe considers an hour later, when we're freshly showered, changed, and ready to fill our grumbling stomachs.

"I don't think so," I say as we jog down the stairs, "I think it's something else entirely." I have a good inkling of what that something–or someone, rather–may be, but I say nothing.

I'd rather *he* told us both, if and only if he feels like it. As we step into the canteen, the smell of delicious curry immediately fills my nostrils, and I can't help but sigh in content.

"Sorry, Phoebs, I know you hate curry," I grimace.

Phoebe rummages through her bottomless bag and lifts the corner of a small plastic tupperware.

"You should know by now that I always come prepared," she whispers, rattling the contents of the green plastic container.

"Is it that barley salad I can never pronounce?" I ask.

"*Byggrynsalat*," she nods sagely in perfect Norwegian.

She cracks me up. I get in line to grab my food and an extra chocolate chip cookie for both Phoebe and Ollie, then make my way to the table Phoebe secured.

I'm almost there, when someone bumps into me with the entire left side of their body–and I can see the vision of what's about to happen so clearly. My food splattered on the marble-like floor, me falling face-first and possibly breaking my nasal septum. Except none of that happens, because a strong arm is holding me upright by the waist, one hand splayed over my stomach, the other gripping the food tray around me. I turn, praying it's not who I think, knowing damn well it's exactly him. Theodore's eyes roam over my face, then he abruptly lets go of my waist but keeps his hand on the tray like he's not sure I can support it on my own. My fluttering stomach would agree. Funny–I don't remember enjoying being the damsel in distress in real life. I feel like a terrible feminist right now. He eyes the tray and slowly loosens his grip

until he removes his hand completely.
"Thank you," I mutter, moving my hair over my shoulder with one hand in what I hope resembles a confident gesture, holding onto the tray for dear life with the other.

"Hey, you," Theodore says somewhere to my back, "Are you going to apologise for nearly making her fall?" he asks, his tone on the verge of authoritative, and I wonder if Phoebe happens to have a mini fan in that bag of hers.

"Price, it's fine, they probably didn't even notice–"

He eyes me, one eyebrow raised. Is he *scolding* me?

I turn and see the culprit staring at Theodore like he's been struck by lightning, then look between the two of us and mumble a *sorry* before sprinting towards a table on the other side of the room. Theodore makes a rumbling sound like he's not satisfied with the boy's answer, so I place a hand on his arm.

"He was clearly a first-year, I'm sure he's been terrorized enough for the day," I say in my most placating tone.

Theodore clears his throat, then nonchalantly gazes around the room, looking everywhere but at me.

"Are we good?" he asks, as if he didn't really care about the answer, and maybe it's presumptuous of me, but I think he does.

"Why wouldn't we be?" I reply with a smile, having decided approximately three seconds ago that I will not be the one to cave in. His gaze drops to me now, as warm as wildflower honey.

"Maybe because we–" he stops. "I just think we should talk about it."

"Not in the middle of the canteen, we shouldn't," I reply simply.

He nods, and when his eyes fall on the table where his friends are sitting at he asks, "Is Oliver good?" His voice is strained, like he would have preferred dropping a hammer on his big toe than ask the question. That makes me purse my lips. "Since when do you care about Ollie?" I inquire, subtly stealing a look at Phoebe. She's staring at us as if we were a movie, and the salad she's stabbing with her tiny recycled-plastic fork the popcorn. Theodore clicks his tongue and shakes his head lightly.

"I don't," he shrugs, then walks back to the table where Devon and some of the other lads are chatting animatedly. What is he acting all mysterious for?

I plop onto my seat at the designated table, my tray clattering as I drop it with a tad too much force.

Phoebe cleans her mouth with the green paper napkin that matches her tupperware, looking as proper as Maggie Smith's character in *Downton Abbey*.

"Well," she says slowly, setting her cutlery down in perfectly parallel lines, her baby pink manicure shining under the cafeteria lights. "The plot thickens, and so does–"

I can't stop the laugh that erupts from me. "*Phoebe*, not in front of my–" I don't finish the sentence, because a near-empty tray appears next to mine, the seat to my left being filled by Ollie.

"Who eats curry with coconut sauce?" he grimaces, eyeing my now semi–cold dinner skeptically. Still laughing from Phoebe's colourful use of semantics, I nudge him lightly.

"You know I do. I'd cover everything in coconut if I could." Phoebe chokes on her water then, and I tilt my head in question. She wiggles her eyebrows, and my eyes grow wide because I can't believe that's where her thoughts went. *Again*. Pervert.

Ollie nods knowingly, crossing his arms over the table by pushing his tray further from him. Phoebe smiles brightly at him and asks, "What's up, Ollie?"

I take a bite of my cookie and look over at him.

"Not much," he sighs. "I found a penny in my shoe, tomorrow will rain, I like a bloke as more than a friend, the usual." He says it casually, but Phoebe and I exchange a look. Wait, what? Just like that?

"You want to talk about that last thing?" I ask carefully, offering the cookie I got for him, which he accepts and starts breaking in smaller pieces.

"What's there to talk about? It doesn't change anything, does it?"

"Of course not," I place a delicate hand on his arm. There's nothing Ollie could do or be that would make me love him any less, least of all the fact that he likes a lad. I'm just … disappointed at myself for not realising sooner. I mean, what happened today at rehearsal had me wondering whether *something* was going on, and perhaps he hadn't figured it out himself until a short while ago, but I always took pride in knowing him better than anyone else. I just wish I could have been there for him.

His silence should tell me not to insist, but I decide to take a leap of faith that he's not going to run away, and ask the question that will keep gnawing at me if I don't set it free. This is not the place, though.

"I propose a walk," I say then, "but first, we pick up dessert."

Phoebe and Ollie look at each other, then at me, then scramble out of their seats. I'll take that as a yes.

Phoebe's arm is linked with mine, which makes it difficult to get the spoon of my single portion of crème brûlée to my mouth. Ollie has been quiet, and I'm sure he's grateful for the silence being filled by our friend's anecdotes about her castmates. When even she runs out of words, I take a deep breath and turn to Ollie.

"Does it maybe have anything to do with Devon? You know, your realisation?"

He doesn't answer for a few beats.

"Is it that obvious?" he grimaces, removing some stray cream from his chin with the back of his hand.

I smile warmly and say, "I probably wouldn't have thought much about it before, but your reaction to that thing Mr. Hackle and Devon said about Tybalt and Mercutio …" I shrug. "The last time I saw that expression on your face your mum was telling you about how she'd caught you making out with Tam on her new couch. It all makes sense now, the time you spend with him."

"Are you upset?" the corners of his mouth pull down.

"Ollie–no, absolutely not."

"I'm not either, in case you were wondering," Phoebe says over a mouthful of dessert. That makes him snort. "Good."

"So … are you going to do something about it?"

"Like what? Just because we've been hanging out, that doesn't mean he's interested," he huffs.

"He wouldn't show his interest if he thought you were into girls *only,* now, would he," Phoebe considers, and fails to stifle a yawn.

"Phoebs has a point," I say as I take her empty plastic bowl from her hands and stack it over mine. "You're the one who's been telling me to take risks for the past fifteen years, yeah?"

"I hate when you use my wisdom against me," he narrows his eyes, but I can tell he's only mildly annoyed. "Truth hurts," I nudge his elbow, and we start heading to the dorms.

Chapter 18

Dafne

"This is … *picturesque,*" I say, the only word I can think of that won't sound outright snobbish. I had almost forgotten that Ethan was going to take me out today, and I'm not sure if it's because my brain is refusing to take in any more information or for some … other reason.

"I know, right?" Ethan beams, sounding so proud of himself for taking me here–and I'm certainly not about to clip his wings, but I also wonder how I never noticed this place before. It's not exactly subtle, and I thought I knew the West End from the inside out.

The Pop Factory, the name in cursive red neon lights, is located at the very end of an alley right next to the Royal Opera House. A giant tin box covered in swirling red and white stripes, filled to the brim with just as much solid plastic popcorn, towers at the entrance. It strikes me as odd, and rather specific, how a lad would take a girl out to a popcorn place on a … date, for a lack of a better term. I wasn't expecting a gourmet restaurant–most students need to put a mortgage on their kidneys just to pay for APDAS' tuition–but I was thinking of the cinema or a pre-dinner (non-alcoholic) drink. Maybe I'm just too old-fashioned and this is the proper way to court someone now. I certainly wouldn't know.

"Come on, I'm a v.i.p in here," he says, and I don't manage to comment on that, because he's pulling me by the wrist towards the pearly white-painted wooden doors. Once we're inside, my jaw drops. I've never seen so many popcorn references in my life.

I reckon not even the person that *invented* the snack has. Ethan walks in front of me as I peel my coat off and stare wordlessly at two walls covered entirely in plastic cases, each of them containing popcorn of every imaginable color–navy blue, lavender, burgundy red, charcoal black.

"Impressive, huh?" he grins, as I remove my wool beanie and pass a hand through my hair to tame the frizz, courtesy of the outside humidity.

"Quite," I reply, already wondering if they'll have even coconut-flavoured popcorn. I know, I have a problem. As my eyes roam over the infinite possibilities,

Ethan offers me a silver tin and says, "Whatever you want, it's on the house–the house being me," and before I can object, he's already moving to the end of the wall and grabbing a load of popcorn with a small shovel. Right.

I notice the different flavours are categorized alphabetically, so I head towards the beginning of the wall, in Ethan's opposite direction. "Caramel apple, carrot, cherry pie…" I murmur, passing over the name tags with a finger, "cilantro–yuck, cinnamon … oh, cinnamon."

My mind immediately wanders to my hot chocolate date with Theodore–no wait, it wasn't a date. It was the result of an unforeseen event, is all. As was that kiss.

As I finally locate the coconut popcorn tank, I grab the small shovel and stick it inside with a bit too much force to be casual.

"Stupid Theodore Price, with his stupid hands and stupid kisses and stupid bloody cinnamon," I mutter to myself.

"Wow, you must really hate it," Ethan appears next to me, an eyebrow raised.

"*What?*" I ask, the possibility that he heard me knotting my stomach up in a matter of seconds.

"The popcorn," he nods towards the steel grip I still have on the shovel.

"Oh," I huff out a laugh, "no, I'm sure it's great. I'm just a little on edge, you know–with opening night coming up and all."

Ethan makes a noise that tells me he wasn't listening, then waves a hand to something behind us. A few seconds later, a pale girl with bleached blonde hair who can't be more than eighteen walks up to us, high-fiving Ethan with one hand, holding a small table scale in the other.

"My man," she says in a thick American, Mid-Western I think, accent. "Shall I put your order on your tab? Pepper and vanilla, the usual?" I try to keep my face neutral, but my brows furrow at the combination. And Ollie calls *my* food choices disgusting.

"You know it, Kay, but add my good friend's order as well," he says, gingerly taking the tin bucket from my hands and handing it to Kay so she can weigh it.

"So you're the good friend. E mentioned he was bringing a lady here but I thought he was joking." *E*?

"Apparently not," I smile, unsure of what else to say so as not to embarrass both of us. He looks perfectly relaxed though, so I tell myself there's no need to look for hidden meanings. I'm supposed to have fun–and not think about Mr. Polo Neck if I can help it.

"Here you go! Enjoy," Kay winks, handing me the bucket back. And it's me and Ethan alone again. As alone as one can be with an army of popcorn looming over us, that is.

"Do you want to sit or eat on the go?" he asks, and although it's cold outside, I think the more fresh air I get, the better, and I tell him as much. He holds my bucket as I fix my beanie back on, then we begin our stroll around the theatre district.

"How did you find out about that place?" I ask, because it is truly beyond me how I never noticed it before.

"I used to work there," he says as he loudly munches his awful snack, so I take it as an opportunity to speak again.

"Can I ask you something else?" I'm rather confident he's not going to say *no, you cannot.* He proceeds to make a *mmh* sound I assume means yes.

"Why did you ask me out?" I ask simply. "Don't get me wrong, I appreciated it, but … why now?"

He swallows, then throws me a lopsided smile. I briefly think it's the kind of smile girls would sigh over, but I can't lie to myself. It does absolutely nothing for me.

"It wasn't a trick question, I'm genuinely curious."

I say with a shrug.

"Fine, I'll tell you the truth," he replies after a beat, as I pop another piece of coconut-flavoured popcorn into my mouth–which is really good, by the way, take that, Ollie–

"I didn't make a move before because I thought you and Price were a thing."

I very nearly choke.

"What?"

"I don't know, everyone knows that you fight. I thought it meant history, dude–"

Everyone?

"History," I repeat, blinking a few times.

"You know, stuff," he says over the chewing, and I want to say that I definitely *do not know*.
I look back in front of me just in time to dodge a lamp post about to hit me dead in the forehead.

If that's what Ethan, the least perceptive person I know, thought because apparently our … disagreements are common knowledge, after what happened between

Price and I, is everyone going to think we're one step away from marriage? This is bad, right?
Ethan seems oblivious to my thoughts, because he goes on, not even noticing my quasi-incident with the lamp-post.

"But if you two aren't kicking it," he resumes.

"Nope," I say quickly. It's not untrue.

"Then this is cool. We could do it again, if you're not like, swamped."

"Sure," I say. And as we walk past the Apollo Victoria Theatre, I imagine my face on the marquee someday.

Theodore

When Devon comes back from the deli, I'm studying Act Five. I'm in the middle of fake-taking the poison vial when I hear the keys rattle in the lock, and I quickly stuff my script under the bed, grab my laptop and position myself to look as if I hadn't been going over lines on a Saturday night while he was concocting who knows what between Dafne and Ethan. If only he knew.
"Theo," he greets me as he removes his bomber jacket and flings himself onto his bed along with the contents of his grocery paper bag. "Enjoying yourself?"

I throw him a bored look. "Not as much as you, I'm

sure," I say, channeling a relaxed vibe my insides truly do not reflect right now. From the corner of my eye, I see him roll onto his side to look at me.

"I'm told the date went great, in case you're curious," he chuckles, no doubt hoping to elicit more questions from me–a satisfaction I simply refuse to give him. "Ethan said he'd let me know more later."

My fingers still on the keyboard where I was pretending to write absolutely nothing, but I can't deny I am itching to know what in the world they could have possibly talked about. I once overheard him explaining to someone that aliens will invade us and make us all wear party hats; I'm not sure conspiracy theories are Dafne's preferred topic of discussion.

However, before I can indeed give in and ask what he means by that, his phone pings with a new notification. "Speak of the devil … he forwarded me Dafne's text."

I clear my throat, still not straying my gaze from the computer screen. Naturally, Devon stretches to shove his phone into my face.

Thank you again for
the popcorn–my friends will be
delighted to know a place like that exists. :)
I've just been so stressed about everything,
tonight was a much-needed distraction.
See you around x
Sent 21:24 p.m.

X? A bloody *kiss*? Did they kiss? No, they didn't. But if they did … hell.

Stressed about everything. Am I part of that everything? Have I been stressing her out? Can my brain be quiet for ten seconds?

"Earth to Romeo," Devon says, pretending to speak into a walkie-talkie. "Nothing happened, if that's what you're trying to decipher, and nothing *will* happen, if you'd put your blasted pride away and asked her out yourself."

I close my laptop, and start towards the bathroom.

"*She's* not opposed to the idea," Dev mumbles, and I turn around as if he'd thrown a brick at me.

"What did you say?"

"You heard me."

"What about *see you tomorrow. Kiss*?" I'm aware I sound like a petulant child. I can't stop it. Devon is smiling so widely that I think his face might split up.

"Dev. Why would you say that?"

"Just a hunch," he shrugs, "but that is an awful lot of interest for someone who claims not to be interested, so if you want to throw in the towel…"

At the challenge, I find my composure again. I smile, give him the middle finger, and close the bathroom door behind me. I won't admit it even under torture, but there is no escaping the bitter taste in my mouth: jealousy.

Chapter 19

Dafne

"*No faith, no honesty in men; all perjured, all forsworn, all naught, all dissemblers*," Ollie says as we practice Act Three, Scene Two in one of the rooms any student can reserve for out of schedule rehearsals. He's reading Isabel's part for me since she stood me up at the last minute.

"*Shame come to Romeo!*" he cries with exaggerated pathos.

He looks over at me when I don't reply.

"Shame come to Romeo?" he tries again, unconvinced.

"I'm sorry," I shoot him an apologetic look. "I can't bring myself to say that 'he was not born in shame'. That's still up for debate," I huff as I sit with my head against the mirror-covered wall, my elbows propped on my knees.

"Is this about that lad who took the last scone this morning?" Ollie offers, only half-joking. I really wanted that scone.

"No," I roll my eyes playfully. "It's not about *that* lad."

"Oh. What did Price do now?"

Of course that was Ollie's immediate thought.

Guilt suddenly reminds me Ollie still doesn't know about the kiss, as I begged Phoebe not to tell him because I wanted to do it myself. I've never not told Ollie something. Especially something this big. I don't know why it's so hard to bring myself to say the words–is it plain shame? Shame that I let Theodore kiss me and kissed him back, after everything that's transpired between us? I should know Ollie would never judge me for it.

I need to get it off my chest. "There's something I should tell you–"

The door opens, Theodore coming in as he sings under his breath, wearing a short-sleeved black shirt that clings to the lean muscles of his chest, and grey sweatpants. Well, that is just unfair.

He abruptly stops and freezes when he takes us in.

"Sorry, uh …" he turns to look at the small plaque on the door with a number four etched on it. "Wrong room." He's about to leave, when Ollie yells, "Hold on!" which makes me wonder whose side he's really on, and I hope the glare I throw him conveys as much. "I have to go anyway, I'm sure Dafne doesn't mind a different partner. Do you, Daf?" he asks innocently, and I can't help but think he and Phoebe have spent too much time together. Theodore swallows and moves from the door to let Ollie pass. Before my soon-to-be ex best friend closes the door, he mouths a *talk to him* at me.

Once we're alone, Theodore grips his rucksack's shoulder strap tighter and says, "For what it's worth I didn't know you'd be here."

"It's fine, Price," I sigh as I get up.

Theodore

Might as well take the bull by the horns since we're at it I think, dropping my things next to the door. "Maybe we can talk now? I know you were rehearsing, and that's what I came here to do as well, but …" I shrug. She considers me for a moment, tapping one foot on the hardwood floor.

"Go ahead," she says then, her brows furrowed.

Right. Not intimidating at all.

I begin rolling up my earbuds cord and start, "Let me just say it was wrong of me to assume–"

I am about to shove it in my pocket, when she steps forward and offers her palm up. I eye her once, and when she nods in her palm's direction, I place the tangle of white plastic in her waiting hand. Unexpectedly, she starts detangling it carefully. It's probably not the best time for me to notice even her hands are fascinating.

"Assume that you'd be okay with it," I resume,

trying not to stare at her meticulous work like a psycho.

"It?"

"Kissing you."

She hums pensively, her gaze focused on a particularly tight knot in the string, and I'm about to drop to my knees and beg her to say something else before I spontaneously combust. Out of annoyance, because I feel like an idiot, but also frustration because how did I ever manage to brush over the fact that she's absolutely beautiful– and I can't even tell her.

"I think we both know I was *more* than okay with it, but I appreciate that," she finally says.

I should be relieved, but I can sense something else is coming.

"Can I ask you something?" she says calmly, handing me the perfectly untangled earbuds.

I swallow way too audibly and nod.

"Did you know some, uh, people think that we were, or … are, together?" It's one person, but still.

"Beg pardon? Who?" I ask, and I realise too late that it came out like an accusation, more than a question.

"Alright, no need to lose your head over it," she purses her lips. "Just someone I know."

"Ah, it must be true, then," I say scornfully before I can think twice.

"What is that supposed to mean?"

"Nothing, Wright, you wanted to rehearse, yeah? How about Scene Three from Act–"

"You're the one who wanted to talk! Is it really so hard for you to have a normal conversation? Do you rehearse in your sleep, too?"

"Some of us have to! Some of us aren't *naturally gifted*, as Ms. Patterson put it," I sneer.

"*Oh my God.*" She articulates it, and I know it's stupid, but that riles me up even more.

"Come on now, I know you love to hear what you already know," I raise my arms and let them fall with a muffled thud against my sides.

"You're the one who told me you were *obviously going to get Romeo*. You should really–"

"I lied, alright? Does this answer satisfy you?" I snap.

Her mouth opens and closes on nothing.

My brain is suddenly in overdrive. I feel like I could cry. I can't remember the last time I cried.

"I wasn't *sure* I'd get Romeo. I'd already started learning Mercutio and Tybalt's parts as well, in case I lost the role to someone else because the truth is that I don't know what I'm doing, Dafne. The clothes, the smiles. I'm a big fucking fraud, and everyone will see that eventually."

It's out.

I close my eyes and desperately try to calm my racing heart, but my breath is stuck in my throat, and I can't think–

"Theodore," she says softly. "Look at me."

I shake my head, wishing I could get out of here, but I drop to my knees instead. I think that if I were to open my eyes this dreadful feeling would crush me completely.

"Theodore, breathe," Dafne's voice says, close, but not enough for it to feel suffocating. "We'll breathe deeply together, yeah?"

I nod once.

"In," she says, "and out."

I follow her instructions one time, two times, three times. The only sounds I hear are our deep breaths and the muffled footsteps of people walking down the corridor.

I can't tell how much time passes, all I know is that once I've calmed down and managed to peel my eyes open, Dafne is sitting on her knees about three feet from me. Her head is cocked, caramel eyes roaming over my face.

At whatever she sees on my face she murmurs, "I think you had an anxiety attack. Was it the first time?"

I want to say it was, but that's not quite true. It's happened a few times before, I've never told anyone, and I'm not really sure why. I clear my throat and slowly start rising when she does the same and steps closer, her hand hovering over my arm as if to make sure she's there in case I plummet to the ground.

"I don't have anxiety. It's just a stressful time," I tell her.

Dafne licks her lips and says, "Maybe. But if you did, there would be nothing to be ashamed about." She's looking at me with softness, not pity, which is infinitely worse. I'm starting to think she's actually perfect and I just have always had a deeply twisted sense of reality.

"You should rest, Price," she adds after a beat.

She heads to retrieve her things, and when I have my back to her she says, "And for what it's worth … I don't think you're a fraud."

I'm still reeling from being at my most vulnerable in front of her twice in the span of ten minutes, her last words echoing in my head.

They affect me more than I'd like.

Chapter 20

Dafne

Phoebe and I treat ourselves to takeaway since we've both been bursting our arses off at our respective rehearsals, and I promptly text Ollie to let him know he's missing out on the delicious sushi piled on our small desk.

About two minutes later he sends me a selfie of him and Devon clinking their glasses, big, goofy smiles on their faces. I laugh softly and show the photo to Phoebe, whose eyes grow wide as she raises a hand in front of her mouth so that her food doesn't spill out when she says, "Devon is cuuute!"

I'd never thought about it, but I suppose he is. I find that my parameters in whether I'm attracted to someone or not have drastically shifted in the past few weeks, and I'm perfectly aware of whose fault that is.

"Oh, that reminds me, I need to show you the romance books I downloaded today," she huffs as she grabs her ebook reader from the floor with her chopsticks-free hand. I make an affirmative sound as I chew on my sal-

-mon roll. I wonder how Theodore's doing after this morning. I haven't told Phoebe about that, and this time it's because it's not my place to do so. But if I don't talk about what he said *before* … it's not going to bode well for my peace of mind.

"Phoebs, before you tell me all about those books," I start, setting my food aside, "can I tell you something?"

She shoots me a curious look, and probably sensing an important topic coming up she all but throws her device on the pillow. "I'm all ears."

"I had a chat with Theodore today," I sigh.

"What kind of chat?" she wiggles her eyebrows.

"Not the kind you'd like to hear about, but … he said some things that got me thinking. This whole speech about how he didn't actually think he'd get Romeo."

Phoebe's face scrunches up. "That doesn't sound like the bloke you've been having verbal boxing matches with for the past three years," she says.

"I know, right?" He sounded so insecure it was like speaking to a completely different person. And I was just shocked, because how does he seriously not know how good he is?"

"Daf," the corners of Phoebe's mouth lift, her eyes twinkling. "You actually care about him, don't you?"

That catches me off guard. *Do I* care about him?

If I'm being honest, and I am, it's a rhetorical question. Instead of saying that out loud, though, I ask her, pointing towards her reading device with my chopsticks,

"Come on. What trope are you reading about this week?"

Theodore

I decide to take a short walk after dinner. I tell my friends it's because it helps digestion, which earns me numerous eye rolls, but the truth is I need space to just *think*. My mind is reeling with all sorts of catastrophic scenarios, but mostly, with the knowledge that there's something wrong with me, and I can't ignore it anymore. I also can't believe Dafne's not losing her shite over what happened, because I am. Maybe she's just better at hiding it.

I take the gravel path that leads to APDAS' garden, which is dimly lit at night, the ash trees' branches swaying gently in the evening breeze. It's cold, the tip of my nose starting to turn red as I shove a hand in my coat's pocket to retrieve the gloves my grandmother crocheted for me–one of the *four* pairs with a slightly different percentage of wool in them, because '*One degree can change everything, darling*'. I sit on one of the few benches scattered in the garden, next to one of the ever-intermittent lampposts under the biggest sycamore. I unlock my phone, tap to recent calls, and press the green phone icon. Barely two rings go by when a bright voice-answers. "Theo! My precious," Grandma Mary says, the affection in her words so obvious it tugs at my heart.

"Did you eat already, love? Do they feed you at all in that school?" she continues, a shuffling sound in the background meaning she moved to get more comfortable in her favorite armchair.

"Hi Gran, yes, I've been adequately fed," I say, unable to keep a smile off my face. "Not that the canteen's food compares to yours."

She makes a knowing sound, then yells a *Robert, quit fooling around and come say hello to your grandson,* making me laugh out loud, huffing out the crisp air.

"So," she resumes in a less deafening volume, "you don't usually call at this hour. Is everything alright?" Sudden guilt gnaws at me for making her worry even for a second.

"Yes, Gran," I say quietly, "I just wanted to hear your voice." Grandma sighs and I hear the clinking of her glass being placed on a table. I must have interrupted her evening soft drink time.

"Has your mother called?" she asks, her voice gentler than when she picked up the call.

"No, she hasn't," I say honestly. If she had, it would've been one more thing to stress over, and I think I've had quite enough for now. "Really, I'm fine. There's just a lot on my plate right now, and I would very much appreciate some reassuring words from my favorite grandmother."

She snorts. "Your only *living* grandmother, child," a wave of relief at her playfulness washing over me.

"Are they working you–" she's interrupted by the deep, husky voice belonging to my other favorite person.
"Son!" Grandpa says, brimming with wonder as if he were about to hear me speak for the first time all over again. "This old lady right here made some weird signs at me, and you know I'm not good at charades, so do me the favour of telling me what is going on yourself," he adds, sounding like he's moving around the room with my grandma probably trying to pry the phone back from his hands or slap his arm for calling her old.
I could keep deflecting, but who am I going to open up to if not them? They have been with me every step of the way without a doubt, without faltering. Even when my parents dropped me at my grandparents' house like I was never even theirs to keep. Maybe someone should have told them that if you bring a child into the world, you're not supposed to discard them like a used toy.

"There are two things, really. Something happened today–well, not just today, but it happened again," I say, scratching a piece of moss off the bench.

"I had an anxiety attack. I mean, that's what I figure it was, since it's happened before under the same circumstances. The … anxious kind."

He must be wondering what he's put me through school for if this is how poorly I express my thoughts.
"Honestly, Theo?" Grandpa murmurs gently, but firmly. "I've had my suspicions you weren't always telling the truth when you said you were fine, given the pressure

you put on yourself. But I'm afraid you get your pride from me, so I understand why you didn't tell us. Either way, thank you for telling me now."

"I'm sorry," I tell him.

"*I'm* sorry we can't be there with you." We're both quiet for a beat, then he adds, "I can look up someone for you to see about it, would that be fine?"

Would it be fine? Because if I see someone about this, it means it's real. I don't have time for it to be real.

"I'll think about it," I offer weakly.

"It's your decision, Theo," he says, and sensing what a massive feat opening up like this has been for me, he mercifully changes the topic by asking what the other thing that's bothering me is.

"Well, opening night is coming up, and rehearsals are going fine, I suppose, but … I'm distracted. Unfocused. This isn't me," and it really isn't. It feels like confessing to a heinous crime, something much worse than suffering from anxiety and not being straightforward about it. Feeling myself fall short in what should be the one thing I do better than everyone. Except, even three years later, I know that's not true. And it cuts me open, because it's all they've ever asked of me, and I'm letting them down. They don't know it now, they would never say it, but throwing their enormous sacrifices to shite because I can't think straight because I'm feeling irrational things all over–for the one girl that has now seen my at my weakest, no less. What a pig's ear of a situation.

As if he just peeked inside my thick skull, Grandpa asks, "What's the young lady's name?"

I groan. "Seriously? Have you been watching those mentalist videos again?" I ask, half-joking, half-concerned whether I'm related to an actual mind reader. He chuckles, the sound reverberating through the phone, then says to my grandmother, "The boy's got the hots for a girl."

I hear Grandma make a surprised sound and chant a string of *who is she is she gorgeous I bet she's positively stunning will we meet her when we come see you oh Theo, darling.*

"The hots? I didn't know you were a fifteen-year-old skater from Los Angeles," I say, uselessly trying to shove the achingly true piece of information he's provided Grandma somewhere I won't be able to retrieve it from. "Her name's Dafne," I admit after a bit, passing a hand over my face. "And I got myself into a big, bloody mess."

Chapter 21

Dafne

Act Three, Scene Two. Juliet finds out from her Nurse that Romeo has killed Tybalt–her cousin–and is now exiled. We're two months into rehearsals, and one month is left. Twenty-eight days, to be precise. The structure of the show has been ready for weeks; we're making sure everything works, smoothing the edges. There can be no uncertainty, no detail left behind. Unlike a usual play, we won't get second, third, fourth chances. It's all or nothing. I'm not worried, that's not the right word to describe how I feel. This is what I do, what I want to do, always; but there is so much at stake. And maybe it's starting to get to me.

"*There is no end, limit, measure, bound, in that word's death. No words can that woe sound.*

Where is my moth–" I'm interrupted by Mr. Hackle's raised hand from the central seat in the front row. "Dafne, do you know where you are?" he asks, his voice neutral, and I can't tell if he's about to hand me an award or tell

me to scram from his stage.
"Juliet's room, she's–"

"No," he interrupts again, "where are *you*? Right now?"

I bite my tongue to get some saliva to circulate in my mouth, which went dry the second Mr. Hackle spoke; it's one of the first things he's taught us for when you're on stage and your tongue feels coated with sand. I know what he wants to hear, and I know I need to keep my wits about me. "I'm at the Queen Victoria Theatre," I reply, "I'm on stage. I'm here, now."

He eyes me for a long moment, then nods once. "From the top," he says.

When Mr. Hackle seems satisfied, we move on to Scene Three, so it's time for Theodore and David to get on stage. I'm about to walk off when Ms. Patterson tells me to move to David's mark while he finishes getting his measurements done backstage so that the light technician can take notes of the position for the show. So now Theodore and I are staring at each other, and it's admittedly a little awkward.

"Funny to meet you here," I smirk in a poor attempt at diverting attention from the elephant in the room. Also known as the ambiguous tension radiating from both of us. He opens his mouth to say something back, but I never get to hear it.

Theodore's eyes grow wide as he lunges for something behind me–when said something hits me in the back of the head, and the next thing I know I am falling face-first on the rough wooden boards of the stage, a cacophony of sounds rushing towards me.

I'm dimly aware of being held in someone's arms, a warm voice saying something along the lines of *I'd like to have a normal conversation when you're awake,* but when I'm fully conscious again I blink my eyes open to the familiar chattering of Phoebe and Ollie, their heads snapping towards me like owls the second I'm able to let my eyes flutter open.

"What the–" I stop myself from cursing, the sparks of what I'm sure will soon turn into throbbing pain radiating from my nape. "Did a boxer take a swing at me or what?" I groan, and a pair of manicured hands grip my own from the left side of what looks like an infirmary bed.

"How are you feeling? Do you know my name? How many fingers am I holding up," Phoebe says on a single gulp of air, which is a testament to the endless hours of breathwork we're put through in yoga classes. I snatch my hands from her surprisingly strong grip and motion turning down the volume.

"I'm fine, your name is Phoebe Nilsen, and if you would just stop waving your fingers perhaps I'd be able to tell you just how many. All good?" I reply to stop her from going all *Grey's Anatomy* on me. Phoebe's shoulders sag in relief, and I shoot her an apologetic smile, even though the massive headache pounding in my head begs to differ with my analysis.

"She was only unconscious for a few minutes, Phoebe," Ollie tells her with a raised eyebrow. "And even then she was mumbling about who knows what."

Ha ha, I mouth. "So," I glance between Phoebe and Ollie on my right, carefully touching the back of my head. "Does either of you know what happened exactly? One second I was on stage with Price and the next I'm hugging the floor."

A knowing look passes between the two across my bed, and it's just for a few seconds, but it's enough for me to notice there's either something they don't want to say or something they've argued over who would have to tell me. In both cases, I'm likely not going to like it.

"A couple of second-year students were rushing to take a ladder off the stage. I assume because they realised you were about to start with the scene," Ollie explains.

"The ladder was too heavy for them to carry," Phoebe continues. "It slipped out of their grasp and, well, hit you," she grimaces, pointing at her nape.

"Right. Who else could have been in the damned ladder's trajectory? At least I managed not to shatter my nose" I consider, followed by a beat of silence. "There's something you're not telling me though. I might've been hit by a deranged wooden construction, but I saw those *looks.* What is–" I urge, when a male voice interrupts my questioning. It takes me a couple of seconds to grasp who that voice belongs to. Ollie gets up from his chair to go open the door, but I jump off the bed, my head swimming for a second at the sudden change in position, just in time to pull on his sleeve and stop him.

I bring my pointer finger to my mouth to tell him to be quiet.

"So you're sure she's alright? How bad is the concussion? Shouldn't she be taken to an *actual* hospital–" Theodore says to Mrs. Digby–the school nurse. There's an impatient edge to his voice, but something else too, something that tastes sour in my mouth, and I could bet my good set of highlighters that it's worry.

"Nothing to fear, darling," we hear Mrs. Digby reply through the thin wall separating us. "She will need to take some aspirin daily and take it easy for a while, but she will be fine. I heard some chatting, would you like to go in?"

"No need, and please don't tell her I was here," Theodore replies in a low voice, but I still hear it.

My heart positively sinks and my stomach immediately churns with a concoction of unpleasant emotions. The sound of receding footsteps echoes through the corridor, and I slowly step back from my eavesdropping position, turning with my back and palms flat on the door. "So *that* happened," Phoebe whispers, breaking the silence. Ollie looks like he's the one who's been hit in the head.

"What we didn't tell you," he starts, "is that when you were barely conscious on the floor, he carried you to the infirmary. We practically ran here together, but he left right after setting you on the bed. I had a feeling he'd be back though."

I don't know if it's the blow to the head, but it sounds like he's articulating the words. Like I'm a teenager and he's giving me the birds and bees speech. My mouth opens and closes once on nothing. but all I manage to utter is a weak, "*He carried me*. You mean …"

Ollie nods, his lips twitching. "Oh, yes, Daf. *Bridal style*."

It doesn't mean anything if I don't give it importance. Right? So why is it that if I allow my brain to picture Theodore rushing me to the infirmary in his arms like a knight in light wash jeans, I feel hot all over?

Before I can talk myself out of it, I snatch the door open and call his name.

Theodore

I hear my name just before I'm about to turn the corner, and find Dafne with her fingers gripping the infirmary's door handle, her lips pressed tightly together. Oliver and her roommate's heads peek at me from either side of her,

but I'm unable to pay them much attention.
"Where are you going?" Dafne yells to reach me on the other end of the corridor. No point in pretending I was just passing by. I start walking back towards her, and her friends disappear from my line of sight only to emerge from the room a few seconds later, hastily telling her that they'll go grab her a tea. The nurse smiles warmly at me while she goes back to typing on the computer at her desk.
"I wasn't sure you'd like me to be the first person you saw," I grimace when we're alone in the room. I close the door behind us gently while she goes to sit on the edge of the bed.
"Always assuming," she says with a smile.
"You scared me for a moment there," I say then, looking at her steadily.
"You need to stop doing that," she sighs.
"You'll have to be more specific."
"Saying things like that," she looks up at me from under her lashes. "I'm going to start thinking you care about me if you don't."
She sounds like she's joking, but also not really.
"What kind of awful person would I be if I didn't help after you fell face first in front of me?" She's quiet for a few seconds that feel like four hours.
"The person you've been until a few weeks ago?" she offers then, not mean or teasing, but as if she were just stating a fact. Which makes me feel infinitely worse,

because I can't really argue with that. As much as I would like to think I would have scooped her up in my arms if she'd needed me to in the past, the truth is, I don't know if I would have. I would have stepped back and let somebody else take charge. I sure as hell wouldn't have carried her here. Fuck, I really am awful.

"So you know," I add.

"Yes, I know you went all *An Officer and a Gentleman* on me. Very dashing of you," she smirks.

I don't even try to stop the smile that forms on my lips at that.

"By the way, I … I realised I never thanked you. For helping me out the other day, I mean." She makes a face that seems to mean, *you don't need to thank me*, and I raise a hand.

"You could have freaked out and called someone, but you went through it with me. It would have been much worse if you hadn't, so accept the gratitude. Please."

"If you insist," she says with a small shrug, which makes her wince in pain a second later. I pick up a gauze from the glass table placed against the wall and start rolling it up. "How did you know how to do that?" I ask, as it occurs to me that not everyone is probably accustomed to witnessing something like that.

"My cousin was diagnosed with generalised anxiety in middle school. We were in the same class, so my aunt had me learn basic notions about helping her with an attack, in case it happened. I'm not an expert but the power of breathing is …" she explains.

I nod, and as hard as it is, I let the notion settle inside me. I repeat the word in my head, let it take a shape. Make the idea bearable, since comfortable seems a bit of a stretch. I can't keep dismissing what I feel. *None* of it.

"I don't mean to be rude, I really did want to talk to you, but I think I'm going to need a nap," she says with a chuckle as she slowly rises, smoothing the fabric of her top where it bunched at the waist.

"No, of course, I'll walk you," I offer, crouching to retrieve her bag from the floor. Oliver must have brought it in earlier. Only when I get up with her bag strapped on my shoulder and see the expression on her face do I realise I might be out of line. What am I thinking, carrying her bag for her like I'm–

"Sounds good." She opens the door and mouths an *after you*, and she's definitely taking the mickey out of me, but it doesn't bother me one bit. We say goodbye to Mrs. Digby after she gives Dafne a note with the painkiller dosage she needs to take, and as we walk down the corridor I say, "Maybe I should get myself a Navy officer suit. You know, make a cosplay out of it."

She snorts, and promises she'll help in court when Richard Gere sues me. We both end up cackling like two proper idiots. When was the last time I laughed so hard?

Chapter 22

Dafne

It's safe to say I look good today. No, you know what–I look *great*. I've slept with my hair in a braid and woke up with pretty waves. My skin is glowing thanks to my meticulous skincare routine. I don't usually wear much makeup to rehearsals–there's really no point when it's going to melt after twenty minutes of warm-ups, but I have a mandatory class this morning and feel rather dainty, so why the hell not. It's important to recognise particularly good days looks-wise. *Affirm that shite,* as Phoebe would say. I pat a shimmery champagne eyeshadow color over my lid, apply a small amount of waterproof mascara on my upper lashes, a soft strawberry red lip with a blotted effect, and blend the usual few drops of concealer over each bag under the eyes–consistent sleeping patterns are still a work in progress, especially with so much to think about. Thankfully the pain from my injury is mostly gone, and I feel lucky it only took about a week. Phoebe left early to get some alleged alone time in the yoga studio, or that's what the note she left on our night stand said. So it's just me, and after deeming the work on my face satisfying, I get up to make myself some tea and honey before my nine o' clock mock audition class. The over fifty hours per week third year-students are subjected to are starting to take their toll, and even though I have a generally good feeling about today, I'm also incredibly tired. The kind of tired that settles in your joints and bones and makes you wonder if your body is supposed to hurt this much at this age.

After the kettle rattles–which manages to make me jolt even though I'm the one who put it on the stove–I pour the tea in my mug and add a generous amount of acacia honey. I'm about to stir the sweetened mixture, when it occurs to me how it looks exactly like Theodore's eyes, save for the green. It also occurs to me that such thoughts should not occur at all, since I'm not sure where we stand. I guess we're not on the warpath anymore, so where are we then? With everything that's happened we didn't really manage to properly discuss what that kiss meant, and he seemed downright annoyed by the possibility of anyone thinking we were together. I shake my head, down the drink as I've seen Phoebe do countless times with her tequila, and grab my things to leave.

I find Isabel, who's wearing cat-eye sunglasses despite the absence of sun and putting together a cigarette, her eyes rolling into their sockets at my chastising expression.

"You know that's terrible for your lungs, therefore for

your vo–"

"Tell me something I don't know," she chuckles, knowing from experience I only wish she'd cut this particular habit off for her own good. I think about recent events and settle on what seems the least shocking thing that's happened to me as of late.

"I went out with someone."

She turns towards me, and her eyes look like they're about to fall off their sockets like in cartoons. I'm not sure if I should be offended by her shock.

"What?!"

"You wanted me to tell you something you didn't know, and I did."

"That was a figure of speech but who bloody cares–who is it?"

I shake my head, and motion locking my lips up with an invisible key.

"You can't drop a bomb like that on me and then not tell me," she groans, her cigarette bobbing wildly between her lips. "I thought you didn't date."

"Who said anything about dating? And you could always guess," I shrug.

"Do I know this person?"

"I think so."

"Is it Mr. Boyd?"

"Why would you say that? I'm not into old men."

"He's barely fifty."

I eye her once, and she shrugs.

"Alright, then … is it Theodore?"

My stomach does something one might see in a parkour demonstration. I did *not* expect her to say that, and I scramble to school my face into neutrality. It's the second person who seems convinced he and I have or had something going on. The second bloody person. That's what I get for saying things out loud and manifesting them.

"How was Price your second choice after Mr. Boyd?" I joke as I hold the door open for both of us.

She squints at me, like I've just said the stupidest thing she's ever heard. "I just thought all that crazy nemesis tension you have going on was bound to blow up eventually. You know, in the *fun* way of the term."

I laugh and shoot a silent prayer to whatever divinity is willing to listen that she'll drop the subject.

The worst part? It doesn't sound half bad. It's not the worst idea I've ever heard. Which clearly means I have a secret penchant for masochism.

Once we get to class, I drop in my seat and notice with unreasonable relief that Theodore isn't here, only to remember this is one of the classes we don't share. Ollie arrives a few minutes later and leans on the edge of my desk, slipping a packet of white chocolate-covered biscuits towards me. "You know that old lady I sometimes meet on my morning jog?" he asks.

"The one with the yellow hat?"

"The very one. She keeps giving me these, and I don't have the heart to tell her I find them disgusting. Please enjoy them for me." That draws a genuine smile out of me, and I stash the packet in my bag. I look up at him and notice he looks like he didn't get a minute of sleep. "Ollie, are you feeling alright? You don't *look* alright–no offense." He smiles weakly, and it seems like I'm not the only one with a tendency to deflect.

"None taken–I think a spring in my mattress broke, there's something sharp stabbing me on the back all night long," he yawns. I let my head rest in my hands.

"A spring."

"You know those sharp metal things that look like one of Phoebe's curls?"

"Hilarious," I reply drily, and a second later Ms. Danson comes in, her new assistant trailing behind her with the equipment cart.

"Have you and Price talked at all this week?" Ollie whispers as he sits at the desk next to mine while the assistant fumbles with the camera settings.

"Not really," I say casually. I feel rather than see Ollie lean closer, pretending to stretch his long arms over his desk.

"Are you going to?"

"Ollie what is with you and–"

"Mr. Hall," Ms. Danson starts, "Would you like to go first today?"

Ollie shoots me an annoyed look, and I blow him a kiss.

"Of course, Ms. Danson, I'd *love* to."

Chapter 23

Theodore

It's been a week since the accident with the ladder, and things have been oddly peaceful. Don't get me wrong, it's not like we can spend too much time without teasing each other, but something's obviously changed. For me, at least. Then all that has to happen for me to feel the insidious pang of resentment is Mr. Hackle telling her the way she delivered a line was perfect. She catches my eye then–she always does. And whatever she sees there puts a look on her face that shouldn't be there, and I hate myself for it, but I also wonder if I'd ever be able to help it. There's also the not-so-inconsequential fact I've told her about my deepest fear, proceeded to have a meltdown, and she didn't even bat her eyes. Didn't judge me for it, not outwardly, at least, which is probably basic decency, but coming from her, it has been making me feel all sorts of things. So yes, things are also rather … tricky.

I start taking my earbuds out and say, "You dropped this," as I offer Dafne a bright pink sticky note, holding it between two fingers. She takes the note as she shoots me a glance, mouthing a *thank you* and probably hoping that'll be that. But it's me, so of course it won't. I lean against the wall with one shoulder and casually cross my arms. "Act Five looks great, huh?"

"Because I'm quiet for most of it?"

Shite.

"I didn't mean it like that–"

"Relax," she snorts. "I was *joking*. Remember, joking?" she smirks as she starts to walk ahead, her hair swishing on her back. Her smile widens as she looks at me over her shoulder. I catch up with her in a couple of strides, and we start walking side by side through the hall. It's not uncomfortable. I guess making out with someone daily takes the awkwardness away like that. I notice she's wearing more makeup than usual, and while I'm trying to come up with a something nice to say, she suddenly speaks again.

"Have you had tea yet?" she shoots me a casual look.

I have. "No," I blurt out. "You want to get some?" The words are out before I can even think them.

"Sure," she raises one shoulder, without looking at me. We don't say anything else as we walk to the nearest hot drinks vending machine, right next to the class where we have our Use of Voice lessons. I rummage through my pocket for the two pounds we'll need for the tea, and immediately shove them in the coin slot. She opens her mouth to speak, but I say, "No more debts, remember?"

She rolls her eyes, but there's a smile tugging at her lips. I ask if she takes it with sugar, and she raises three fingers. "Someone's got a sweet tooth," I consider as I press the buttons.

"I don't trust people who don't," she tilts her head as I chuckle, but my vision zeroes on the thumb she's stroking on the back of the book she's been carrying around. "What's that?" I ask, nodding towards it, the machine whirring in the background.

"*The Power of the Actor,*" she explains.

"Ivana Chubbuck," I muse. "Classic."

"I suppose you might have heard of it," she drawls, extending the contents in her arms to me to hold while she extracts the first white plastic cup of tea out of the shutter.

Naturally, I notice two things: one, she's being sarcastic. I remember discussing chapter five of that book–interior objects–at length during one of our joined lessons last year. I remember it so clearly because she felt it necessary to specify the importance of the emotional value of the object we chose, as a metaphor for what our character wanted to achieve. I argued emotions were a double-edged sword, which is obviously still true.

Two, she had to lower herself just enough to retrieve her tea that her black square-neck shirt exposed the dip of her cleavage. And most of her clavicles. Since when am I attracted to bloody clavicles?

Christ. I shake my head subtly to get the image out of it,

and if she notices I'm being weird, she gracefully doesn't comment on it. I'm still holding her book and script when she takes the first sip, then passes her tongue over her bottom lip. Get a grip, Theo.

"Also," I suddenly remember why I wanted to talk to her, besides making sure her head was still attached to her neck. "Ms. Eisner said we can use her class to practice the dance after lunch. Would that work for you?"

She's about to answer when someone yells a *Yoooo, Dafne* somewhere to our left.

The howler approaches us and swings an arm around her shoulders. Ethan. "What's up, babe?"

Babe? He's known her for what, a week? It takes every ounce of strength I have in me not to roll my eyes and settle on a tight smile instead.

"I'm good, Ethan," she grimaces, because he forgot, or doesn't care, that even though she's healed, her neck probably hurts when he weighs on her like a boulder. "I'd be better if you put your arm elsewhere, though.

"Also, please don't call me babe?" she chuckles, and my head snaps towards her.

She has no business being this hot when she's telling someone to essentially piss off–especially if that someone isn't me.

Is this where it's gotten? If I had a mean kink we'd be married by now. Alright, that's not fair. She's assertive, there's a difference.

I find that apparently, despite myself, I'm into it.

"Oh, shit, sorry," he says, removing his arm and placing a more careful hand on her shoulder instead. Is it just me, or is he already acting like she's his property or something? He's also completely ignored me, so I decide to change that.

"Photography, yeah?" I offer one hand, the other still holding Dafne's belongings.

"Yeah, dude," he shakes my hand, and even though I'm looking straight at him now, I can tell Dafne's eyes are on me and not on this beach boy cliché.

"Can I call you Romeo?" he smiles broadly, and before I can say *God no*, he turns to Dafne again.

"I've got a class I'm already late to, but I'll see you at the canteen for dinner? I'm having lunch with the boys."

"I'll see you, I'm sure," she replies, not sounding ecstatic at the prospect, but of course, he doesn't notice.

"Cool, later!" he plants a quick kiss on her cheek and flees down the hallway, his white sneakers nearly glowing. So they're on a cheek kiss base. I have the pressing urge to sucker-punch the bloke.

"Your tea must be cold," Dafne points out a tad stiffly, pulling lightly on her book and script I'm gripping with my right hand. I glance at the small cup, take it out, and drink it in a single gulp. Yes, it was in fact rather cold and gross. She lowers her head as if not to let me see the soft laugh that escapes her at the way I squint my eyes after drinking the tea. The plastic creaks under the pressure of my fingers, and I start, "Seems like–"

"What were you listening to? Before taking your earbuds out."

I was not expecting that question.

"*Songbird*," I reply, suddenly reminded of her Fleetwood Mac shirt. And our kiss. And all the ones after that, even if they weren't real. Her eyes widen and her eyebrows shoot to her hairline.

"You're not serious," she laughs, like it's a fact and not a question.

"Why would I not be serious about that?"

Her smile falters. "That's my favorite song," she says simply.

"It's a lovely song," I say, like the least slick person on planet Earth.

She takes on a thoughtful look, and I wish I could know what's going through her mind, but then she says, "Let's do that. Dance rehearsal, after lunch. Two-thirty?"

I nod wordlessly, and she leaves with a firm step. I find that I don't enjoy watching her walk away from me.

Chapter 24

Dafne

We have an hour for lunch break, so Ollie and I bring our food outside and sit at our favorite spot in the garden. Despite the near absence of sun, the weather is somewhat mild by London's standards, spring slowly making its way forth.

"Please tell me the story again," Ollie says, extracting his turkey sandwich from his rucksack. I release an exasperated breath and take a sip from my canteen.

"He took me to a popcorn place. Think *Charlie and the Chocolate Factory*, but it's popcorn."

"Amazing," he says slowly, and I all but throw his water bottle at him.

"Why do I allow you to bully me like this?" I sigh dramatically as he chugs the contents of the bottle so greedily, I'm not sure it's water.

"I'm serious! It was a genius idea, I have to hand it to him. I would have never thought of taking someone out for popcorn. Caramelised almonds, perhaps, but not–" he says, expression serious, but obviously taking the piss.

"Maybe I'll do it again," I say before taking a bite of my apple.

Ollie's nose scrunches up. "Why?"

"Why not?"

"Because you clearly don't like him, and it has nothing to do with popcorn. It's not like you to settle."

"Ethan is a good bloke. He has …"

"The emotional depth of a children's swimming pool?"

"I was going for 'an interesting sense of humour'", I smile. Ollie isn't entirely wrong; not that I'd want a potential boyfriend to talk to me about Proust all day, but Ethan also used the world *cool* more than fifteen times in the span of one hour. There should be a middle ground. Besides, why am I thinking about boyfriends at all? So much for swearing love off, Dafne.

I suddenly think of the mind-blowing kiss Theodore and I shared and my breath hitches in my throat. Then I think about how we're going to be alone and sweaty in a room in approximately twenty minutes.

"Okay, cards on the table," I sigh then, setting my food aside. "I have to tell you something, but you have to promise not to be mad at me."

He gestures for me to go on, and I look down at my lap. "I, well, not exactly *I*, but Theodore, rather–he kissed me. Uh, we kissed. I kissed him back. Not at rehearsals, I mean."

Ollie stares at me unblinking, his half-bitten sandwich long forgotten.

"When."

"I don't know," I say quietly–which is a lie, because I know precisely what day it was. "A while ago, but it's not like we're having an affair or anything, I mean, even saying it out loud is–"

Ollie waves a hand in front of me, which promptly shuts me up. "Does Devon know about this?" he asks, and I can't tell if he's shocked or something else.

"Uh, unless Theodore told him, which I assume he didn't, then no."

Ollie nods a few times, then goes back to gobbling his lunch down. I eye him suspiciously because I cannot believe he has nothing else to say. The bomb I just dropped on him should have him losing his shite.

"Uhm, did you miss the part where I told you Theodore Price stuck his tongue down my throat?" I whisper in disbelief.

"I heard you."

"You're not upset with me for not telling you sooner?"

"Have I ever been upset with you in my life?"

"I guess not," I say.

"But now I see exactly what is going on. I know who I'm dealing with."

I look up at him with a questioning look, so he starts to

elaborate.

"You entertain this Ethan idea because you're afraid of what the other option means for you. Except the Dafne I know doesn't play safe. She never did," he adds a little sadly, throwing me a metaphorical punch in the gut.

"Well, that's not how I was expecting this conversation to go," I huff. Ollie chuckles and unexpectedly offers me his hand. I curl my fingers around his and he squeezes once before letting go.

I'd honestly be lost without him, even if I don't like what he has to say.

"Either way I'm meeting him for a quick dance rehearsal after lunch, so that should be fun," I grimace.

"Ethan dances?" he smirks.

"Price, Ollie, I'm talking about Price," I say as I rub the back of my head, just to confirm it barely hurts now.

"You know, maybe it could be a lovely opportunity to chat," I ponder, an idea forming in my head.

He blinks twice, then raises both hands in surrender. "I know better than to ask for details," he declares, but I can tell he's more amused than anything else. I stuff my things in my tote bag and mess up Ollie's hair with one hand before jogging inside to get changed.

Ollie's right. I don't play safe.

Theodore

"Where is she?" I mutter to myself as I wait for Dafne just outside the dance studio, only to glance at my phone and find out I'm fifteen minutes early. The fact that I couldn't eat anything other than crackers and a sip of Devon's disgusting energising drink might have something to do with that–long lost are the days of smooth Theo, who didn't have to worry about talking to a girl. With this specific girl, all I had to think about a good enough retort to whatever argument we'd end up having.

Luckily or not, Dafne turns the corner exactly four minutes before the designated time.

"Hey, sorry I'm late, I met Ethan again on the way, he needed–never mind," she says, a little breathless, her canteen's handle dangling from two fingers.

Does the bloke follow her around?

"Did you run?" I ask instead.

"*No*," she glares. She definitely did.

I smirk, opening the door as I nod for her to go in. I put my rucksack next to the door, and as I reach to grab the cable to connect the loudspeaker to my phone I say, "Let's start with–"

"How about we practice one of the duels instead?" she interjects as she secures her hair in a high ponytail.

"Uh, shouldn't you take it easy? Besides, you don't have any fight scenes in the play–"

"I'm fine, and I know the sequences," she insists,

challenge clear in her tone. "I'm a fast learner."
"Fine by me," I nod. I'm not sure what the point is, but I can't bring myself to not see where it goes.

She walks to the small cabinet in the far left corner of the spacious room and extracts two wooden practice sticks, all but throwing one of them at me. We stand a foot apart from each other, bow, and the duel begins.

"Why don't we–" she huffs as she ducks to avoid my first jab, "make it more interesting?"

"Do tell," I reply, my gaze focused on her mock weapon.

"A truth for a truth," she rotates her stick in a half-circle motion, which I intercept, and our sticks clack when they meet above us. "You answer a question honestly, and I'll do the same."

The sticks slide apart as we push back.

She takes two retreating steps back, just like the choreography requires. She really has been paying attention, and I should be impressed–but this is just the kind of thing she would do. Which is perhaps somewhere between slightly annoying and quite admirable.

"I'll go first," she says, and I know we're both holding simple sticks, but for some reason it looks like hers could actually pierce me if she willed it to.

"Does anybody else know what you told me that day when you walked in on me and Ollie rehearsing?" she asks, no trace of teasing in her voice.
Bloody hell.

"Cutting right to the–" our weapons briefly clack again as I follow her across the room, "chase." Not long until Romeo stabs Tybalt now. Will that provide an excuse for me to end this game before it gets dangerous?

"No," I breathe. "My turn."

She moves her fingers in a forthcoming gesture, a few strands of hair having escaped her ponytail brushing over her forehead. I rotate my pretend sword until it collides with hers again.

"Do you still hate me?" I blurt out.

"That's a question you should ask yourself," she grunts, pushing against my stick with hers so that I find myself retreating a few steps.

We circle each other, not exactly following the original duel's choreography. When I point out it's her turn to answer, she says that she'll give a proper one, but only after I answer my own question first. It would be fair, if not for the fact I don't really want to talk about this, and there's no way I can get out of it again; I should have known my luck wouldn't last. If I've learned anything about Dafne, it's that she knows what she wants and she'll do whatever it takes to obtain it. Not so differently from me, after all. Before I can add anything else, she's running towards me with much more force than expected, and when she acts on Tybalt's last blow, the pretend sword held high in both of her hands, I mimic Romeo's fatal strike to his–her chest. She slowly drops the stick and pretends to fall to the ground, and I find myself scrambling to throw my weapon behind me and stop her from hitting the floor with her knees first. Now I'm keeping her upright with my arms securely planted on her back, our chests nearly pressed together.

We're both breathing heavily, and her eyes flicker to my lips for such a short moment I can't be sure I actually saw it. I should really step back, but I'm rooted in place and she's not backing away either. I wouldn't be surprised to know she's never backed away, literally or metaphorically, from anything in her life.

My next words flow out of me as if they'd been tied to an invisible string and pulled out of my mouth.

"I've told you before, I don't hate *you*. I hate that I'll never be as good as you. I hate this jealousy, and I hate that you've seen all the ugly parts of me, but you're still here. And I don't understand why."

Fuck my life.

It's the second time since I've known her that she looks taken aback; the first time was when she heard my stupid interview. She nods slowly.

"Ask me again," she repeats firmly, her fingers digging into my arms.

"Do you still hate me?" I ask after swallowing. Can bravado be passed by osmosis?

"I hate that you hate that I'm good," she whispers. "I hate that you should *know* how good *you* are, but still spent the last three years taking out your senseless frustrations on me. I hate that you didn't let me see the good parts sooner. And I hate that you chose the worst possible moment to decide to kiss me like that."

Fuck Fuck Fuck.

She suddenly pulls away and turns in one swift motion.

"Next time you kiss a girl, make sure it's for the right reasons," she says as she tugs the hair tie off and lets her hair free. She starts gathering her things, and I'm exactly where she left me.

I figure I have a choice: I can let her walk away again, or I can change this narrative once and for all. She has one hand on the door handle, and I reach her in a few strides, placing my hand over hers from behind.

"Am I out of time?" I ask in a low voice.

When I think she's about to elbow me in the stomach and wrench the door open, she turns around and lets her bag slip off her shoulder to the floor. Dafne looks up at me, something bold flashing in her eyes. She reaches to thread her fingers in my hair and pulls my mouth to hers.

Have I said fuck? Because now I understand what giving a drink to a thirsty man really means. I don't think I realised just *how badly* I wanted to kiss her again.

Dafne

I part my lips to allow his tongue in, and his hands move

to my hips as we retreat. He effortlessly lifts me to sit on top of the small table next to the stereo, a pen and a note pad clattering to the floor as I adjust myself on the surface with one arm draped around his neck and the other hand gripping the hair at his nape.

"Are you–mmh," I breathe as he moves to kiss my neck, "going to keep acting like-like I'm not the Juliet you wanted?" I detangle from around him to snake a hand under the hem of his shirt and trail my fingers over his abdominals. Holy Bard, does he have great muscles.

"No," he says before pressing another kiss to my jaw. "No, Dafne."

I tug lightly on his hair so that he pulls back with a small groan, just enough to look at me in the eyes. He sweeps a thumb over my bottom lip, brown eyes infused with gorgeous green roaming from my own to my mouth. "I don't know how to just *stop*," he admits. "In everything I do. I'm not built to feel things halfway." He licks his lips and squints a little, like he has to focus extra hard to say what he's thinking. I find that I'm not displeased by the notion I do that to him. After a few moments where the only sound is our breathing, ragged from both practicing the duel and kissing, he says, "But I really want to try." There goes honest Theodore again. Making my heart go to Zumba class.

"Good," I say quietly, the haze of the past few minutes clinging to every part of me.

He drops his head, his hand still cradling my face.

Now I'm having other kinds of thoughts entirely. He kisses me again, this time slowly. Deliberately. In a way I didn't think about being kissed, but that I enjoy way too much, if the heat spreading down my belly is of any indication.

"What about Ethan?" he asks then, his lips an inch from mine. "Are you still going to see him?"

Of course something had to ruin the moment.

"We're not in a relationship," I breathe, and I could swear his shoulder slump a little bit. "You and me," I clarify. Not even these stupid feelings coursing through my whole body, and the knowledge that no one can understand why I do what I do like he does, are enough to make me drop everything else in my life to be his groupie. History doesn't erase itself unless we do something about it.

His jaw works, then he takes a small step back, and his hands move to envelop the sides of my legs. It's quite the dominant gesture, and I find I enjoy it. A lot.

"I suppose not," he agrees. I can't tell if he's upset, but I'd be lying if I said I didn't feel the taste of disappointment. That's not what I wanted him to say. Ollie's words from earlier ring in my head like an alarm.
"That'd be too much now, wouldn't it," he continues.
"Wouldn't it be better if we shared you? You go out with Mr. Yo on the first and third day of the week, and we can make out every other day."
Upset it is, then. His hands are still on me though.

"I'm sorry, what do you want me to say? That I'll tell him to piss off because you don't like me talking to him?" I know I'm being harsh, but I want him to tell me the truth again. Because I know he's holding something back.

"He's an idiot, Dafne, and we both know it. Are you even into him? Because it sure didn't look like it earlier today."

He's not entirely wrong, but he doesn't need to know that right now.

"Why are you acting like I owe you something?"

"You *don't*. But it's going to be really hard to fix *this*," he gestures between us, "if I know that you spend your spare time with him."

"I went out with him on–" I sigh. "I don't understand you. You *just* said you'd try. You don't want me to see other people, and you've told me something about you that no one else knows. You've got nothing else to say?"

"Don't do that," he grimaces. Why is he so eager for a fight, even after everything we've just said and done, is beyond me. Well, here goes the million pounds questions. "You want to date me, Price?" I look him straight in the eye.

His mouth opens and closes without saying anything. His shoulders are clearly tense now, in such contrast to how he was melting into me mere minutes ago, it seems impossible. He closes his eyes and takes a breath, his brows furrowing. I'd like to smooth them with my thumb, but I don't move a muscle.

He eventually settles on, "It's complicated."

Of course.

"I've heard that one before," I say bitterly, hopping off the table so that he has to take another step back to make space for me. My hair is probably absolutely wild right now, but I can't bring myself to care. A truth for a truth, was it? Even if he doesn't give one back now, mine will have to do.

"I'm nobody's pastime, Theodore. I have been once, and I won't do it again. So make no mistake: I didn't kiss you twice because I was desperate for it. I did it because," I use my pointer finger to move his chin ever so slightly–I want him to really look at me when I say this,

"I wanted to kiss *you*. I can look you in the eyes and tell you that even if it makes me ten kinds of crazy, I *like* you.

A troubled expression hardens his features at the words.

"Why is it so hard for you to do the same?"

He doesn't answer.

"You want us to be more? Own it," I say then.

I fix my hair back into a low ponytail as I lower myself to the stereo. I can see from the corner of my eye that he hasn't moved.

"We've got a dance to practice now," I remind him as I turn on the music. He doesn't say anything else, and we rehearse in perfect, silent synchrony.

Theodore

How do you tell someone that your head has *got to be* to be wired up the wrong way, because you made a very stupid decision that could potentially make them hate you and it's not right to pretend you didn't? How do you tell them there is so much they don't know, and I see now that none of it is a good excuse for everything that you've put them through?

When Dafne leaves, I glance at the clock on the wall and see I have exactly fifteen minutes before I need to get to the theatre. I tidy the room up, make sure it looks as if no one had just been here. As if I hadn't kissed Dafne on that table. As if I hadn't tried, and failed, to get four simple words out: *I like you too*. Maybe one day I'll be the kind of person that can accept good things and never look back. And maybe trying isn't enough; sometimes the people we care about need us to show up and do the thing.

I make my way to the locker rooms for a quick change of shirt. I wash my face, too, and when I turn the water off I take a moment to breathe deeply. A buzzing energy envelops me as soon as I set foot in the theatre, my castmates chatting or stretching. Naturally, my attention is caught by Dafne's ponytail and the easy smile she throws Margaret as they talk. Someone's pale arm suddenly weighs on my shoulder and Devon says, "You look stressed, Montague. I'm taking you out one of these nights."

Chapter 25

Dafne

The next day, Mr. Hackle's voice echoes through the first row of seats where I'm sitting. "Ten-minute break before we go over Act Four," and as he scratches his eyebrow with his thumb adds a muttered, "and that means *ten* minutes, Thomas." Thomas throws him a covert glare, but we all know he's the tardy one. I'm about to get off stage to drink some water, when Ms. Patterson signals me to come over to her seat next to Mr. Hackle. "Aya is in the backstage taking measurements, Dafne," she whispers, making sure we don't bother the evidently tested man sitting on her left.

"Off you go," she smiles pleasantly, and I nod and thank her for letting me know before making my way backstage as quietly as possible. Aya, one of the school's tailors, is finishing taking someone else's measurements–Theodore's, of course.

"You are all set," she says, rolling up her measuring tape and scribbling on her tiny leather notebook. He thanks her warmly, and it's like getting hit by a cricket bat in the stomach. I shake the feeling off, pretending to stretch my shoulders–perks of being in a theatre, where no one will question random exercising. He doesn't notice me, and as he slips his APDAS sweatshirt back on, the movement is slow enough for me to notice how firm his skin looks under the few delicate yellow lights in the backstage area. Not a single lock of his chestnut hair is out of place, and in this precise moment in time, he looks exactly like he did the day we met, just outside the audition room. My head spins at how drastically things have changed since then. When he looks up and sees me, he nearly trips on the powder blue jacquard bag where Aya keeps her tools.

"Careful, or your understudy will dance on your corpse," I say, and I wish the floor would open and swallow me whole. Really, Dafne? Is that the best you can do? You're not supposed to joke with him. You're mad at him, remember?

Theodore huffs a laugh, and he opens his mouth, but takes one look at Aya and stops himself.

"I'm not the one the show needs to sell out," he says then, like he's just pointed out water is wet. We stare at each other for a second too long, then a rustling sound of fabric coming from behind him makes me break eye contact. He shoots Aya a look, then clears his throat before disappearing through the curtains.

"That was adorable," Aya sighs, handing me her notebook to hold as with one fluid movement she starts taking my waist's measurements. "I didn't know you were dating on *and* off stage," she adds before I can comment on it, a playful smile on her thin lips. My eyes grow wide at her assumption, her measuring tape circling my forearm. Alright, where are the cameras? How is this happening again? It's like there's a glitch in the simulation, as Ollie would say.

"Why would you say that?" I feel more than see Aya shrug, as she snatches the notebook from my hand and with one of the numerous pencils she keeps on herself at all times starts scribbling numbers.

"For one, he asked if I'd already seen you today," she starts, and why does it sound like she's about to give me an actual *list* of reasons? "And then, you know, we made small talk. I said I thought you were spectacular in last year's *Titus Andronicus*, and he agreed. Something about you outshining everyone else …" she says absent-mindedly, the scratch of pencil on paper almost unbearable. "… I think."

You think? I want to yell, but Aya's patting my shoulder and saying something that sounds a lot like "All done." I wouldn't bet my life on it, though, because I'm not listening anymore. Even sweet Aya thinks we're a thing. Wait–I didn't *correct* her on it. I really should. I turn around from the spot I'm still rooted in, but when I turn Aya's gone, her bag and pencils with her.

"Yes Dad, I've been repeating the mantra," I mumble into the phone as I'm balancing a cupholder with three steaming-hot coffees in one hand and adjusting my ever-slipping tote bag on my shoulder with the other. My father has self-proclaimed himself as my personal motivational speaker ever since I decided I was going to be an actor at nine years old after seeing *Macbeth* at our local theatre. As such, he comes up with new life mottos on a monthly basis for me to recite. This month's is an acronym–*PEA*, which stands for Positive Energetic Attitude–and I can picture him perfectly, sitting at our round cherry wood table, scribbling in one of his many notebooks.

"Good, good, good, and tell your friends to use them, too!" he says, pride lingering in his voice.

I assure him I will have the message delivered and ask him to kiss mum for me as I hang up–then stop dead in my tracks. Theodore is standing a few feet from me, hands in his pockets, looking perfectly relaxed. I take a couple of steps back and try hiding behind a low wall. He's chatting amiably with someone I can't see as they're blocked by a pillar. If I want to know who it is I can't turn around and take a different route; I have to pass right next to them. *Do I* want to know who's the mysterious girl? Why am I assuming it's a girl at all? I grimace at myself. Is this the reason he won't–

"Hey, stalker," Phoebe whispers in my ear and I let out a yelp the entire neighbourhood probably hears.

"What are you do–" I push the coffee tray in

Phoebe's hands hoping that will make her be quiet. "I'm not doing anything," I say quickly, reaching for my water bottle from my bag and taking a long sip. "I was waiting for you." Phoebe raises a blond eyebrow. "So you crouching behind a wall has nothing to do with the fact that Theodore is over there, talking to a pretty second-year student?" she asks, the smile on her lips expanding with each word.

So it *is* a girl. Probably the girl Ollie mentioned. Fine. He can talk to whomever he pleases. I have been seeing Ethan after all … one time and a half. Even though the thought of kissing him hasn't even crossed the threshold of my mind.

And Theodore knows that.

"Of course not," I raise one shoulder, and slowly link my arm with hers so as not to make the coffees drop. "In fact, we are going to walk past them right now." We start walking, and when we reach their proximity, Theodore turns towards us as if I'd called out to him. I say nothing and can't stop a nod in acknowledgment, but repress the urge to greet him like a normal, unfazed person–which I would have done if he hadn't been talking to this girl. *Hey*, he mouths, eyes lingering on me for that extra second. As for the girl … she *is* pretty. I've never seen her before, and I don't know where she could've met him but–Nuh uh. Stop. Rewind. Not a problem. Comparison kills joy. Insecurity? I don't know her. I'm amazing. Phoebe downright yells, "Hello Theodore!" flashing him a toothy smile, and I pull her a little more vigorously than intended. Coffee has definitely been spilled now.

"Was that necessary? Whose side are you on? I mutter as soon as we're out of his hearing range, snatching my coffee from the tray.

"Was it, Dafne?" she asks innocently, peering behind us. "And we're both on your side, given his eyes are totally glued to your back, babes."

I narrow my eyes at her, willing my body not to turn around to see for myself.

"I know what you're doing, Nilsen, and it's not going to work." I gulp half my coffee down, and Phoebe snorts before taking a sip from her own cup.

"But what if this whole nemesis thing is more than just that, Daf? What if all the tension and fighting and *kissing* between you two has all been leading up to a *glorious* riva–"

I stop abruptly in the street, raising a finger in warning. "If you say the words rivals to lovers I'm going to put in a request for a new roommate," I threaten, to which she gasps.

"You wouldn't," genuine worry in her eyes.

After a moment of suspense, I confirm that I wouldn't. "But enough of this, yeah?" I plead.

"We kissed. I'm not delusional–it was great. Bloody magical. Did I think things could be different after finding out that he has actual *emotions*, and is funny, and is capable of warmth and–" I sigh.

"I've made my feelings very clear, and he's had the opportunity to talk to me today and he didn't, so he's obviously determined to ignore whatever is going on between us. He's confused about what he wants, and I can't have that. Besides, he's probably seeing that girl now, and I'll be dead before I pine over another man. Okay?" I'm out of breath, out of energy, out of sorts.

Phoebe nods sadly and links her arm with mine, giving me a gentle squeeze. As we resume our walk back to APDAS, I can't help but doubt my own words.

Chapter 26

Dafne

"For the third time," I shout into the phone to let myself be heard over the pouring rain, "I don't know where your red bra is. Have you checked under the bed?" I tell a distressed Phoebe, who sounds on the verge of losing her mind over one very specific piece of lingerie.

"*Why would it be–*" a beat.

"You were saying?"

Phoebe lets out a nervous laugh. "See? I'd be lost without you. *Now*," she quickly changes topic. "What are you wearing tonight? You should go for that gorgeous lavender dre–" Phoebe's deafening squeal hits me from the other end of the phone then, and I figure it can only mean one thing: Peter, her boyfriend, has just entered the room. When he and Phoebe first met, he'd accidentally splattered his scone-on-the-go on her brand new coat on a particularly busy day in Piccadilly Circus, and immediately offered to buy her a new one.

"I'll even add a bag of scones as interest," he'd said. He'd held true to his word, and on their first date, much to Phoebe's delight, he brought her a cotton candy-pink tin box filled to the brim with strawberry jam scones, as well as a beautiful bouquet of peonies. One of those peonies is dried and framed in our room, even two years later.

I've heard the story eleven times. I counted them. But the light in Phoebe's eyes whenever she talks about their literal meet-cute is so bright, I could never stop her from telling it again. Unfortunately, he's had to move to Doncaster for work, and their time together has been drastically reduced. He's only in town for a few days at a time, and Phoebe wants him to decompress and enjoy himself.

"Say hi to Peter for me," I'm unable to keep the softness from my voice.

"He says hi, I'll see you later babes!" she squeals again and makes an obnoxiously sweet kissing sound before hanging up.

I throw my phone in my tote bag and make a quick run for a covered archway I can shelter myself under from the unwavering rain. It's not that I'd forgotten about our monthly gathering at *Glinda's*–the pub all the Musical Theatre kids go to for karaoke night, where Phoebe kept dragging Ollie and I again and again until it became a habit to go there–but with the crazy amount of rehearsals, regular classes and Price's, well, everything, I haven't really taken any time to just stop and be. I should do that.

About three hours later, I'm about to reach the handle to *Glinda's* door, when a hand bats my own away.

"Allow me," Ollie says, and I'm surprised he's on time. We would have come together but he said he and Devon were rehearsing. Is that what it's called now?

As we stroll inside, the too-sweet scent of the pub fills my nostrils, and above the crowd, a head of blonde hair jumps up and down, a hand waving frantically.

"That would be Phoebe," I chuckle, but just as I'm making my way to the table she and Peter reserved for us, someone bumps into me.

"Yooo, what are the chances!" Ethan shouts.

"Hey, I didn't think I'd meet you here," I say honestly. He doesn't really paint the average musical theatre fan picture.

"They make the best tacos here," he shrugs with a huge smile. I wonder how he manages to always look so happy. Ollie clears his throat, and I quickly introduce them.

"Well, we were about to meet up with our friends," he says after they shake hands, starting towards our designated table. "If you don't mind–"

"I'd love to meet your friends," Ethan pats Ollie on the arm, the latter staring at the point he touched like he just burned him with a lighter. I shoot Ollie a look to make sure he's not about to tackle Ethan to the ground for the boundary overstep. I don't want to be the bad guy and I figure there's no harm in introducing my friends to him, so I lead the way and wave to where Phoebe and Peter are.

"Congrats on landing Juliet, Daf," Peter says, offering me his knuckles to fist bump.

"Thanks Pete," I smile at him while Ollie greets Phoebe with a nod. Weird.

I introduce Phoebe and Peter to Ethan, who goes straight for bear hugs with both of them by way of greeting. Phoebe looks only mildly shocked by the gesture, and Peter mutters a weak *right* as Ethan lets go of him.

This is fine.

"We took the liberty of ordering for you," Phoebe says then, shimmying with her shoulders and chest as the first notes of L*ady Marmalade* play in the background.

"Wait a second," I gasp with my palms flat on the table, "It's *Moulin Rouge* night?"

Phoebe's squeal of excitement erupts at my left, making me jump in my seat.

"You bet it is," Ollie says, nodding approvingly. I groan, because I know what he's going to say next. "Who's forgotten about Dafne's drunk rendition of *Your Song*?" he muses after a few seconds, and a pair of *Not Mes* rises from the table.

"It was *one* time," I hold up a finger, "and I was *semi*-drunk," I nod in Ollie's direction. He shrugs a half-arsed apology, and I shake my head at the memory of my little incident, which I reluctantly tell Ethan about. It'd been Phoebe's birthday during our first year and mind you, I had never gotten drunk before in my life, and never again since. I'd been so excited for the surprise dinner Ollie and I had put together at her favorite place, that I'd chugged two pints of beer on an empty stomach. The rest is history. Ethan thinks it's cool, of course.

"So," Phoebe claps her hands to gather our attention, "who is duetting with me? And my love, before you volunteer, please don't," she says, throwing a guilty look in her boyfriend's direction. Peter narrows his eyes and scowls at her. "I have other talents," he huffs, looking genuinely offended by Phoebe's lack of faith in his singing skills.

"Of course *min kjærlighet,*" she chuckles what I'm sure is some affectionate nickname as she pats his cheek.

"I will," I provide, because although Musical Theatre is not my field, I've always loved singing, and I can hardly miss a chance of performing; the one place I feel completely at home is a stage, even if it's a crammed karaoke one. A waitress wearing a green and black Wicked-themed uniform brings our non-alcoholic drinks, and I barely have time to take a couple of sips that Phoebe is dragging me out of my seat, yelling a, "You better clap for us!" at our friends. Phoebe signs our names on the song sheet–apparently, no one has signed up for *The Elephant Love Medley*, which is mine and Phoebs' specialty. I can't count the number of times we've belted it in our room, earning us many angry knocks on the paper-thin walls of our dorm room. Worth it. As I'm turning towards the stage to listen to the next singer, an impatient huff makes me raise my eyes and–no way.

This must be a conspiracy. He's here too? Is there a reunion of all the blokes from literally any department except for the one where they actually study the subject? Is my ex going to stroll out of the toilet next?

"Look what Elphaba dragged in," I joke dumbly, because I'm not sure where we stand after our last … close encounter. I am simply unable to ignore how something stirs in me whenever I see him, cast in the new light of the knowledge that he feels something for me, even though he refuses to let it out. I wonder what's going on in his head. If he thinks about it as much as I do.

Theodore releases a breath when he takes me in–he probably hadn't seen me or was enjoying himself and my presence interrupted his peace. Which would be hysterical since he's stuck his tongue in my mouth and had his hands all over me multiple times now. Willingly, I mean.

I've never seen him here before, so I can only assume that one of his friends might have dragged him here with force.

That being said … I am not here to stress tonight. That's going to be the mantra. I turn towards Phoebe, who smiles at me weakly, and as we wait for our turn, I nonchalantly glance around us. No more Theodore in sight. That's good. As the two girls currently singing *Come What May* at the top of their lungs finish their duet, the red-haired owner of the pub dressed in a sparkling white and pink dress with a tiara precariously propped on her head hops on stage and taps her microphone twice. "Alright, everyone, a big round of applause, great job darlings," she smiles politely as they stumble off stage giggling. "Let's welcome our lovely Dafne and Phoe–oh, sorry dearies," she stammers, and I shoot Phoebe a confused look. "Dafne and Theodore, who will surely delight us with *Your Song*!" My jaw goes slack so fast I think it might detach from the rest of my face, Phoebe whispers an *I don't know, just go,* into my ear before nudging me towards the stage.

"What in the–" I turn around, but Theodore is already being pushed on the other side of the stage by Devon, the latter looking at me like he's afraid I'm going to hit him with the microphone that's just been shoved into my hand. He isn't wrong to be. A second later, the music starts. I have two options: I can either get off the stage and leave him to sing the song on his own just to spite whoever is responsible for this, or do what I really want to do and be here. With him.

I search for Phoebe in the crowd and find not just her, but all three of my friends staring at me with wide eyes. Ethan looks like he's at an amusement park and shoots me a thumbs up.

It's almost comical, really. Almost.

You've got this, Phoebe mouths to soothe whatever must be transpiring through my eyes.

It's only one of the most romantic love declarations in the

history of music, but it's no big deal, right?

I decide to turn my brain off for the few minutes of the song and just enjoy this. It. Whatever it is that we're about to do. When I finally look at Theodore, the lights casting him in green and blue, all thoughts quiet down. He looks surprised, but not as on edge as I'd thought.

Just like that I'm singing, and so is he, and Sweet Caroline, does he *sing*. I shouldn't be surprised, but it seems all he ever does lately is surprise me. Three minutes and thirty-nine seconds later, we've just sung the last verse, and I wouldn't be able to tell you when or how it happened, but we're standing close. Way too close for comfort. Under the dim lights above the stage, the green of his eyes greedily makes its way among the brown; I think this might be the moment I have no doubt, it's the prettiest pair of eyes I've ever seen. They're flickering between mine, and my brain is screaming to move out of the way before he sees anything I might regret showing, but my body is planted firmly in the stubborn eagerness of being close to him.

As the music ends, a thunderous clap explodes through the crowd, and as if a spell were broken, I snap out of my rapture. Ethan is clapping enthusiastically, I see Phoebe and Peter share a knowing look, and Ollie's towering figure as he lets out a whistle and a whoop. Theodore clears his throat, taking in the ovation, and leaning in ever so slightly, he says, "Not bad for two amateurs, huh?"

I can't help but smile. "Yeah," I whisper, "not bad."

When we hop off the stage, and a few people I don't know tell us we were great as they pass by. Not to gloat, but our voices do sound really nice together.

"So *that* was unexpected," I say to Theodore.

"I'm afraid Devon might have had something to do with it," he replies with a resigned shake of the head.

I guess both of our best friends have been getting ideas, then. He looks like he's about to say something else, but the music gets obscenely loud, and on some unspoken agreement, we wave each other awkward goodbyes as we turn opposite ways to reach our tables. I don't know what I was expecting, but I don't like the space we've put between us. Not that it's my job to get him to talk, anyway. Never mind our bloody High School Musical moment. It's Troy that looks for Gabriella, not the other way around.

When I join my friends, who had already scurried back to our table, their chatter abruptly stops.

I sit in my chair and turn to Phoebe, who's folding a napkin and pretending I'm not staring right at her. "Any idea how that just happened?" I ask. They all turn to look at me in one robot-like movement. For a split second, I regret not pretending nothing happened and imagine sprinting out of the door, because some part of me isn't sure I want to hear whatever they're going to say. Ollie would probably tackle me like a rugby player to prevent my escape, though.

"Elizabeth must have messed up with the names on the list," Phoebe shrugs, referring to the pub's owner. *With Devon's help*, I think to myself.

"That was …" Ethan starts, shaking his blond mane, "… awesome, dude!"

I blink once, my head suddenly empty. Peter eyes him as if he'd just insulted his mother. I've told my friends about every single skirmish or fight I've had with Theodore, so I don't blame him for thinking at least one of us is insane.

One corner of my mouth lifts involuntarily at the sheer absurdity of it all.

"I thought you, uh, strongly disliked each other?" Peter asks then, and I think about how if I'd been murdered by the imaginary burglar, I could have spared myself this.

"Don't let the lights and the song fool you," I say as vaguely as possible and wave a hand towards the stage.

"Baby," Phoebe drawls. "Haven't I forced you to watch enough rom-coms to know *that* was a *lot of things*, but hate–" Peter coughs loudly enough to cover her next words; Phoebe is probably forgetting that Ethan is here. To be fair, he's still smiling as he orders another drink, seemingly oblivious, or at the very least unfazed, by the situation. Bless his heart. Before his next drink even arrives, Ethan says, "Bathroom break, y'all! Don't tell more funny stories without me," and disappears through

the crowd.
"I know what you said, Daf, but I think *you* know I'm right," Phoebe adds the second he's gone, rolling the straw of her drink between two fingers.
I press my lips into a thin line, turning towards Ollie, pleading with him with my eyes.

"A little help?" I mutter expectantly when he says nothing. He breaks into a seemingly innocent smile, before saying "Do you want me to lie or do you want the truth?" My face falls. I've known Ollie the longest, he's seen me at my lowest and knows me inside out. I already know what he's going to say.
"Lie, please," I say, crossing my arms on the table.
Ollie snorts.
"I stand by what I told you, Daf." It's such a simple sentence, but the serious tone he reserves for delicate conversations–which is somehow discordant with the fairy lights dangling above our booth–is enough to make me close my eyes and wish things were easy, once in a while. Besides, why is everyone suddenly on team Price? It'd be so much easier if they just agreed that the best thing would be to forget about him altogether.

I sigh deeply, pressing my fingers to my temples and suddenly finding a spot of grease on the table extremely interesting. "None of it excuses the fact that he's been an arsehole for the past few years, mind you," Ollie adds then, and when I shift my gaze up again, they're all looking at me fondly.

At least I know that whatever happens, the people at this table have my back.

I'm lying in bed, and as predicted, that traitor organ I have in lieu of a regular brain won't shut off even for what could've been a blissful few hours. Phoebe promised she wouldn't sleep until I did, but the poor thing always had the enviable ability to fall right into Morpheus' arms the second her head hit the pillow. It's a few minutes past one a.m. when I'm in the thick of combing through a hundred questions all crammed in my head that my phone lights up on the night table. I assume it's going to be Ollie, resorting to his never-ending archive of acting memes to make me laugh, but it's that unknown number again. Well, it's not unknown anymore–it's Theodore. I realise I still haven't saved his contact. I know from experience it's easier to let go of things if you don't let yourself get attached to them.

> I don't know if you're up, I'm not familiar
> with your sleeping patterns.
> I just wanted to tell you it was fun,
> singing together.
> *Sent 1:04 a.m.*

I consider pretending I never read the text, after all I could be sleeping, or studying, or doing whatever else one does at night, but some masochist part of me is determined not to get any sleep at all. Besides, is he really not going to mention yesterday? Or is he just ignoring it, hoping it will go away?

I'm awake. For the record, my sleeping patterns are nonexistent. But yes, it was fun. Not full-house-on-opening-night kind of fun, but still.
Sent: 1:06 a.m.

Having trouble sleeping again?
Sent: 1:07 a.m.

Yeah, you could say that. How about you? Mr. Hackle will have our heads if we're late tomorrow.
Sent: 1:09 a.m.

Just a lot of thoughts. I should try to, though. Devon will throw a shoe at me if I don't turn the phone off. Have you tried one of those rainforests sounds apps? I'm told they work wonders. Goodnight.
Sent: 1:11 a.m.

Goodnight. Maybe I've actually managed to fall so deeply asleep that I'm having a very vivid, albeit absurd dream, because that single word makes me want to shove my face into the pillow and scream, which I understand is not a reasonable reaction–but I guess that's what emotional damage and years of depriving myself of affection that wasn't my family's or my best friends' did to me.

Let's not upset our Tybalt, then.
I'll give those a try. Night.
Sent: 1:14 a.m.

I must have completely lost my mind, because I actually do end up downloading one of those apps, and above Phoebe's soft snoring, the sounds of tropical birds and of waves lapping on a shore eventually, incredibly lull me to a dreamless sleep.

Theodore

After texting Dafne goodnight, I'm left alone with the stream of my thoughts. Tonight really was fun. I'm not used to having genuine fun anymore, and it left me a little breathless, on that stage. And maybe it's selfish of me, of even just imagining how much fun we could have together.

All I'd have to do is stop worrying. Accepting that it wouldn't be a betrayal to myself. Just a change of perspective. Taking a chance. Which I realise is easier said than done, especially when there's a voice in the back of your head reminding you of everything that could go wrong.

I think it's time I start thinking about what could go right, even if it costs me.

I need to talk to her soon. Because the only truth is she couldn't have been more straightforward if she'd tried, and the least I can do is be the same.

I just need to find the right moment.

"Theo?" Devon mumbles in the darkness.

"What?"

"You're welcome."

Chapter 27

Dafne

Ollie has the weirdest look on his face as I go through my vocal warming exercise for vowels. He's staring at his phone's stopwatch, but I don't think he is actually seeing the seconds tick by on the screen.

"E-E-E-E-your hair is on fire–" I attempt to get his attention, with no results. "Ollie?"

"Yeah?"

"What's going on?" I laugh. "You look a million years away."

He cuts me a look, then slumps on the nearest chair. "I kissed him," he says as he pushes the heel of his hand in one eye.

"Devon?" I ask, throwing myself on the seat next to his. "How was it? Was there tongue? No, you don't have to tell me. But I did tell you, so it's only fair."

He's quiet for a few seconds, then nods.

"Oh come on," I groan, "you've got to give me more than that."

"I just … did it, Daf. I didn't think about the implications or consequences, it just felt like the right thing to do in the moment. And he definitely kissed me back, so … glad I took the risk," he says.

"Ollie, I'm so happy for you. Truly." I pat his knee twice.

"I'm so weak for redheads. Male *or* female, apparently," he considers. We share a look, then burst out laughing. Truth be told, Tam was a redhead, too.

When we've sobered up he says, "We could go on double dates, you know," implying something that ought not to be implied.

"These vocal cords won't warm themselves–" I start to bolt off my chair, but Ollie rises with me.

"I would normally advise you against making the first move, but are you really okay with staying in this limbo forever?"

"There is no limbo, Ollie," I absently pick at the corner of my Use of Voice textbook. "I don't know why you and Phoebe are so attached to this idea of me and Price together, but all I can see myself getting out of everything that's happened is polite conversation. No amount of romantic singing can change that. I'm not going to beg for more, if that's not in the cards."

My hand hurts from transcribing the whole of my lines, but as I've always found it helpful for memorisation purposes, it's worth the momentary pain. I should probably be using this time to do something good for me, like, I don't know, actively try to get some sleep–but if I don't keep myself occupied, I'll think about Theodore, and that shouldn't be number one on my priority list, should it?

It's almost nine, and Phoebe is already yawning on her bed. "Whoever said actors don't know what strain is, clearly didn't know shite," she mumbles, and I smile in agreement.

"You can turn off the lights, Phoebs, I've got my reading light," I offer.

"Shouldn't you sleep too? You've been getting half of the recommended eight hours. More like a third of that," she scowls. She takes sleep very seriously.

"You know I can't, not this early at least."

She sighs dramatically, and extends her arm to the light switch, bathing our room in near darkness. I release a deep breath and roll my shoulders on our far from ergonomic chair, debating whether I should actually try to rest. Before I can make a decision, my phone lights up with a message notification.

Are you up?
Sent: 9:03 p.m.

My heart rate goes up in the time it takes me to read who

the message is from and what it says. There's no reason a simple question should make my heart speed up so much, but I'm quite sure that if I smoked, I'd need an entire packet of cigarettes right now.

My every waking thought used to be occupied by acting, and studying, and rehearsing, over and over. What's happened to me?

I cover my phone under the desk as to not wake Phoebe, who is already snoring softly. I really don't need a third-degree questioning session right now. I panic a little, because if I don't answer soon it'll look like I'm thinking too hard about what to say, and if I answer immediately I'll just seem desperate. So, of course, I type the stupidest thing I could have possibly thought of. The king of the friendzone.

The thumbs-up emoji.

"Shite," I hiss at myself, slapping a hand over my forehead. To my surprise, an answer still comes.

Look out your window.
Sent 9:07 p.m.

I frown at the screen, fervently hoping he's not one of those *I saw the moon and it made me think of you* blokes. Or maybe I hope that he is, so I have an excuse to forget about him as quickly as possible. I get up quietly, then walk to the small window overlooking the garden. There are only a few lights still on downstairs, but it's enough for me to see Theodore looking up and waving his fingers at me.

Another notification buzzes.

> I'd like to talk.
> *Sent 9:08 p.m.*

Are you really going to
make me wear shoes again?
I thought I was shoe-free
until morning.
Sent: 9:09 p.m.

> The nerve. Socks, too.
> *Sent 9:10 p.m.*

That makes me snort, and I turn towards Phoebe to make sure she's still snoring. I look down at him again in time to see him pocket his phone and tilt his head in a forthcoming gesture. I sigh, think this is a very bad idea, yet still find myself slipping my shoes on, grabbing my keys and jacket and silently slipping out the door.

Once I reach him, he looks at me wordlessly for a second, then starts walking down the graveled path circling the garden. "I followed your advice, about the app," I start. "Slept like a baby."

"I'm glad."

He's *glad.* Grand.
"You know," I continue, since it looks like he won't, "you could've climbed the wall. What kind of second-hand Romeo are you?"
He breathes out a laugh and shakes his head lightly.
I am so not prepared for his next choice of words.

"Would breaking my neck be enough of a declaration?

My smile falters. "Declaration of what?" I ask quietly, looking everywhere but at him.

"You know what."

"Nuh-uh." He'll have to give me more than that.

I nervously rub at the inside of my jacket's pockets where my hands have been tucked the whole time.

"I'm tired, Dafne." he sighs, turning towards me. "It's exhausting, not being able to bloody think anymore without your face coming up in my head. I can't stand the mention of coconut or the sight of *rain* because it makes me think of you. We're in London, Dafne! It rains *all the time.* It's–" he clenches his fists at his side, and I'm sure that if he had a punching ball in front of him he'd have a hell of a time with it. "You wanted the truth, so here it is. It wasn't in my plans. We were supposed to keep up the bickering until the year was over and we could *finally* go our separate ways."
"Supposed to? Is there a contract I haven't been told about on the nature of our relationship? I ask, aware of how bitter I sound, but I can't help it.

Besides, what is he even saying? That him willingly seeking me out is somehow my fault? I haven't changed around him. I'm the same person I was when he *didn't* like me. The only thing that's changed is this gnawing feeling in my stomach that I can't shake when he's around, and it's not hate. It's a hundred times worse because I should have known better.

"Did you make me rush down here so you could essentially tell me you're repulsed by the feelings you have for me?" I add.

"Christ, Dafne, no," he groans, so I rush to him and whisper, "Maybe keep your voice down?"

And now we're at two inches from each other again.

His eyes roam over my face, and there's both softness and frustration in them.

"I need to show you something," he says after a few moments.

He extracts his phone from his back pocket and swipes his thumb on the screen to unlock it. I take a step back, but he grabs my elbow to tug me back to him. I'm not completely opposed.

"These are my grandparents," he starts, and I immediately recognise the photo as the same one I saw the night we got stuck in the prop room. Something tells me he's always had that specific lock screen and has no intention of changing it, and for some reason it makes my heart drum louder in my ribcage.

"My grandmother's name is Mary, and my grandpa

is Frank," he explains as we both look at the picture he must have scanned a long time ago, tiny, sparse white dots giving its age away.

"And they are–" he clears his throat, and I dare a glance at him, and his brows are furrowed in concentration; he's always so careful not to let too much emotion show.

I'd like to change that.

"They are my parents as far as I'm concerned, and they are the reason I bust my arse off. Every good thing in my life, I owe it to them. They have sacrificed so much for me to be here today, while my parents are just … barely in the picture. Which is not to say I blame them for my mistakes, because I don't."

I had no idea.

"When I actually managed to get into APDAS, I made my grandparents a promise. That I'd be the best, no matter what. I owed them that much."

Realisation strikes me like a slap in the face.

"You need us to be perfect," I say, echoing his words from not so long ago, on the day we first kissed.

He looks at me then, really looks at me, nodding slowly.

"And you–you are. Always have been. While I always felt a step behind you."

I release a deep sigh and close my eyes. I feel like I could cry. Out of sadness, but also anger, because we could have talked this through, if I'd known. Stabbing disappointment, both at him and myself. I thought I'd made it clear that I was never out to get him, that my work was about me and me alone. That I fought back be cause I was never in the business of being quiet if I felt wronged–and I *did*. And I'm mad at myself, because I waited until a few months ago to even ask for the first time, while I could have been the bigger person. But this is where we're at now. I consider my next words carefully.

"I understand what it means to make sacrifices, Theodore. I understand what it means to want to make someone proud. And while I don't know what your parents have put you through, what I do know is …" I click my tongue, scouring my head for the right words. Something tells me this is a now or never moment. I take his free hand and squeeze his fingers. They're warm, of course, much warmer than mine, and he squeezes back, never taking his eyes off me. I wonder if he can read everything I'm thinking on my face.

"I don't enjoy it, you know. The fighting. I never have. I just felt like you didn't deem me worthy of being here, and it made me lose my head," I huff out a breath. "So I reacted. I'm just sorry we didn't figure each other out sooner, you know."

He nods, something wistful tugging at the corners of his mouth. I refrain from kissing it away.

"I've been such a prick," he laughs sadly. "You had every right to act the way you did. I just got so caught up in this idea of perfection that I," he swallows. "I lost sight of everything else. I looked at you and all I saw was something to best. That's awful and … I am sorry."

"Thank you. I think that a man who knows when to apologise is very sex–" I start with a smirk, but he interrupts me by tugging at my hand and wrapping his arms around my waist, pulling me close for a hug.

We are hugging. I don't know how, but this is setting a small fire alight in my chest even more so than when we kissed. But *this* hug–oh dear. I wrap my arms around his neck and bask in the moment, suddenly unaware of the cold. I like this version of Theodore, but most importantly, I acknowledge how monumental this moment is for me. Trusting people is not something I take lightly, but right now I feel like maybe it would be okay to trust him.

So on the walk back, I tell him everything.

About how I had a boyfriend all through college–Noah. How perfectly wonderful he was at first. How in the summer after college ended, he'd been acting distant, but every time I'd ask about it he'd just say school had tired him out. How the day before I auditioned for APDAS, we were in the car, and he got a text and my eyes fell to the screen. The text said *are you still with the second-hand actress?*

Theo has a troubled look, his brows lowered.

"When I confronted him about it," I keep explaining, "after denying it for a bit, he came clean. He'd been seeing that girl for months behind my back. I felt *so* stupid.

Because after I left for APDAS it would have gone on and on with me counting down the days until I could see him again while he was shagging someone else.

"So you see, that's why I can't afford not to be able to trust you. To not know with absolute certainty that you want *me*. I can't do that to myself."

He shakes his head almost imperceptibly as he once again holds me impossibly closer. "I'm sorry you had to go through that. I *want you* to trust me," he says.

I don't say that I do, but I hope he knows now.

I guess we both feel guilty for a lot of things we've said in the past.

"Well, that's all you needed to know," I smile, trying to redirect the conversation. It's supposed to be a happy moment. I believe I should be expecting a question no–

"So," he pulls back just enough to look at me. "Are we doing this? Would you like that?"

I grin up at him so quickly that my mouth hurts.

"Yeah, Price. I'd like that," I confirm. My stomach is doing vertical loops. I love it.

And I've been a fool for believing I could let it go like it was nothing.

"But the day you stop making me laugh, it's over," I add with a teasing curve of my mouth.

He snorts and leans in for a peck, and I find I enjoy it just as much as the other kinds of kisses we've shared. I bury my face in the crook of his neck then, and I can't remember the last time someone held me like this.

When we break apart, he loosely intertwines our fingers. "Wait," I say quietly as we get to the stairs. "What about that girl you were talking to? I mean, you're obviously allowed to talk to girls but Ollie told me he'd seen you with her before and I–"

"Erica? We share a few classes. All she talks about are her back problems," he chuckles. "I promise you don't have any competition. You've ruined all other women for me."

Is it bad that I like that a lot?

As we say goodbye, it finally sinks in. It's like I'd been aimlessly searching for something, something that was once blurry and unclear, but that some part of me I insisted on keeping under lock and key hoped existed out there.

A feeling like light hitting water and making it sparkle, like pastel sunsets greeting you at the end of a long day.

A thought tucked in a corner of my brain, of my heart.

And here it is.

Chapter 28

Theodore

Opening night is a little over a week away. Dafne and I grab lunch together in the school's garden the day after finally clearing things up for good, which is still surreal if I'm being honest.

It also blows my mind how *interesting* she is, and it seems the Theodore that could barely stand her voice is an entirely different person.

According to Devon, Oliver and he are keeping their dating 'lowkey', but I know my friend. He is whipped. Still, they want to figure things out on their own time, especially since Oliver's only recently realised he's bi, so I completely understand and respect that. The thing is, I haven't exactly told Devon that Dafne and I are official. We haven't told anyone, really, but I'm sure it won't take long for most people to figure it out. I can't take my eyes off her.

Oddly enough, Devon hasn't asked anything nor

made any comments about me coming back at an admittedly odd hour last night. I wouldn't be surprised if he'd placed a hidden microphone in my jacket, though.

And then there's the blasted bet. I'd nearly forgotten about it until this morning, when the thought started randomly creeping in the back of my mind, reminding me I can't keep it from her forever. I'll tell her as soon as we're alone again and there's no possibility of people eavesdropping on us.

We're about to go grab coffees before afternoon rehearsal, but Isabel intercepts us, script in hand, and asks Dafne if they can sit and go over one of their scenes before we get back to the theatre. Dafne shoots me an apologetic look, and I offer to bring the coffees back for both of us.

Twenty minutes later, when I step back into the garden, I immediately spot her gorgeous hair, even with her back to me. I take a few steps towards her, only to realise Isabel's left, and she's now talking to Ethan. I lean casually on the nearest tree and balance the coffee tray in one hand so I can get my script out of my rucksack and do something instead of staring at them like a creep. She said she'd tell him things couldn't go on between them, so I assume that's exactly what she's doing. I repress the urge to walk over there and put an arm around her shoulder just so it's clear she's not available. After a few minutes, I notice Ethan nodding in my direction by way of greeting, so I nod back. Dafne waves goodbye to him and walks over to me. When our eyes meet, I've forgotten all about my script.

"How'd it go?" I ask as I hand her the coffee.

"It went something like *'Aw that's cool, dude. I mean you're cool and really hot but it's chill,'"* she says in an impeccable Californian accent. "He's also on his way to ask Sandra Higgins out, I believe."

"That was quick," I grimace. "And he told you you're hot?"

"Do you disagree?" she wiggles her eyebrows.

"Absolutely not. It's just a weird thing to say to someone who's essentially rejecting you," I shrug.

"He also said his spider senses," she makes air quotations with one hand, "weren't wrong."

"About …?"

"He's the one who thought you and I were a thing all these years," she says as she stares at her cup. "When I went out with him, he told me as much."

Isn't that ironic.

"If I had a penny for every time Devon mentioned you and I should have slept together," I sigh as I place a hand on the small of her back, "I'd be filthy rich and with a yacht docked at Brighton Pier."

She laughs then, and I think it might be my new favorite sound.

Dafne

Later in the evening, we finish rehearsal for Act Five. Theodore and I had to lie 'dead' for quite a long time, and it's been really hard to resist the urge to thread my fingers through his hair with him so close. Lord help me, I don't even recognise myself anymore–in a good way, that is. I kept the softest part of me hidden for too long. And the little surprise I've put together for him … he'll never see it coming. I can't wait.

I'm debating whether to show him already, but I'd sort of like for it to be a special moment. I could ask him to get dinner and–

"I'll meet you in an hour, yeah?" Ollie asks, scattering my thoughts.

"Hhmm?"

"It's Cartoons Night," he reminds me.

Of course. One night every month, Phoebe, Ollie and I meet in my room and watch an animated film. We use a random generator to choose for us from our list, and it's ridiculous, but also fun. It suddenly strikes me how it's going to be our last Cartoons Night at APDAS. An unpleasant feeling completely opposite to the cloud I was walking on knots my stomach.

Theo's surprise can wait. I explain that I can't see him tonight, which he doesn't seem too happy about, but he understands. I plant a kiss on his cheek before darting towards my dorm.

Chapter 29

Theodore

"I'm an idiot," I say solemnly, and Devon turns to me with a raised eyebrow.

"I mean, I'm sure you're right, but why?" he chuckles.

I sit up straight on my bed and let my legs swing over it so that I'm sitting on its edge and facing him.

"You win," I sigh.

"Come again?"

"I kissed her, Dev. Twice. Both times were spectacular," I admit, eyes on the navy-blue carpet of our room. "And we are now … together."

"I cannot contain my shock. I would have never seen it coming."

When I look up at him, the arsehole is smiling.

"Are you going to say anything else or let me wallow forever?" I groan.

"Theo," he laughs, slapping my knee. "I don't give a shite about the bet. I mean, I knew I'd win, and don't get me wrong, you'll never live it down, but I'm happy for you, man. It was time you got your head out of your arse."

"I don't know how you're so calm about this. Don't you understand the implications?"

Devon extends a hand to place on my shoulder.

"All I understand is you've got something that can make you happy, now. Something that you don't have to lose sleep over. Something good."

"Yeah, and I'm also a hypocrite," I shake my head.

"Because of the bet? It was just us being dickheads, alright? It won't be a prob–"

"Yes, it *will* be a problem!" I stand from the bed, my hands clenching into fists. "She told me just how badly she despises being lied to, Devon. I should have never let you convince me."

"Oh," he drawls. "So now it's my fault? Honestly, Theo–"

"You just couldn't let it go, could you?"

"You're a grown arse man, you can make your own decisions."

"And you're my best friend, and you're supposed to look after me and stop me from making terrible decisions, not encourage me," I snap.

"What's so terrible about having fallen in love?!"

"That's the point!" I throw my arms in the air. "Do you even care about Dafne? Or does this whole thing not bother you because you've gotten Oliver out of it? I'm starting to think that was part of the plan all along," I say bitterly. The Devon I know doesn't do things for his own gain, but I'm so frustrated I can't leave any possibility out. I need to calm down.

Breathe, Theo.

"Wow," Devon huffs. "You've lost your mind for good, haven't you? You know what–fuck this, Theo, I'm out of here," he grabs his jacket and keys and storms out of our dorm room.

Chapter 30

Dafne

We all show up at rehearsal even earlier than usual, as Ms. Patterson told us she had an announcement to make. Hopefully, she's just going to tell us she's bought a new earthenware ceramic teapot online.

When we're all in a circle on stage, she claps her hands lightly to call us to attention, which she really didn't need to do as Mr. Hackle's presence in the background is enough for us to know we'd better keep the chatter to a minimum.

"As you know," she starts, fixing her tortoise glasses on her nose, "opening night is coming up, just over *one week left,*" she thrills, a pleased expression taking over her entire face, and a few whoops rise from our circle. I look at my castmates, a bubble of pride surging in my chest, because at the end of the day, we're doing something very special–and I think everyone knows it. Theodore is standing straight, listening to Ms. Patterson with a small smile on his lips. When he notices me staring, he

shoots me a look and winks.
I wish I had my phone on me to immortalise Theodore Price winking.

"Yes, it is very exciting, but being so close to the show also means it's time for our …" she drum rolls with her pointer fingers on her thigh, "actors weekend retreat!"

Ollie and I exchange an excited smile; the weekend retreat is a something of a myth around here, that one experience only third-year students get to have as a way of bonding before their last opening night at APDAS. I'd honestly forgotten all about it, but I suppose it'll be a little adventure. While the law-abiding part of me thinks it's two days of time we could use to work on our scenes, I'm also glad to have a few days to recharge, and find an excuse to spend more time with Theo. Plus, I'll be rooming with Ollie, which I'm looking forward to. I don't mind the time he's been spending with Devon, but I can't help but miss him a little.

"I don't want to spoil any surprises, so you will find out what we have in store for you once we get there."
We? As in, Miss. Patterson and Mr. Hackle? No way he's coming along. I figure he'd rather drink rotten milk for a year than be stuck with us for a full weekend. I'm also sensing that whatever *is in store* won't be as fun as she made it out to be.

After rolling out of bed at five-thirty in the morning and Phoebe's half-asleep mumbled *"Have fun and don't get murdered"*, I snuggle against Ollie's shoulder on the bus taking us to our destination: Ashwell, Hertfordshire, population 1,870 poor souls. We might as well be the only guests they've had in years and be welcomed with a parade and balloons.

"Aren't you tired?" I groan against Ollie's cotton shirt.

"I went to bed at eight, unlike someone else," he says, poking me in the stomach and making me jump in my seat.

"Oh, shuddup," I yawn. "I wanted to make sure I wouldn't have forgotten my lines by the time we get back," I say as I pass my hands over my face. I didn't bother wearing makeup–this group of people has seen me at my sweatiest, they can handle a pair of dark circles. My attention is snatched by a pair of arms stretching above a seat a few seats ahead to our right.

"His hair looks so soft, huh," Ollie whispers, and I narrow my eyes at him.

"I don't know about that," I blatantly lie. "Don't you have a boyfriend of your own to ogle at?"

"I'm lucky said boyfriend loves to sleep, since you coerced me into sitting with you," he smirks, and I move my head back just to glare at him.

"It seems Price and Devon aren't on speaking terms at the moment, has he told you anything about it?"

I tell him what Theo told me this morning when they

didn't arrive at the meeting point in the courtyard together, which was a vague, "We disagreed on something."

"Well, then, why aren't *you* sitting with him?" Ollie asks, looking way too interested.

"I can't. I've got a surprise for him, and if he gets me talking I'm afraid I'll accidentally spill it," I whisper.

Ollie gasps as if I'd told him I was going to dye my hair green.

Mercifully, Theo has earbuds plugged in, so he doesn't seem to hear any of it.

"I swear both you and Phoebe need a crash course in speaking at a regular volume," I hiss, and he pushes his shoulder against mine, taking a small packet of candy out of his pocket–which I promptly snag from his hand. He knows I can't stay mad at him for more than fifteen seconds, but he also knows I'm easy to bribe. When we were in seventh grade, during an afternoon of vigorous background painting for our school play, he accidentally dropped an entire can of blue paint on my head. Scarce minutes of scowling later, he convinced me to forgive him solely with puppy eyes and the promise of an unlimited supply of hot chocolate.

Needless to say, all was well.

"Are you not going to tell me what it is?"

"If I don't trust myself to keep quiet, I can't trust you either," I reason.

Ollie pouts, but I'm sure Devon will be enough of a dis-

traction for him to get over it.
I was joking, of course, I trust Ollie with my life. But this specific surprise, as simple as it is, is something for Theodore only.

Theodore

Dafne has been avoiding me all morning except for the quick chat we had before hopping on the bus–I assume mostly due to the fact that we were all half-zombies–but my gut tells me there's something else. Our driver is parking in a small, graveled courtyard, so I figure I can ask her as soon as we get off. While everyone's collecting their bags from the overhead compartments, though, Dafne is the first to dart out, Oliver following shortly after. I hear him tell a sleepy Devon that Mr. Hackle is going to make him run laps if he doesn't get his butt off the bus. As I make my way out, I immediately spot Oliver's tall figure a few feet from the bus, his arm draped over Dafne's shoulder as they chat about something. I start towards them, but a heavy hand clasps my shoulder and stops me in my tracks. "Ms. Patterson is about to make her welcome speech," Mr. Hackle says. "You're going to want to listen, lover boy."

"Yes sir," I nod. I eye Dafne one more time, then step closer to where Ms. Patterson is frantically scanning

the sheets on her clipboard.
"Right, everyone, welcome to sunny Ashwell, which will be your sanctuary for the next two and a half days."
My castmates exchange dubious looks. The sky looking like it's about to fall over us doesn't really scream sunny, but Ms. Patterson is nothing if not an incurable optimist.
"First things first, we'll take care of your bedroom arrangements," she adds, and a worried chatter spreads over our small group like wildfire. We thought we'd be choosing our own roommates, as forced cohabitation almost never bides well, and wait–why did Mr. Hackle say *I* would want to hear this?

"I thought it would be interesting to let fate decide! Isn't that fun?" she muses as she extracts a small glass bowl filled with ripped sheets of paper from the craft bag dangling from her elbow.

I swallow as she rummages through the bowl to extract the first pair. "Our Mercutio will room with ..." she says, wiggling her eyebrows in Devon's direction, "ahh, Tybalt! How fitting, don't you think?"

Nobody answers.

I see Oliver shoot Devon a lopsided smile, but don't turn to witness Devon's reaction. I'm not prepared for the glare he'd send my way.

The next extraction ends up pairing Thomas with David; apparently, there is a triple left as well as a pair, meaning there's a good chance I'll room with Dafne after all. A few months ago I would have put a fight with Ms.

Patterson to change that in a heartbeat, but now, well, the thought is far from bothersome. Ms. Patterson readjusts her glasses on her nose. “Next, we have Isabel, Jack, and …”

Chapter 31

Dafne

I didn't think Theodore and I would be sharing bunk beds literally two days after getting together, but I gingerly take the keys Ms. Patterson is handing out with a pleased smile on her face and walk at a brisk pace towards the keep where we're spending the weekend. I step down the corridor, counting through the room numbers, and I find my–*not just yours*, my brain reminds me–door. The dark mahogany is covered in scratches, looking straight out of a horror film. I notice the small nameplate at eye-level next to the door frame, which lets me know this is *The Lovers' Room*. The bloody lovers' room. I fail to stifle a snort just in time for Theodore to hear as he catches up with me.

"Hey," he starts, "what are you star–oh."

"Not a word," I laugh, the door all but opening wide and creaking loudly when I twist the key into the lock and push it open, which makes me wonder if we're actually here to enjoy ourselves before opening night or if it's a survival trial and only one is meant to make it out alive.

The room isn't exactly small, but not spacious either; I don't have time to pay much attention to the dusty pieces of furniture or the one-too-many paintings adorning the walls, because my vision zeroes on the bed. The one, queen size bed, mocking me from its placement under the one window in the dead centre of the room.

"This is great," I say sarcastically.

"I don't snore, you know."

"I don't care what sounds you make at night," I blurt out before I can think twice, and Theodore shoots me an amused look. Okay, that came out wrong.

"That's … good to know?" he adds, carefully bemused, and I notice the feeling of wanting to slap the smile off his face I used to get is truly dead and buried.

"If you're thinking about asking Ms. Patterson to change rooms, save your breath. David already tried and she said something about room swaps being strictly forbidden in order to protect the balance of the group–whatever that means," he tells me, walking around the room and swiping a finger on the top of the only wardrobe, which comes out covered in chalky dust. I walk towards the left side of the bed and place my travel bag on the embroidered duvet cover.

"I don't want to change rooms," I say distractedly, and although my attention is on the bag I'm zipping open, I can tell he's looking at me. I'm thinking about how flattering that is, but then he asks, "What are you doing?" as he still holds his bag by the handles.

"What do you mean?"

"What are you doing *there*? That's my side of the bed."

My hands still on my bag's zipper. "I beg your pardon?"

"I can't sleep on the right side."

"Ah, but that sounds like it's your problem, though," I raise one shoulder in mock helplessness.

"Hhmm, let's see if I can change your mind about that." He rushes around the bed and towards me and I roll over to the opposite side just in time for him to miss me, a shriek escaping my lips.

"Nice try Price," I say, a little out of breath. "You've got to catch me first!" I yell as I run outside, giggling like a bloody child.

Theodore

"I hope everyone has settled in nicely in your respective cocoons," Ms. Patterson says, delighted as ever.

"*Cocoons*?" Oliver mouths, and I chuckle.

"We'll have our first activity after lunch–yes, I know you're tired and you'd rather gossip in your bedrooms, but it is scientifically proven that engaging in group activities on a full stomach is far more beneficial for all parties involved."

"Someone needs to take the internet away from her," I hear Devon mutter from Oliver's other side, and Mr. Hackle must hear him because he gives him a light clip around the ear. Lunch consists of a roast and seasoned potatoes, as apparently the one person living in the keep besides our group is a cook, who looks positively thrilled about having company. He keeps asking us if we're enjoying the food, if our rooms are nice, if we are excited to be here.

"Do you happen to know why Dafne's been running away from me? Literally. Anytime I go hear her she makes up an excuse and flees," I ask Oliver, who's not-so-subtly throwing glances at her a few seats from us on the other side of the table.

"I don't know what you're referring to," he says before gulping down a forkful of potatoes.

"You honestly expect me to believe that?" I whisper.

"Look, Price, I don't know, and even if I did, I wouldn't tell you. It's best friend code," he says, a hand hovering in front of his mouth.

"Best frien–alright, you know what, it's fine." I just hope it's nothing serious.

"On another note," Oliver adds as Devon gets up to refill the pitcher, "when are *you* two going to sort your shite out? I'm already tired of playing buffer."

"He told you?" I ask, any appetite I might have had

instantly dissipating. If he told Oliver, then Oliver told Dafne, and she knows about the bet before I've had the chance to talk to her and–

"Yeah, he told me you had a stupid fight. Surely it's nothing you can't get over a mere week before leaving APDAS for good, is it?"

Oh.

I feel like he's scolding me, and it should bother me, but it really doesn't. I know he's right and I should talk to Devon and fix this mess. And then talk to Dafne once for all, so maybe, just maybe … we can move on. Start over.

The afternoon passes by between interpretative dance exercises and group meditations, which probably sounds odd, but is actually quite cathartic. Dafne is still avoiding me, and trying really hard not to make it look like she is, which naturally has the opposite effect.

A half-hour after dinner, which I spend sitting on a log around a small fire Mr. Hackle managed to light up after several unsuccessful attempts, Ms. Patterson claps her hands and gathers us around her.

"For tonight, we'll go with something simple. I want you to pair up with the person to your right and look at them in the eyes for a while. Mr. Hackle and I will be timing you, but you don't need to concern yourself with that. I want you to try to communicate whatever you're feeling to the person in front of you without using any words. You'll then switch partners and repeat. All clear? Good!" she says giddily, and even if someone hadn't understood, the directions they wouldn't have been given the time to say so.

Margaret is my designated partner for this exercise, and we sit close to the fire one in front of the other, both of us crossing our legs. We've done this before in class of course, but never in the open, with only the sound of the fire crackling and the gentle breeze making our hair sway.

I'm not sure Margaret needs to know what I'm feeling–and I'm aware that defeats the exercise's goal–so I focus on trying to understand her instead.

I find that it's near impossible to think about anything that isn't Dafne. The way her eyes light up when she talks about the play. The softness of her skin. How she twists her favorite ring around her finger when she's lost in thought.

My thoughts are abruptly interrupted when Mr. Hackle claps once, and we know it's time to switch partners. I'm about to pair up with David, because even though I'm itching to know what could be so bad that she feels like she can't just talk to me after everything we've shared, I don't want to oppress her. Isabel gets to him before I can, so I turn around to find that the only person left is Dafne. She gives me a soft smile and gestures for me to go to her. We sit as before, and unsurprisingly, she looks at me straight in the eyes and doesn't falter for a second. She doesn't even blink.

For the time we spend sitting in front of each other, my mind blanks. Her mere presence is so soothing now, it takes everything I have not to slap myself for everything we've said to each other in the past. Her gaze is so intense that I think she might be having the exact same thoughts.

Ms. Patterson claps again, and Dafne brushes her knuckles against the back of my hand before we part ways to switch partners again.

Chapter 32

Dafne

I close the bedroom door behind me as quietly as possible while I hear Theodore shrug his jacket off. I turn and lean on the door, my arms behind my back.

"So," Theo says.

"So," I repeat, my lips quirking to the side.

Come on, Daf. You're no coward.

"You've probably been wondering why we haven't really spent time together today," I offer as I step closer.

"You could say that," he mumbles, but he doesn't sound upset. More like curious, and slightly worried.

"Remember when you told me that you feel like you don't know what you're doing? Like, and I hate that word, but–a fraud?" I ask carefully, stepping into his space. He stiffens imperceptibly and nods, his brows slightly furrowing. He clearly wasn't expecting me to bring it up again.

"Well, I wanted to prove to you that's not true. You know, in case my word wasn't enough."

He blinks rapidly and swallows, so I gently caress his cheekbone with one knuckle, and he relaxes ever so slightly.

I take my phone out of my jeans pocket and ask, "May I?"

He nods again, his hands coming to rest lightly on my hips, and we're close enough that the back of the phone in my hands rests against his chest. "Theodore is the best goddamn actor I've ever seen IRL. He's a hottie, too," I read from my screen, and smile at the extra comment.

"What?" he breathes.

"TP was brilliant in *The Comedy of Errors* last year. Couldn't take my eyes off him," I keep reading the next slide, and swipe to another. "My mum saw him perform at the open doors event the school did last summer and told me it was only worth sending me to APDAS if I turned out to be half as good as him."

I turn my screen so that he can see it and rapidly scroll down dozens of little boxes with my thumb.

He's clearly struggling to believe it, but it's all there.

"I put up a question box on my Instagram," I tell him. "'*If you've ever seen Theodore Price acting, what are your honest thoughts about him?*' I promised they'd stay anonymous. That last part was only half-true," I smirk.

His eyes roam over the screen for another few seconds, then he takes the phone from my hands and carefully places it on the bed behind him.

"Theo? Are you–"

He moves a messy lock of hair with his index finger to tuck it behind my ear, rich brown and beautiful green flickering from my eyes to my mouth. The simple gesture is so gentle it makes me weak in the knees.

"Thank you," he breathes. "For this, for being able to get past everything. Just–thank you."

"Do you believe it, now? That you're anything *but* a fraud?"

"I believe I can't believe my luck," he says with a little shrug. I try extremely hard to reign in a smile.

"Can I kiss you?"

"Permission granted," I laugh softly before he cradles my jaw and plants the most incredible kiss on my mouth.

Chapter 33

Theodore

There will never be a good moment for what I have to tell her. The more I mull it over in my mind, the worse it gets. Waking up next to her this morning after what she did for me was the best damn thing I've ever felt. I *just* got her. I can't lose her like this. But isn't it because of what she did that I should wait? She looked so happy that I could see what people really thought of my work. I have to protect that, even if I'll regret it later.

After breakfast, our teachers take us for a walk in the surrounding area, and once we reach the core of the village, we are instructed to spend the rest of the morning as our characters. Mannerism, inflection, whatever the meticulous character work we've done for the past months entails, we need to apply it–which would probably be embarrassing if we were anywhere else, but there are so few people in this place it's unlikely we will even get to talk to anyone beside our group. I keep stealing looks at

Devon, because everything would be easier if I could at least talk to my best friend. Dafne must sense me looking at him, because she inclines her head as if to say *go talk to him*. I look up and squint at the pale sky with a sigh. When I turn in Devon's direction she conveniently steps up to Oliver and drags her friend away with an elaborate Juliet-like turn of phrase, giving me a window to walk up to Devon.

"My friend, shall thou give me the opportunity to walk where honest men walk?" I try in my best Romeo attitude. He cuts me a long look, then huffs out a breath and gestures for me to lead the way.

"What an idiot hast life made of me," I continue, "to forget thy heart resides in the map of honor and loyal–"

"Alright, shut up, mate," Devon cuts me off, definitely not as Tybalt would.

"I have a talent for mucking things up," I add in regular English, kicking lightly at the gravel.

Ms. Patterson clears her throat a few feet from us, so Devon pretends to extract a sword from its sheath and practice basic lunges.

"You know, *good Romeo*," he says as I join him in the air duel, "your life would be so much easier if you counted to ten before speaking." he dodges my fake dab at his ribs.

"Believe it or not, you're not the first person to tell me that," I grunt as we switch places, a few of the townspeople walking by and looking at us with a mix of excite-

-ment and curiosity.

Devon pretends to throw his sword in the middle and bows. "Lucky for thee, I shall exchange peace for a free meal. Because you called yourself an idiot, I deem meself satisfied."

"Well, that's–"

Devon raises an eyebrow at me, crossing his arms.

"Indeed," I concede, bowing back.

"I'm sorry too, by the way. I admit I haven't handled the situation as well as I thought I would."

I nod, appreciating the sentiment. "There's something else I should tell you," I sigh as we make our way towards the one tiny bakery in the village. Devon gives me his full attention.

"I had an anxiety attack not so long ago. Well, it wasn't the first, and I wanted to say something earlier but I also didn't want to make a big deal out of it. I know it is, though, so … I'm going to see someone about it soon. Apparently being easily irritable can be part of it, so I guess that explains *some* things."

Devon's brows lower as he nods and he places a hand on my shoulder, squeezing it for a second.

"I'm sorry, mate, that must've been awful. I'm glad you're taking care of yourself, though," he says, more serious than I've ever seen him. "I can come to the appointment if you'd like? For moral support," he winks, even though I can tell he's not happy I didn't talk to him about it.

"Sure," I smile.

Later, when we regroup with everyone else, Mr. Hackle lets us know we're free to do as we please until late afternoon.

Dafne finds me and smiles warmly as she walks up to me, and I'm suddenly so mad at myself for all the times I could've been the recipient of that warmth.

"So," she says, practically bouncing on her heels, "what plans do you have?" she asks as Devon starts to retreat and head towards Oliver.

"I was thinking of…" I grimace, "you know what, never mind, we're supposed to have fun."

"You want to rehearse?" she asks simply, no teasing in her tone.

"That *was* my first thought, yes. It's not like there's much to do around here anyway," I shrug.

"I agree," she beams, which sends an electric jolt running through my body.

"Yeah?"

"Yeah."

She grabs me by the wrist and leads me back inside– towards the bedroom.

Dafne

I press Theodore against the closed door with a little too much force, which draws a groan out of him that I know here and now I'd pay good money to hear again.

"I thought," he breathes, "we were going to rehearse," his hands belying his words as he haphazardly removes my blazer, his lips hungrily parting mine.

"We are," I say against them. "It's a scene that didn't make it to the final cut," I say before moving my mouth to place a kiss on the side of his neck. I feel powerful and I *love it*. I love that he loves it too, if his ragged breath is of any indication.

I practically rip his jean jacket from his shoulders, letting out a frustrated grunt when the cuffs get stuck at his wrists. Theodore looks all too amused by my efforts, and gently pries my hands away so he can do it himself, throwing the jacket on the gray carpet at the bed's feet. He slides his hands through my hair and pulls me closer for another kiss, backing up until I hit the footboard, and he places a hand on the small of my back to prevent me from losing balance.

"Thank you, good pilgrim," I whisper, resting my forehead against his.

"Tis' my honour."

"So, are–

I'm interrupted by Theodore hooking one arm under my

knees, the other wrapped firmly around my back so he can sweep me up–in more ways than one, I think–and carry me to bed like we're a pair of newlyweds.

I slap one hand on my mouth to keep a surprised sound from escaping, but I just feel so *excited* it's bloody ridiculous. He places me carefully on the bed and hovers above me, a smile twitching on his lips.

"What?" I ask, tracing the veins on his toned arms with my fingertips.

"If someone told me at the beginning of the year we'd be in this position I would have had an aneurysm just thinking about it."

"You mean with you on top of me?"

He drops his head and huffs out a laugh. "*Very funny.*"

"You're right, though," I say. "I would have withdrawn from public life altogether–joined a witness protection program in Tennes–"

"Alright, smart mouth," he says, dipping his head to wipe my smirk away with a kiss. He lowers his forearms so that we're closer, and I take the opportunity to bring our bodies flushed and roll us around so that I'm on top of him.

"I hate to be the killjoy," I whisper, peppering his jaw with kisses, "but… what if Ms. Patterson barges in? Or someone else?" I ask quietly against his cheek.

"Then it's her fault for putting us in this room together," he says simply, a lazy smile on his lips.

His hands are resting on my hips now, his thumbs brushing back and forth doing absolutely nothing to stop the craving I've been feeling all morning.

"But if you're not sure," he adds, "that is perfectly fine, Dafne."

I hold myself up higher so I can look in his eyes. *My favorite eyes*, I realise with no shortage of wonder.

"No," I say, tracing his bottom lip with my thumb. His expression is so open and soft, even though his eyes are lined with a sparkle of lust.

"I don't have the proper words for how sure I am." I push myself up to straddle him so I can grab the hem of his jumper and undershirt and push them over his head, revealing the firm planes of his chest.

I trace a finger on a small mole on his right peck that immediately snags my attention. I know I'm being a tease, but I can't help it. I want to memorise every centimeter of him. When I don't move he says, voice hoarse, "You're killing me, Wright."

I hold onto his shoulder with my free hand to urge him to get closer, so when he rises to rest on his elbows, my knees on either side of him, I say, "Let's not waste any more time, then," and close the distance between us.

Chapter 34

Theodore

It's after dinner now, and for the whole evening, after getting cleaned up and trying to muster as much innocence as possible, I find that we can't keep our eyes off each other to save our lives. It's like an unspoken fear between the two of us–that the other could disappear or turn into someone else if we got distracted for too long. Ollie and Devon immediately figure us out, of course, which leads to more than one embarrassing comment and results in just as many glares from Dafne.

Ms. Patterson suggests the whole group walks to a clearing which the village's people have assured her is the best place in a twenty-mile radius to look at the stars. The cast gathers in the keep's parking space before making our way towards the designated area. There are already a few people there, sitting on cloths, gazes up at the night sky.

Dafne and I sit side by side, but we haven't been touching, or holding hands, or whatever it is that couples do. Which is sort of ridiculous considering what we did barely a few hours ago.

She elbows me gently, probably sensing I'm lost in thoughts, but doesn't comment on it. I give her a small smile, and she winks.

"I've always wanted to know more about constellations," she says then, eyes roaming above.

"What do you want to know?"

"Well, it would be fun to be able to name them, for one. I know it's not *that* hard, but it's just one of those things I never got around to learning," she explains.

"That," I say, pointing upwards to our left, "is the Ursa Major." I trace my fingers in the air so that she can hopefully see the little chariot pattern. "Also called the Big Dipper, although to be precise, the stars that make it aren't a constellation, but something called an asterism–what?"

She's looking at me, her chin resting on her knees. "You're such a know-it-all," she smiles. "Keep going."

I clear my throat, and it doesn't go unnoticed by me how many times she's called me that before, but in a completely different way.

"That's, uhm, Venus, the planet, of course."

"Of course."

"And, oh, over there," I point, "that's Sirius. One of my favorites."

"What did Sirius do to be deemed worthy of such honour?" she asks, her eyes so bright they reflect the stars.

"It's one, if not the, most luminous stars visible from Earth," I tell her. It's nearly pitch black, the landscape illuminated by a few lanterns planted in the ground, but I can see her looking intently at the patch of sky I pointed to.

"That's you," I add so quietly I'm not sure she's heard me.

She takes her gaze off the sky, and her eyes are wide when she looks at me again. Her lips part on an exhale, then the right corner of her mouth goes up.

"You know you can't tell me that and expect me to not want to kiss you, right?" she breaks our eye contact by taking a look around us, none of our friends seemingly having noticed our closeness. She closes her eyes.

"It was worth the risk," I laugh softly.

"You're not allowed to change your mind in a week, Price," she says half-heartedly, but I know better now. I know now that behind the snark and the wit and the strength with which she carries herself, she's also been hurt and she doesn't want to again.

And I'm transported back to reality.

The blasted bet.

My stomach turns upside down. I've been so caught up in her today, and I just …

I need to come clean about it before she has the chance to learn it elsewhere. I just *have to*. And maybe she'll understand.

I mean, the conversations we had set the record straight

on the fact that I'm not *actively* trying to hurt her. I realise that's the bare minimum, but given everything that's happened, it has to count for something, right?
I might end up hurting her worse than ever after all, and the thought makes me want to be sick. I'm in too deep, in every possible way.

I tilt her head towards me again by gently pushing under her chin with one finger,
"I won't," I promise. That much she can count on.

I can't remember if there was ever a time I felt like I do now, in this specific moment in time. Completely, perfectly happy. It's such a foreign feeling, off a stage, that I briefly think I might not be equipped for it; but Dafne's back is against my stomach, my arm draped around her, and she begins to stir, drowning out my thoughts.

Last night she essentially collapsed in bed, and I figured I'd let her get a good night's sleep before talking to her.

"Morning," she mumbles, and I press a kiss to her shoulder.

"How'd you know I was awake?" I ask, resting my chin in the crook of her neck. I smell peaches.

"You think too loudly," she yawns, which makes me snort. I'm about to tell her I want to talk when she tries to wiggle free of my grasp. I hold on tighter. "Are you

trying to run away already?" I joke.
"This is not a film, Price," she says, prying my hands away from her stomach. "I'm not kissing you until we both brush our teeth," she says, padding toward the bathroom.

"Point taken," I sigh. Might as well go for it now.

"Also, I need to talk to you about something," I add over the sound of the water running in the sink and get up. Each passing second she doesn't know threatens to draw an impassable line between us for good. She makes a noncommittal sound as she finishes up in the tiny bathroom, then walks back to the bed with a grin. I take my turn at the sink, taking a moment to collect myself. When I get back to the bed, she pushes me down with one hand and falls next to me.

I swallow, and I'm about to speak again when she asks, "How'd you get this?" She touches the side of my chin with her pointer finger.

"Uh, the scar?"

She nods as she looks at it intently, fingers caressing my jaw.

"I fell from the table I was using as a stage," I explain. "I was six."

"Really? Poor thing."

"Yeah. My parents never paid attention," I fail miserably at keeping harshness out of the words. You could say I've never really forgiven them for essentially pretending I don't exist.

"If you ever want to talk about them, I'll listen, you know."

"There's not much to say. They hadn't planned for me, I … happened to them, I guess. So at some point they decided I'd be better off with my grandparents. They were right."

"They're the ones missing out," she says confidently, like it's an irrefutable truth.

"You never speak about your parents. I hope it's not because they suck," I say to shift the topic. She gives me a look that means she knows that, and smiles.

"No, they do not suck. They're really fun. They keep a copy of the speech I wrote at nine when I announced I was going to win an Academy Award in their wallets. Always said I was '*born for great things*,'' she licks her lips.

"They're not wrong, you know."

She looks at me like she can see inside my brain. I hope that's not the case.

"I really do need to ta–"

She gets up and plants a palm firmly on my chest as she straddles me.

"Daf–"

"Yeah?" she lowers herself to press a kiss between my pecs. Then another lower. And lower. Christ.

"I really–"

"I have another idea," she says against my stomach.

"We also have to meet the others in–hmm–fifteen…" I can't seem to formulate a full sentence when her tongue and her teeth are doing *that*. She stops to look at me through thick lashes, and smiles coyly. I want her so much, but I can't let her go on. I don't want her to regret it, although at this point, there is already too much to possibly regret.

"I only need eight," she whispers, and before she can slip under the covers, I gather any remnant of willpower I have left and pull her up by her forearms. "Please, it's–important." I say roughly.

"Fine," she sighs, clearly annoyed at the interruption. "You want to pass up on a perfectly nice blowjob, suit yourself. What is it?" she asks, sitting back on her knees.

"It's about, well, you and me, and–"

Three sharp knocks on the door suspend my almost confession.

For fuck's sake.

Ms. Patterson's shrill voice lets us know we need to be in the courtyard with everyone else *right about now.*

"Sounds like it'll have to wait some more?" she chuckles, completely oblivious to how unfunny this whole situation is. I roll off the bed after her to get dressed.

Chapter 35

Dafne

After we hurry out of bed and try to make ourselves presentable, Ms. Patterson and Mr. Hackle have the whole group gather in the courtyard. The sun is bright despite the chilly air–it seems like the sunshine we were promised a few days ago is pulling a prank by coming out just as we're leaving.

"I know it's not time for goodbyes yet," Ms. Patterson starts, fixing her glasses on top of her head.

"But Mr. Hackle and I have been working with you for the past three years, and whether you believe it or not, we care about each and every single one of you."

I'm taken aback by the veil of emotion coating her speech. She's right–we hadn't been expecting one at all.

"Whatever happens once you have that diploma in your hands is up to you," Mr. Hackle adds, scratching his bearded chin with a thumb. "But we sincerely hope we, as well as the rest of your teachers, have given you the means to navigate what is waiting for you out there."

Oh, boy. Ollie and I exchange a look, and he nods at me. Ms. Patterson is about to say something else, but our director claps his hands instead. "Enough with the pleasantries, tomorrow you've got your dress rehearsal, which I expect you to be ready for. You're so close to the finish line, but there's still the biggest chunk to go." He meets each of our gazes individually, and I hope he has confidence in what he finds there. "I hope you've already gathered your things, APDAS awaits."

Barely ten minutes later, when we're all about to get on the bus, Ms. Patterson approaches me. "Dafne, a word?"

Ollie shoots me a questioning look and I subtly shrug. I have no idea what this could be about.

"I just wanted to tell you how glad I am that you and Theodore have been getting along so well," she chirps, her hands pressed over her heart.

"Oh, uh, thank you, Ms., I–"

"I knew you'd make a perfect match!" she squeals. I don't fail to notice that with the way she just scrunched her nose, and her new bob haircut, she suddenly looks even younger than her thirty-four years. But there's also something *else*. And I know she's enthusiastic by nature, but this level of zeal regarding Theo and me is suspicious even for her.

"Forgive me for speaking plainly, but did someone tell you Theodore and I are…"

"I didn't need anyone to tell me, Miss Wright. I have an eye for matters of the heart," she says with no shortage of satisfaction. "I like to think I've helped a little. Nudged the both of you in the right direction, so to speak."

She's not making sense. Nudged us in–wait.

No, that's not possible. Is it?

"The handkerchief," I articulate. "Theodore came in looking for a practice sword after rehearsals, but those are not usually in the prop room."

"Guilty," she beams. "The room placements were a welcome coincidence, well, I sort of color-coded–"

"Did you know the lock was broken?" I know I'm still speaking to a teacher, but I honestly can't believe she'd have us spend the night in a room with no windows, no heating, and no *beds*. And what if one of us was claustrophobic? Have Phoebe's romance novels gotten to her, too?

Her smile falls. "The lock? In the prop room?"

I nod faintly and sense Theo's eyes on me through the bus window. *What?* He mouths as I glance up at him, and I shake my head.

"Oh my," Ms. Patterson whispers, a sudden wave of panic in her voice. "No, Dafne, I did not. Oh, that's really bad. Robert, I mean, Mr. Hackle–"

"Won't know if we don't tell him," I finish her sentence, giving her a pointed look. Her eyes are wide, but she nods. I don't want her to get in trouble, even though she was trying to play bloody matchmaker with her

acting students.
"You're a good girl, Dafne. I'm really sorry for meddling. It just pains me to see two people who would be great together not see it themselves," she sighs, and I don't miss the look full of longing she throws somewhere behind us. I don't need to turn to know who she's looking at.

"It's probably not my place, Ms., but … the past few months have taught me that you'll never know if you never try," I say before I get on the bus, Mr. Hackle oblivious to the conversations she and I were just having as he shakes hands with the keep's only staff member.

"Just a thought," I add to her, and hop on the bus.

"What was that about?" Theo asks as I take my place next to him, Ollie and Devon right behind us.

"Turns out we have a groupie," I laugh before explaining what Ms. Patterson just confessed.

On the ride back I nap on Theo's shoulder for the majority of the time, slipping in and out of consciousness as he sings *Dreams* under his breath. He nudges me gently when we're almost back at APDAS, letting me know if I don't get up we might be stuck here forever.
"That's not such a bad idea," I mumble, which makes him laugh. He retrieves both of our bags from the compartments of the bus, as Mr. Hackle reminds us he'll see us bright and early for dress rehearsal in the morning.

Our whole group starts walking towards the dorms, and while I'm attempting to pry my bag back from Theo's hand, I hear it.

"I'm telling you, they're shagging. Must have been all along–one of them probably got the other in," someone says, half-whispering, but close enough for me to hear. Theodore's expression hasn't changed from a few seconds before, so I assume he hasn't heard, but then he grimaces, and before I have time to react he lets go of my bag and turns to go stand in front of Jack's face.

"Say it again," he prompts, sounding incredibly calm.

Way too calm.

Jack chuckles nervously as he shrugs, his palms facing up. "Say what, mate?"

Theo huffs, then starts backing away. "You're a spineless arsehole, you know that?" he says, turning to pick up the bags he'd dropped on the gravel. I place a hand on his arm and try to look at him, but he averts my gaze.

"Why so defensive? Is she not a good lay or–" Jack adds then, and I can see in the twitch of his jaw that's when Theo truly loses his patience.

He reaches for Jack in a single stride and grabs him by the collar. As he's about to hurl a fist at his cheekbone, Devon and Ollie rush to drag him back with them.

"Fuck you, Jack," Theodore shouts, the rest of our castmates staring in utter shock.

"You talk about her like that again, I'll–"
"Oy," Devon tries, "it's not worth it, Theo, alright? Let it go," he pulls on his left shoulder.
Theo is breathing heavily, but he allows them to take him away. I look over at Jack and say, "Jealousy's not a good look on you, dickhead," and hurry after them, taking both of our bags with me despite the fact that my knees are suddenly wobbly. I couldn't give less of a damn about what Jack thinks of me or Theo, but that doesn't mean he gets to disrespect us and get away with it.

Theo takes the stairs two at a time, stomping to his room without sparing me a look, and it hurts more than I can say. I start to follow, but Devon puts a hand on my arm and cuts me a pleading look. "It's best to leave him be for tonight," he tells me gently, taking Theo's bag with his free hand. "I'll have him text you later, yeah?"

I nod wordlessly, shooting one more look at the stairs where Theodore just disappeared, and let Ollie walk me back to my room.

"Daf, you okay?" he says softly.

"None of that was okay, Ollie. Jack is such a dick, and-and Theo was *so*–" I start, choking on whatever I was about to say next. My head is swimming with the events of the past ten minutes, and I don't know what I should be worrying more about. The very way Theo was ready to make Jack shut up with his fist or that his reaction to what that idiot said might get him into trouble?

"Do you want me to stay? I can squeeze myself into Phoebe's bed. Or in the bathtub." Ollie suggests, knowing well we don't have a bathtub, but trying to get a smile out of me. Maybe for the first time since I've known him, he fails miserably.

"No, you should go. Tomorrow's going to be a long day," I sniff.

He steps closer and squeezes my shoulder. "Text me if you need me, yes?"

I nod once, and pass a hand over my face, crouching to unzip the pocket where I put my keys.

I get the door open, and Phoebe jolts from her bed. "M'wake," she yawns as she props herself on one elbow, waking up completely as she takes me in. I'm fairly sure I look like I'm going to throw up.

"What's that face for?" she says, sitting up straight so suddenly the book propped on the edge of her bed falls with a muffled thud. I drop my bag and walk to my bed, plopping down on the light pink comforter.

"Jack, uh, one of the cast members," I start, "started talking about Theodore and me and Theo, well, he didn't like it."

"I … see?" Phoebe says, clearly confused by my less than brilliant summary. I tell Phoebe I'll explain later, that I need a steaming shower first. She says a wild berries-infused tea will be ready when I'm out.

I don't know what I'll do without her.

About an hour later, I'm telling Phoebe all about the retreat, and when I get to the sex, she officially loses her mind. I'm about to get to what happened when we got back, but my phone starts to buzz. Theodore's name flashes on the display.

"Is it him?" she asks, trying to peer at the screen from her bed.

"Yep," I breathe, staring at the phone.

"Are you not going to answer?"

"Yeah, but I can't talk to him if you're staring at me," I smile.

"No staring, I promise, but if I happen to overhear something, it's not my fault," she turns with her stomach on the bed, her head propped in one hand, while the other starts scrolling through her Instagram feed.

"Hey," I pick up the call. "I wasn't really expecting to hear from you until tomorrow."

"Dafne, I'm sorry. I shouldn't have reacted like that. I hope I didn't scare you," Theodore says roughly, my heart breaking a little at this tone.

"It takes more than that to scare me, Price. And Jack, well, I always thought him an idiot. I was just … surprised," I admit. "I've never seen you so angry, and I'm fairly sure I've seen various degrees of your anger before." I try to keep my tone light now, because I know, and feel, he's probably been beating himself up for letting his control slip up.

A beat of silence passes, so I continue, "I do want to

make something clear, Theo. I appreciate you standing up for me, but I don't need you to fight my battles. Physically or metaphorically. Besides, you could have gotten hurt."

"No, I know that," he replies quietly.

"Alright," I add, waiting for him to say something that will kill the paranoia I'm trying to smother. Like that he'll talk to Mr. Hackle first thing in the morning before things escalate negatively. I'm about to suggest I could go with him, when he asks,

"Are we good, then?" He sounds unsure, and I don't like hearing him like this.

From the corner of my eye, I can see Phoebe's head is tilted towards me, so I abruptly turn to look at her and meet her eyes. She stifles a laugh and goes back to scrolling.

"Yes. We are *good*."

"Right. I'll see you tomorrow, then. Goodnight," he says, weariness clinging to his words.

He's not a child, Dafne. He'll feel better in the morning, and everything will be fine.

I press the red circle button that ends the call and throw my phone on the comforter before letting myself fall on the bed.

"Okay?" Phoebe asks, without raising her gaze from her screen this time.

"Yeah. Okay."

Chapter 36

Theodore

I wake up feeling like utter shite, my head buzzing from what happened last night. I can't believe I did that. I have never almost hit anyone before. I didn't know I had it in me, to be honest. How could I lose it like that? My grandparents would be so disappointed. The mere idea of them finding out makes me dizzy with worry. Not to mention, if Jack reports me, Mr. Hackle will have no choice but to remove me from the play. APDAS doesn't tolerate any kind of violence. The one thing I have worked towards tirelessly for three years, gone in a heartbeat because I didn't stop and think. And Dafne's face– God. She said we're good so I have to believe that. Except I know we won't be for long, since I still have to tell her about the bet.

"I'm going to the theatre," I tell Devon as I put my shoes on and hastily stuff my script and water in my backpack.

"Wait for me, Theo–"

"I don't have all day, Devon, I need to go now." I grab my keys and fling myself out the door, the feeble hope that I can still fix this propelling me to where I need to be, sure that Dafne is going to be there, and hopefully Jack too.

But when I get inside and reach the front row, only Mr. Hackle is in the theatre, his arms crossed over his stomach as he looks over at the stage. When he hears me approach, he casts me a sideways look and gestures for me to sit beside him.

"You know, Theodore, when I was your age, I thought this," he waves a hand toward the stage, "was all that mattered. That my life didn't have meaning beyond it, because only on a stage was I truly alive."

I don't know where this is going, and I don't have it in me to say, "*Isn't that how it's supposed to be?*" so I keep quiet. Jack must have gotten to him first, and this is probably the speech where he tells me he's kicking me out of the play. I know I deserve it, but I still feel sick.

"Then life happened, and you know what I found out?"

I close my eyes and shake my head. I don't really want to hear it.

"Acting–it's a necessity for some. It is for me, and I know it is for you. But you won't have that heart forever. And when it stops, you don't want to regret having lived for one thing only."

I try to process what Mr. Hackle is saying, and the more

his words seep in, the more it feels like my heart is going to crack open in my chest. If he expects me to say something back, he doesn't let it show. He shifts in his seat so he's finally looking at me.

"You'll have time to think about that. Now, I would like to hear your version of last night's events before I make any drastic decisions."

I feel the color drain from my cheeks, my mouth drying by the second. My heart is beating furiously as his words echo in my head. Drastic decisions–replacing me in the show.

"Mr. Hackle," I start, shaking my head. "I don't–I don't have a good explanation for my behaviour," I say honestly. "Jack said that Dafne and I both got the leads because we're together, and he said something else about her and it just … made me so angry. Because I know how hard we both have worked for this–which I realise is no excuse."

He purses his lips and nods slowly. "Your understudy would be ecstatic to take your place, you know."

I take a deep breath, trying not to pass out. "I know. He probably deserves the role more than I do right now."

"Perhaps," Mr. Hackle says as he gets up with a grunt, motioning for me to do the same.

"But I have faith in the Romeo I chose."

I look at him, my mouth opening and closing on nothing.

"But Jack–"

"Hasn't filed a formal complaint. He's come directly to me since no actual damage was done. I believe you have to thank your friends for that."

I nod wordlessly as my shoulders slump.

"I postponed dress rehearsal for half an hour so we could have this chat, so get your arse backstage. Your castmates will be here any minute," he adds.

I shake his hand once. "Thank you, sir," is all I can muster. He nods, rubbing on his short beard, then takes the stepladder that leads to the stage, disappearing behind the backstage curtains.

"Alright, Theo," I whisper to myself, "on to make things right."

Chapter 37

Dafne

Ollie picks me up on his way to dress rehearsal. Once we get to the theatre, I quickly make my way to the backstage area where our costumes have been pressed and hung by Aya, each of them in its plastic bag to protect it from dust and labeled with our characters' names. I take my first costume to the dressing room I share with Margaret and Isabel, who are helping each other with their hair. "Dafne," Isabel offers a small smile. "You ready for today?"

"Why wouldn't I be?" I say, perhaps a bit too defensively.

"Your new boyfriend almost sucker-punched our Friar Lawrence," Margaret chimes in, and Isabel snatches from her hand the hairspray can she was shaking like a cocktail with a glare in her direction.

"Jack only has himself to blame," I reply drily as I quickly undress to get the costume on.

"No, I agree, he's a proper idiot," Margaret yawns.

"It was just a lot, you know?"

I make a noncommittal sound and tie the back strings of my costume up.

Focus, Dafne.

Twenty minutes later, we're all on stage and Theodore quietly slides between Isabel and me so that we're standing next to each other. "Don't forget I've been meaning to–"

He's interrupted by Ms. Patterson, who looks as excited as ever–I'm afraid she'll have a stroke tomorrow on opening night. "Alright everyone, dress rehearsal time! That means no interruptions, our lovely sound technician is in place," she says, pointing to the soundproof cabin above the highest row of seats where a small figure waves awkwardly down at us from his position, "as is the lights department. Now, does anyone have doubts, things you'd like to ask?"

I shake my head lightly, but I feel, rather than see, a few of my castmates staring at Theo. I raise my eyebrows at them in question, only for them to take their eyes off him and suddenly find the floor all too interesting. I glance at Theodore, who looks jumpy, and I wonder if it has to do with nerves–which I doubt–or what he was about to tell me. He probably just wants to apologise more, and while I appreciate the sentiment, it's unnecessary.

"We can talk when we're done here, okay? You're first up," I whisper to him, squeezing his hand as I go prepare backstage.

Two odd hours later, we get to the final bow, and a small crowd of students from other departments scattered among the seats–including Phoebe–claps enthusiastically.

Mr. Hackle hops on stage with us, joining the applause with a subtle smile.

We all look at him expectantly, a little breathless, definitely sweaty, but those are all good signs.

He starts flipping through his notebook as the noise dies down, but before he speaks, he turns towards the audience. "You lot, off to your classes now," he orders, and everyone immediately obeys. His reputation truly does precede him.

"David, I want slightly bigger movements, we've talked about this," he lists, "Devon, pay attention to the footwork in the duel, Isabel make sure the plank where your mark is in the bedroom scenes doesn't catch on your dress, but if it does, keep going," he continues. He gives last minute notes to everyone, then finishes with a, "Dafne, I want all of *that* tomorrow night, just a notch brighter. You know what I mean," he cuts me a look, and I nod. "Theo … great work. Bigger smiles to your lady, though. Now go rest up everyone–and *no* gym lads, I will kick your arses if I find out you worked out before the play. I don't want any sore knees on my stage. Off you go," he finishes, gesturing for us to get out of here.

I shoot Theo a look, and notice he looks absolutely exhausted. We all give each other a round of applause and head back to the dressing rooms, Aya waiting backstage to make sure our costumes are put back where they belong.

I hastily run my fingers through my hair before leaving the dressing room, and when I get out Theo is there, in his regular clothes, the corners of his mouth pulling downwards.

"I get we're drama students, but I didn't think *everyone* in this cast was a gossip," I laugh weakly, trying to make the tension leave his face.

"Not here," he replies, guiding me down the back and out the stage door. When he's made sure we're alone, he looks at me again, his breathing heavier. *Now* I'm worried.

"I have to tell you something. I've been trying to tell you for the past few days, and it just can't wait anymore."

"Is this the part where you tell me you're the kind of person that leaves video reviews on the internet?" I joke. "Because if that's the case–"

"Just *listen* to me, okay?"

I blink.

"There was a bet."

My smile falters slightly, his words not making sense. "Excuse me?"

His jaw works, and he lets his backpack slip off his shoulder so he can rest his hands freely on my arms. "Devon and I made a bet. Not for money or anything like that, but … he bet that I'd kiss you before opening night."

I let out a breathy, unconvinced laugh. "I guess you lost."

He looks at me like he's about to burst into tears.

"That's not all," he says, swallowing. "We also bet he'd find someone who would ask you out. That'd I'd get jealous and–

"That's how Ethan already had my number," I realise. "For how long did it go on, Theodore?"

"I told Devon about us just before the trip," he replies quietly.

A few days ago. It went on until a few days ago. And we were already together. That means not only he let me believe Ethan's interest was genuine from the start, but that–

It's complicated, he'd said.

"I know it sounds bad, but–"

"It doesn't *sound* bad, Theodore," I flinch away from him. "It's…" I close my eyes, and a supercut of everything we've shared in the past months flashes behind them. I told him how important trust is to me. I *told him.*

"Was Ethan in it too? Did you kiss me just to prove to him that you could or–Am I a joke to you?" I feel ill.

"No, he didn't know, and of course not. *Never*," he pleads. "I wanted to call it off so many times, but I kept pushing it back and then things got out–"

"All you had to do was tell me the truth after our

first kiss. Maybe I would have been angry, but this–you had me wrapped around your finger for *weeks* before you decided you were going to try. And for what? Because you couldn't lose a bet?"

I place a hand on my neck, trying to still myself. Theodore is shaking his head, but as an ugly thought forms in my mind, I can't stop from letting it out.

"Was it actually some sort of elaborate ruse to distract me from the play? Is that it or did you think you could just have fun with me? What's the plan? Staying with me until you get bored–

"Dafne, I wouldn't do that, please–"

"Why should I trust a word you say?" I shout, effectively losing my calm.

I can feel my heart pounding in my ears.

His expression is part sadness, part something I really don't want to think about, and I sure as hell don't want to hear his next words, so when he says my name again, I cut him off. "No."

I won't let him make me feel ashamed. For playing with my heart. For believing him. For thinking he wanted me for *me*, and that was it.

I was so naive for thinking I was heading somewhere safe.

I shake my head once, twice, then start backing away.

My throat is constricting, and I know I'm going to cry if I don't leave right now. He raises his hands in a placating gesture, which does nothing if not make my anger spike.

"I don't want to hear it. You know what, perhaps I should congratulate you on the performance of a lifetime," I laugh bitterly, keeping my chin high despite feeling like I could punch him into oblivion. "You really are a brilliant actor."

"If you'd just let me–" he steps towards me again, but I stop him by raising one hand.

"I don't want you to touch me. In fact, I don't want to see you at all." I get back to the stage door, and this time, he doesn't follow. I pull on the handle and take a deep breath before I say, "We'll get through the play tomorrow, and then we never have to speak again.

"I hope it was worth it," I add quietly, and slam the door behind me.

Chapter 38

Theodore

"Come on, mate, cheer up," Devon says. "We'll find a way to fix this mess, yeah? I promise."

I keep my eyes on my beer–yes, I'm breaking my sobriety-during-rehearsals-period a day before it's all over. I honestly can't bring myself to care. I went straight to Devon after telling Dafne the truth, and while I wanted to go back to the dorms and sleep to avoid reality, he dragged me to the pub instead.

"There is nothing to fix, Devon. You didn't see her face when I told her. She's through with me."

He sighs and taps his phone screen once. "Any minute, now," he mutters, and I furrow my brows.

"Any minute to what? Me ordering another beer? Because that's a great–"

The bar's door swings open, and a drenched Oliver comes in, looking for someone left and right.

Devon waves a hand to catch his attention and he makes his way to us, slipping his jacket's hood off.

"I don't have a lot of time," he says as he sits next to Devon. "Dafne needs me. What is it?"

"I take it you know everything?" I ask.

"Oh, I do. Still not *not* mad at the two of you, but unlike Dafne, I'm willing to listen."

Devon gestures to the waitress to bring another beer.

Both Oliver and I look at Devon, who apparently got the both of us here for some sort of intervention. I don't want to hear it, but I also don't have the strength to get up and back under the pouring rain.

"Alright, look," Devon starts, passing a hand over his mouth. "Cards on deck. We mucked up. I mean, I mostly have, but Theo here is taking the brunt of it, and I feel terrible. Do you think you could tell Dafne it was completely my fault?"

Oliver shakes his head. "She doesn't care whose alleged fault it is. Price here shouldn't have agreed, or at the very least not let it go on for as long as it did. She thinks everything between she and him was either a plan concocted to get her guard down, or worse, that he never cared enough to be honest with everyone, and himrself. Like a stupid bet was more important than her feelings," he explains, his tone serious.

"Not to mention the whole Ethan thing–that was messed up," he adds. He turns to me then, such protective fierceness in his eyes, I am glad that if anything, Dafne has a friend like him.

"You're right," I tell him. "Devon shouldn't excuse me.

It's my responsibility."
"She trusted you."
"I know," I say, and my stomach churns with how badly I wish I could make this right.

"I swear to God, Price, if something happens during the play–"

"I would never, ever, jeopardise her performance."

"Because it would mean to jeopardise your own?"
"Because she's *important* to me."

Oliver's eyes become slits, as if he could see right through me if he tried hard enough.

Devon looks between the two of us, then clears his throat. "Then we agree. We all care about Dafne, so we should find a way for Theo to–" Oliver presses a finger over Devon's lips.

"Let us do the talking, hmm?" he says without taking his eyes off me while Devon's cheeks turn a bright shade of pink.

"I am rarely wrong, Price. And if I had the slightest inkling you weren't being genuine, I wouldn't have let her get close to you, so I'm going to ask you something. Have you told her that?" Oliver says as Devon nods in thanks to the waitress that brings his drink.

"Told her what?" I ask, keeping my hands around my empty pint to cool me down.

"That she," he makes air quotes, "is important to you."
"No. No, I was about to, but she … didn't want to hear

it."

"Maybe–" Devon starts, but Ollie covers his face with his entire hand.

"Ssshhh, I'm thinking," he hisses. Devon and I exchange a glance, and now I really need another beer. Or two. Or seven. Because all those months ago, she was right.

I *am* a coward.

"Alright," Oliver says, placing his palms flat on the table. "I think it's quite simple, what you need to do."

Dafne

After my fight with Theodore, I make my way to my room and wait for Phoebe to be back from class. When she opens the door I'm sitting on the edge of my bed, my suitcase open behind me, my clothes sparwled around the room looking like they were chewed and spat back by a grizzly bear.

"I thought I'd start organising my things, since–since it's our last week in here. But I couldn't remember that method you taught me to fold my shirts and–" I take a breath so deep my ribs ache trying to reign the tears in. The puffy eyes probably give me away, though. Phoebe starts towards me, not even taking her bag off before she comes to sit beside me. "The Dafne I know doesn't have breakdowns over Japanese clothes-folding techniques," she says, rubbing a stray tear off my cheek with her thumb.

"Did the dress rehearsal not go well? I thought you were all great," she says with a pout.

I swallow thickly and try to calm the pulsing in my head, the result of crying and stress I've been piling up since forever finally getting the best of me. I explain to Phoebe what Theodore's told me, her jaw slack in disbelief as she takes everything in.

"I'm going to kill him and bury his body where nobody will find it," she declares after a few quiet moments. "I'm going to go *Peaky Blinders* on that moth–"

"Phoebe."

She stops her eloquent gestures in midair. "Yes?"

"Why does it feel like I'm expendable?" I ask in genuine, utter heartbreak.

Her hands drop and she takes on a pensive look, like she's willing the proper words to come to her.

When she speaks again, instead of making a list of all the reasons Theodore is not good for me, she lists the reasons I'm too good for him. Which are many–at least in her eyes.

"You're not for everyone, Daf. You shine so brightly some people are … afraid to be blinded," she ends sadly.

A few minutes later there's a knock on the door, and Phoebe eyes me once before getting up to see who it is.

"Did the star of the show order coconut pastries from

the bakery down the street?" Ollie asks, bearing a brown paper bag in both hands. I chuckle wetly, relieved to see him instead of–someone else. Phoebe closes the door behind him, and they both come to sit next to me, as she rests her chin on one of my shoulders, Ollie's hand on the other.

"I've gotten through much worse, haven't I?" I ask them after a while.

"I know for a fact you can jump back from anything," Ollie says simply. "That being said, Phoebe and I have to tell you something."

Phoebe makes a choking sound, and shoots Ollie a surprised look. "Now, Ollie, really?" she hisses.

"Now," he confirms, eyebrows raised.

"More life-altering secrets, splendid," I mumble as I pinch the bridge of my nose. Why can't anyone seem to just *talk* to me?

Ollie gets up from the bed and moves to sit in front of me with his legs crossed, his hands massaging his ankles; Phoebe stays rooted in place next to me.

"A few months ago, Devon told me Theodore had a crush on you, and that it would be nice if I … nudged you in his direction. You know, to encourage him to finally make his move." I turn to Phoebe, my eyes wide in shock, and she mouths an *I'm sorry don't hate me.*

"As you know, all either of us," Ollie nods at Phoebe, "have ever done in that regard was trying to make you see that perhaps getting closer to Price wasn't such a terrible idea."

I'm about to tell him it definitely *was* a terrible idea, but he raises both hands to ask me keep listening, so I swallow my anger and cross my arms instead.

"Sure, we put the karaoke thing together, but Daf–we would never do something we didn't think was the absolute best thing for you. And when Devon told me about Theodore, whether or not it was true at the time he did … it got me thinking. The past few years, the two of you have been at each other's literal throats too many times to count, and yeah, he's said some ugly stuff but, to be honest, so have you.

"I'm not trying to justify him, and I know you were acting in defense, but–"

"I'm not a fan of the whole 'he was mean because he liked you' story. He was mean because he *didn't* like me, Ollie. He told me as much. And I know why now, still–"

"I know. And it sucked, alright? But the passion I saw on stage from you two … it can't be faked," he shrugs. Like he's not saying things I don't want to hear. "So at one point, I told Phoebe because this boulder of a secret was driving me insane–"

"But you have to know babes, we had no idea about the bet. *None*. I would have personally kicked both Price and Devon's arses if I'd known, and I mean it in the literal sense. Probably would have asked Peter to lend me his gumshields and boxing gloves," she smiles weakly. "Devon just confessed that *he thought* Price had a crush on you. Apparently Price denied it at first. I think Devon's heart was in the right place, but don't think that I'm not furious at him. I just want you to be happy, Daf. And I know you don't need a man for that, but I also know that light in your eyes means something," Ollie says.

I'm too stunned to speak, too sad, too everything. So I just extend my hand for him to take.

"We know you're tough as nails and don't need us to protect you," Phoebe says as she tentatively rests a hand on my arm. "But we'll always look after you like you've always done with us. Maybe sometimes it's … it's okay not to feel like a bad bitch if you're hurting. Doesn't mean you're not one."

No matter how much I try to refrain, that last bit makes the corners of my mouth pull upwards. Of course they didn't know about the bloody bet. Of course they really thought Theodore and I could be something. Too bad we were all wrong.

"I know that you don't want to talk about it, but … have you thought about what you will do?" Ollie asks as we take a stroll in the gardens after dinner, Phoebe having fallen asleep in the middle of our rewatch of The National Theatre's *Midsummer Night's Dream* production.

"About that ugly orange jumper you found under my bed? Well I think I cou–"

"Daf."

"Ollie." I look over at him, and we share a small smile.

"What do you want me to do? "I'm a professional. I will go on stage, and no matter my personal feelings for whoever is there with me, I will be exactly what Mr. Hackle told me to be. The bloody brightest."

Chapter 39

Theodore

It's… chaos. Everyone is, admittedly, losing their wits. Which is understandable, considering how high the stakes are. There are people that came specifically to our show to find new talent. To change our lives, possibly. And at any other time in my life, I would have been ecstatic, buzzing with the excitement of stepping on stage and giving it blood, sweat and tears. But how can I, when I've ruined what could have been the best thing to ever happen to me? There are probably no good answers to my question, but at the same time, I know I can't throw tonight away because of what happened. I can't do this to my grandparents, who have come here to cheer for me and see their sacrifices weren't in vain.

If Dafne never forgives me, all I have left is to try and forgive myself. But if there's even one chance that what I'll try to do later tonight works, perhaps not all is lost. I can't think about that now, though; it's ten minutes until show time, the backstage is utter madness of people going back and forth to make sure their props and costumes are into place. Someone is making *brrr* and *mmmm* sounds to warm their voice up. Devon is taking deep breaths next to the small table right behind centre backstage where a script is left open for everyone to check in case of last-minute empty-headedness–yes, it's a thing. Completely forgetting our next line happens to the best of us.

Oliver and Dafne are holding each other's hands, their eyes closed in quiet concentration. She looks beautiful with the soft lights hitting her collarbone and the tip of her nose, her long hair half up and half down, but I avert my gaze before they sense the intrusion.

Our stage manager lets us know there's three minutes left until show time, and Mr. Hackle gathers us in a tight circle.

"Alright, I want you to be sharp, be ready, be present. Listen to your castmates, remember what these three years have been for, and most of all," he clears his throat, and for the first time since I've had him as a teacher, I could swear there's a hint of emotion in his voice, "have the bloody time of your lives. Yeah?"

A chorus of *yeses* and whoops rises from our circle, and we start stacking our hands in the middle, Oliver placing his over mine, so Dafne doesn't have to. We push down three times, then as one, our hands soar towards the ceiling, the bell that announces the beginning of the play ringing its first toll.

I should probably refrain, but I can't stop the words that make their way out of my mouth when Dafne accidentally bumps into me.

"Break a leg," I tell her quietly.

She looks at me like she's never heard me speak before. "Break a leg," she says back, not warmly but not angry, either. Defeated, perhaps. Sad.

"I love you," I whisper when I'm sure she can't hear. Not yet.

The second bell rings, echoing clear and bright through the theatre as all sound from the expecting audience dies, and the play begins.

There's a five-minute break after Act Two, and we quickly gather backstage. "You're doing so well, everyone, truly," Ms. Patterson beams, clearly bursting with pride. She hands each of us a water bottle. I take a small sip, then notice Oliver's breathing a little heavier than normal. I look over at Dafne, but she doesn't seem to notice. I try really hard not to think of how kissing her here, on this stage, felt like, because I know it might well be the last time. Trying to draw as little attention as possible, I walk up to Oliver. "You alright?"

"Yeah," he says, pressing two fingers to his temple. "I'm just a little lightheaded."

"You need some sugar in your water? I think I have a packet in my–"

"It's fine, Theodore," he interrupts, as he looks over my shoulder to Dafne, her eyes closed once more in concentration. "I'm fine," he says again, more to himself than to me. I nod, letting it go, as it's time to get back to work. Act Three and Four go by in a flash, and it's time for the Final Act.

Dafne

I'm dead–well, not really. I look dead, but Paris finds me and Romeo and thinks it was my lover who killed me. I lay motionless on my pallet while they duel, until Paris falls to his demise, and Romeo walks towards me.

His monologue begins, and when he reaches me I feel his warm fingers tremble on my cheek, caressing one with his knuckles. If I weren't supposed to be in a drugged sleep, I'd probably cry. Or punch him.

He pulls me up gently as he continues, trying to squeeze the life back into Juliet as he holds me in his arms. I should be hating this, instead all I can think is that we could have had this. Minus the poison. That would have made Theodore laugh.

"*The doors of breath, seal with a righteous kiss a dateless bargain to engrossing death*," he says, prying the plastic vial I'm gripping in my left hand and throwing it

away from us.
"*Come, bitter conduct, come, unsavoury guide! Thou desperate pilot, now at once run on the dashing rocks thy seasick weary bark! Here's to my love,*" and he chugs the contents of the poison he brought with him. "*O true Apothecary! Thy drugs are quick. Thus with a kiss I die.*"

I wake up from the apparent death when Friar Lawrence arrives, and I will my voice to echo through the theatre when I realise Romeo lies dead next to me. "*Drunk all, and left no friendly drop to help me after?*" I say as I take in the empty poison vial he brought with him and just drank, thinking me truly gone. The thought that this is truly the last kiss Theodore and I will ever share crossed my mind for a second, and I refocus immediately.

"*Thy lips are warm!*" I exclaim after pressing my lips to his.

Hearing voices calling from behind me, I hastily grab Romeo's dagger. *"Then I'll be brief. O happy dagger! This is thy sheath; there rust, and let me die,"* I say, as I stab myself and fall next to Romeo so we can sleep together forever.

Clamorous applause spreads and echoes through the theatre as soon as the last line is uttered by Thomas, and Theodore helps me up while the rest of my castmates join us on stage for the final bow. He doesn't let go of my hand as we step forward to get our moment of glory, and I'm so overwhelmed with emotion I simply let him. An ear-shattering *whoop whoop whoop* coming from where I know Phoebe is sitting with my family makes me smile as I look over at Theodore to coordinate our bow. Instead, he kisses my knuckles and smiles warmly as he claps for me along with the rest of the audience, effectively making my heart burst inside my chest. I'm so angry at him, but I could also kiss him right now. Which makes me even more angry.

I tilt my head to encourage him to bow. It's the last time he'll ever be on this stage and despite everything, I don't want him to miss it. He looks unsure, but eventually surrenders and bows to his chest, taking my hand in his again as we retreat to let everyone else have their spotlight.

"You were magnificent," he whispers without looking at me once we're back in line.

"As were you," I reply honestly.

I'm pleased to see I'm still capable of objectivity. Ollie steps forward to bow next to Devon, and I clap so hard my hands hurt; I don't care, he deserves it. I notice he gets back in line on wobbly legs, his gaze unfocused, but I assume it's the rush of adrenaline wearing off. We all take each other's hands and bow together once, twice, three times. The applause doesn't falter. It's pure magic. As we retreat backstage, everyone's complimenting each other. Margaret is definitely crying into the crook of Isa--bel's neck, who's rolling her eyes in affectionate annoy--ance; the guys are patting each other's backs, and Ollie is standing next to Devon, his hand clutching a nearby stool. He looks unsteady, so I start towards him, when a hand taps me on the shoulder.

It's Theodore. He's flushed, something a little wild shining in his eyes, and lord help me–he's never looked so beautiful.

"I know you hate me," he starts, nearly breathless, "but would you listen to me just one more time before you erase me from your life completely?"

"I don't think I should."

"Please," he says quietly, eyes flickering between mine.

"I'm sorry, I really am. I can't, Theodore."

"Dafne–"

Whatever he's about to say is interrupted by a loud thud behind me, and I when I turn around, Ollie's on the floor, his eyes rolling back. I scream.

Chapter 40

Dafne

"Alright, I'll meet you there, thank you, Eleanor." I end the call with Ollie's mother and pocket my phone in the jacket Isabel retrieved for me from the dressing room while I followed the paramedics who carried Ollie on a gurney to their truck, still in my stage costume.

"So, what did she say?" Phoebe asks, worry creating a line between her eyebrows, Peter rubbing a comforting hand on her arm as he envelops her shoulders. They barely allowed Ollie's parents and little brother on the ambulance, so there just wasn't space for us to join them on the ride to the hospital.

"He regained consciousness on the ambulance, thankfully, but they need to check him in because he's having trouble breathing properly. She said she'd call me if there were any updates in the time it takes to get there," I explain as calmly as possible, when in truth I am barely holding it together. If something happens to Ollie I don't know what I would do. The few times he had seizures in the past, they didn't last a whole minute and he was okay after, just shaken up. I wasn't prepared for what happened tonight.

"Why is the bloody cab taking so long?" Phoebe groans, straining her neck to see whether the car is arriving. A perfect whistle sounds from behind us, and the three of us turn only to find our director and Ms. Patterson making their way to the parking lot. What I assume are his car keys dangle from his fingers in one hand, while he holds Ms. Patterson's in the other.

Someone's having a good time, at least.

"Come on, I'm taking you to Oliver."

I have never liked him more.

"Dafne," Theodore's voice calls as I start towards Mr. Hackle's mini truck. Phoebe eyes us warily but I give her a reassuring nod and she walks ahead of us.

"I have to go," I tell him, a desperate edge to my voice.

"He'll be okay. I know he will." He extends his hand as if to comfort me, but takes it back after I make no move to get closer. Devon jogs to us, his breath labored, and he rests his hands on his knees as if he'd just run the New York marathon.

"D'you have a spare seat?" he asks, exhaustion blurring with worry in his tone. I shoot him an unconvinced look, then tilt my head in the direction of Mr. Hackle's vehicle. Ollie and I are both mad at him, but I think he would want Devon to be there. He nods gratefully, pats

Theodore on the back, and sprints to reach Phoebe and the others.

"I know you don't want me to come, but I'll be here in case you change your mind. All night, if that's what it takes. Give Oliver my best when you see him," he tells me.

I scan his face for another second, then head to the truck.

We sit in the packed waiting room; more than a few people cast us skeptical looks as if we were a bunch of aliens when we arrived wearing our costumes, but I suppose it's not something you see on the daily. My dad texted me to let me know he and mum took a wrong turn and are stuck in traffic, which is less than ideal, because I'd feel better if I could hold my parents' hands. But it is what it is.

My right knee is bouncing up and down wildly, Phoebe is torturing her thumb nail, Peter looks lost in thought, Devon nervously paces back and forth in front of us. Ollie's family is in a smaller waiting room outside his room; his little brother texted me shortly after we got here, but hasn't been answering for a while, and neither has his mother. To say I'm a ball of nerves is the understatement of the century. We have been here for exactly fifty-four minutes when a nurse enters the room and asks, "Oliver Hall's friends?" We all rise in one synchronized motion, Devon practically jumping the nurse. "Is he okay?" He asks frantically.

My cheeks are still stained with the tears I shed when I rushed to Ollie in the backstage, begging for help.
"I'm sorry we kept you waiting so long, it's a busy night," the nurse tells us politely. "His parents asked me to tell you their phones died, something about taking too many videos?" That checks. They'd want to record every second of Ollie's big night.

"They're in with him now, but you can go in a few minutes. Be gentle, hmm? He's had a big scare," he says as he hands Devon a note with Ollie's room floor and room number. The relief that washes over me the second my brain realises Ollie is *fine* is unlike any I've ever felt. After getting lost a few times we finally end up in front of his room, his parents and brother just coming out.

Eleanor walks up to me and hugs me, whispering that she's proud of me for tonight and that she's grateful I am here for Ollie. Eric, Ollie's dad, squeezes my hand, and shoots a curious look at the small crowd we've gathered. "I know Phoebe, but are you two friends of Oliver's as well?"

Devon all but hides behind Peter, who in turn raises an eyebrow at him. Phoebe smiles sweetly and quickly introduces Peter and Devon as I greet Ollie's brother.

"Make sure this lot doesn't tire him, yeah? He needs rest," Eleanor whispers to me, and I nod in earnest.

I rap softly on the door before entering, just so Ollie isn't startled by our sudden presence.
"Heeey you," he drawls, opening one eye after the other.

"What's up?"

I glare at him as I take the empty chair next to his bed. "You scared me to death, that's what's up," I mumble, and I feel the sting of tears behind my eyes threaten to fall again.

"What happened?" asks Phoebe, holding onto Peter's arms as if they were a lifeline.

"I think I need to take it easy for a while. I also might have been ignoring some … signs."

"*Ollie*," I sigh.

"I know, I know," he places a hand on my wrist. "Between classes and so many rehearsals and everything happening with you … I think my brain went in over-drive. Literally," he chuckles.

My mouth opens, but nothing comes out. How can he joke about it? This is all my fault. I should have paid more attention, should have made sure–

"Whatever you're thinking, and I know you're thinking it, stop," Ollie warns me. "I'm not your responsibility, okay? You've taken care of me all our lives. This is on me. And I'm perfectly fine, as you can see."

I pout skeptically.

Devon steps forward then, fidgeting nervously.

"No one's ever almost died to get out of dating me," he starts half-jokingly, half miserable. "But I am really glad you're alright." I may not know him well, but I didn't think he had it in him to sound so small. Scared. I guess love brings everything out of us. Ollie smiles

broadly at him and gestures for him to get closer.
"Let's give them some privacy," I whisper as I turn to Phoebe and Peter, who nod knowingly as they make their way outside. Ollie calls for me a second after I've started walking away, so I stop in my tracks.

"About Price," he says, and I immediately shake my head, not keen on engaging in that kind of argument right now. "No, listen to me," he pushes up on his elbows to straighten himself on his cushion. "Remorse is far better than regret. I know you feel betrayed, and you have every right to. But I promise that whatever happens I'll be there, and Phoebe will be there, and Peter and even this lad," he points a thumb to Devon, who smiles sheepishly. He's probably forgetting he's just as responsible for this mess, but that'll be for later.

"You're not free falling. You've got a damn good safety net." Now I'm definitely crying again.

"Okay," I whisper, squeezing his hand.

"Okay," he repeats. "Now go talk to your man!"

Devon does a thumbs up, and I shoot them one last look before walking out the door. I shut it behind me, Peter and Phoebe and Ollie's family all turning to look at me.
"Everything alright, darling?" Eleanor asks from her seat.

"Yeah," I breathe, before turning to Phoebe.
"Is Mr. Hackle still here?"

Chapter 41

Theodore

She's not coming. There's no point in spending the night here with Mr. Davies, who I'm helping inspect all the seats in the audience for gum, still in my Romeo clothes; I promised Aya I would make sure all the costumes would be returned in pristine conditions, since three of the cast left in a rush wearing them, for obvious reasons. My grandparents are waiting for me at the café down the street, as I told them there was something I needed to do before we could go to dinner. I didn't explain the details, only that there's a good chance Dafne might not forgive me. Grandpa would probably kick me in the shins if he knew the real magnitude of the mess I made. I might have left out a few details during our last conversation about her.

"You make up for whatever it is, you hear me son? Heaven knows how many times your grandmother forgave me for being a licensed idiot."

It's what Grandma said me that really got to me, though.

"I don't know what happened, darling, but I'm sure you'll be able to make amends for it. You do know we are proud of the man you are, right? A man that can recognise his failings is worth more than a man who owns millions, never forget that. And look at you!

"My grandson is the most brilliant actor I've ever seen, my word." She patted my cheek and left on Grandpa's arm.

I don't know if it's everything that's happened in the last few days, but as I watched them go, it finally struck me.

I could be a shite actor and it wouldn't make any difference to them. They'd still love me to pieces.

I know I've come a long way, but there's still a lot of work I need to do on myself. Learning how to manage the work, and the stress, and the expectations that I ingrained into my own head that I needed to meet doesn't happen overnight. Still, if in their eyes I kept my promise, then there's one more thing I need to do.

Unfortunately, it looks like it's too late.

I get a text from Devon telling me Oliver will be discharged soon and will just need to rest. I'm grateful Oliver will be fine, but still no word comes from Dafne.

She's not coming back. I have to accept that I blew it.

I look in the sound technician's direction where he graciously waited for me in the sound booth and make a cut-throat gesture. He raises his arms in exasperation.

I turn to go backstage, but someone emerges from the darkness beyond the burgundy tents, eyes glossy and flushed cheeks, a jacket over her Juliet dress.

"They're lovely," Dafne says quietly as she makes her way to the proscenium, twirling a bouquet of roses and white tulips in both hands.

Grandma once told me white tulips symbolise forgiveness. And roses … well. I can't believe she's actually here, and I swallow the emotion.

"I'm glad you like them," I reply, my mouth suddenly dry. I left them in her dressing room a few minutes before the show, when I was sure she wouldn't go back; I didn't want them to upset her before she got on stage.
I slowly make my way up the stepladder and ask, "Have you read the note?"

She shakes her head, avoiding my gaze.

"Can I read it to you?"

That makes her raise her eyes to mine, full of weariness and something I could swear is longing, but I don't let myself hope. As we come to stand a foot apart on stage, she unclips the note from within the flowers and hands it to me, careful to avoid touching me. That's when I know I won't get another chance.

"*I am no pilot, yet wert thou as far as that vast shore wash'd with the furthest sea, I should adventure for such wonder*," I start reading Romeo's words, to which I've made some changes.
"*And were I to take thy hand once more, I shan't ever*

relinquish it," I go on, taking a tentative step towards her. She doesn't move. *"For I wasn't able to make it known before, that–*Dafne," I take my eyes off the note and place a finger under her chin so she looks at me.

"I'm in love with you."

She bats her eyes rapidly, a sheen of tears in her lovely eyes.

"I want you, and they're not just pretty words." I cradle her face in my palms, and she lets me.

"How can you be sure?" she asks.

"Because I see you. And I like all of it. All the time." She shakes her head.

"I can't take what I've done back. All I can do is tell you how deeply sorry I am for taking your feelings for granted and making that stupid bet–"

"It's not just the bet, Theodore. Don't get me wrong, that was despicable and I am so angry about you lying to me, but … there's a reason you went through with it, isn't there?"

"It's different now," I promise.

"It's different, until it's not," she sighs. "Until I get a role on the West End, or on a tv show, and you begrudge me for it. Because I'm afraid you might love acting more than you could love anything else, and I can't be with someone I can't trust with everything I am. Someone who won't put their pride aside–who won't wear their love for me on their sleeve. I won't make myself smaller. Not for you or anyone else."

I let out out a shaky breath, refusing to let go of her. "I've made a mistake. I've made *dozens* of mistakes, and I will spend however long it takes to make that right, if you'll let me. But Dafne, you have to know. I *want you* to have the success you deserve. I want to be in the audience when you win your first bloody *BAFTA*! I want my phone to melt from all the pictures of billboards with your face on it I'm going to take. I want everyone to know that this belongs to you," I say with a hand over my heart.

"All the time I spent feeling jealous is time I could have spent working on me. The truth is I'm a work in progress, Daf, and I've finally realised I can't promise you perfection, and I can't promise some days will not be harder than others for me. But I can promise to give you my all. I'm not Noah. I'm just someone who made the wrong call, and all I ask is that you trust me one last time.

I meant what I said. You are a star. And you don't need anyone's permission to shine. You certainly don't need mine."

She's looking at me intently now, as if she were deciding whether I'm being truthful. I don't think I've been more honest in my life.

"As for the Ethan situation," I resume, stroking her cheekbones lightly, hoping she understands how deep my regret is. "It was stupid and immature. I didn't have it in me, to face the facts. And the facts were that you are amazing in every possible way, and I was afraid, and selfish. I will never be the man that doesn't step up for you again. Let me prove it to you."

She wets her lips, and ever so slowly, she raises her hands to cradle my own as they hold her lovely face.

"If we're going to do this, I have a few conditions," she says after a while, and my heart gallops in my chest.

"Anything."

"No more lies. I mean it."

"You got it."

"No more following Devon's idiotic plans."

"Done."

"Kiss me."

She doesn't have to ask me twice. I close the distance between us and she holds onto my back.

This kiss–it tastes like possibility. And if she always kisses me like this, I know I will be fine.

I faintly remember I was supposed to make some sort of signal upwards when the music starts echoing through the theatre.

Dafne detaches herself from me with a wobbly smile. "*Songbird*," she breathes, as her favourite song envelops us. I shoot the sound technician a grateful look.

"Care for a dance, my lady?" I bow to the waist.

She rolls her eyes and takes my hand so I can spin her around in a twirl before pulling her close.

"Theo?" she whispers after a little while, her nose brushing mine.

"Hmm?"

"I think we have company."

We both turn our heads over to the audience, only to find a besotted Mr. Davies looking at us with eyes shiny with unshed tears. We both break into a laugh, and he goes back to swiping the floor.

"Oh, uh," I start, not daring to break contact with her, "would you like to meet my grandparents?" I ask, suddenly remembering I left the poor souls without giving them further instructions. Although knowing my grandmother she's probably ordered her third Coca Cola by now.

The skin around Dafne's eyes crinkles as she flashes me a big, beautiful smile.

"I'd love to," she confirms before cupping my face in both hands. "And even though you drive me *mad*,

I love you."

She shakes her head lightly as if she were surrendering to the fact. And I think that's what I needed to do all along. Surrender.

"Like never before," she repeats the words to the song that just finished playing.

I feel so light I could soar.

Chapter 42

Dafne

After meeting Theo's grandparents at the designated restaurant, who shower me in kisses and compliments–my family only gets there in time for dessert, because apparently, my dad got into a fistfight with his sat-nav on their way there–the reality of our last days at APDAS finally hits.

The rooms need to be cleaned, luggages need to be packed, goodbyes need to be said. Thankfully, a couple of days after our play, it's time for Phoebe's final showcase. I'm so excited for my Fantine. Her part in APDAS' version of *Les Misérables* is going to bring the house down.

I'm supposed to wait for Theo to pick me up, then meet with everyone else outside the theatre. I nearly stab my eye with my mascara's wand when there are a few raps on the door. I snort to myself and grab a spoolie from my makeup bag to get the excess mascara off as soon as it dries, and zigzag through the various piles of clothes and shoes Phoebe and I have yet to pack. When I open the door, I'm met with my favorite jean jacket draped over a well-known shoulder.

"The good thing about you moving out of here is that you might finally get yourself a proper weapon," Theo says, eyeing the spoolie in my hand. I ended up telling him that the night of our first real kiss, I thought there was a murderer outside my room, hence the plastic Academy Award.

"I could very well crush an eyeball with this, you know," I chuckle, "and there's always the classic knee to the lower regions." He nods and laughs as I open the door wider for him to come in.

He plants a kiss on my cheek and says, "I see packing is going … somewhere," as he scratches his head and takes in the mess that is currently my room.

"I told you," I say, plopping on my bed, stray mascara on my lid seeming not so urgent anymore. "It's hard to put everything away and pretend nothing major is happening."

He sits next to me and places a steady hand on my ready-to-bounce knee. I never knew that was something I wanted someone to do for me until Theodore did it.

"You know this is just the beginning, though, right?"

"Yeah," I agree, and when I look at him, his top button undone, no trace of guard up on his handsome face, I can all but lean into him and let him wrap an arm around me.

"Oh, by the way! You need to tell me about the ap-

-pointment," I tell him, referring to his first meeting with a psychologist he had today.

"She was nice. She did ask about my family's history, how I see myself, a lot of things I'd been trying to avoid thinking about at all, but … it was time. Baby steps, right?" he says with a small smile.

"Baby steps," I confirm.

"Also," he starts after a few moments of comfortable silence, "I got an interesting call from a certain Theatre about a half-hour ago."

My head immediately snaps up, my eyes growing wide. "You mean–"

"They saw me in the play, and they want me in the National's new *Tempest* production."

"Yes they bloody do!" I launch myself at him and we fall backwards on the bed as I pepper his face with kisses. I'm so proud I could burst.

"Say you deserve it," I grin at him.

He takes a deep breath, "I bloody deserve it."

"We have so much to celebrate," I say.

"We do, but come on now. Phoebe will murder me if she thinks I'm responsible for your tardiness," he chuckles as he stands straight, and pulls me up with him.

As I grab my bag to leave, I think that the sadness I'd been feeling over leaving APDAS for good can turn into something hopeful. Something better.

Epilogue

Two Years, seven months later

Dafne

"I'm going to throw up," I whisper.
"No, you're not. Deep breaths, Daf."
"If I take another deep breath It'll be the last–"

"The Rising Star Award goes to…"

I am fairly sure my heart has stopped. I'm squeezing Theo's hand so hard it just might pop off his wrist.

"… Dafne Wright for *Violets in the Snow*!"

"Oh my God. That's me! O*h my God*–" I start, rooted to my red seat, my hands flying to my cheeks in complete, bloody disbelief. Because I'm at the *BAFTAs* and I just won an actual award. I'm in such utter shock my legs seem to have retired from work until further notice.

"You have to go on stage, Wright," Theodore says, pulling both of my hands away from my face as he helps me get up. There's thunderous applause all around, so many people looking towards us, towards me, and all I can do not to pass out is focus on my partner's face-splitting smile. He kisses my cheek, lingering there for a second longer than strictly necessary. "I'm so proud of you," he whispers against me. "Now go and give the speech your parents have been keeping in their wallets for the past fourteen years."

I nod a few times, rapidly blinking the tears that are already threatening to ruin the two-hour work of art that my makeup is. I squeeze Theo's hand one more time and turn to head towards the stage, holding the gown of my sparkling off the shoulder deep red dress up with both hands, so that I don't trip spectacularly on the velvety carpet that leads up to the stage. I pass a sea of clapping people in their seats, some standing and smiling warmly at me, and I barely register that Dame Judi Queen Dench is among them, her serene yet sharp gaze trailing on me as someone offers to help me walk up to the steplad–it's Pedro bloody Pascal. I am having a very vivid dream again, aren't I?

"Thank you so much," I tell him as he holds my right hand to help me up, as I no doubt look a little on edge.

"Of course, amazing work," he replies, and I don't have time to gape or ask him to marry me–Theo wouldn't mind, I'm sure–because I'm on stage, being handed a shiny turquoise mask, its empty plaque ready to be etched with my name. I babble a thank you to the hostess who gave it to me and take a few seconds to stare at it before I settle it on the shiny black stand at centre stage.

"Can I just say–*wow*, my mind is officially blown," I joke as I lean into the small microphone, hoping that will ease my own tension. "Thank you from the bottom of my heart to every single person who voted for me for this incredible honour," I continue, gently biting my tongue to get my salivation going. "I could lie and say I didn't have a speech prepared, that I'd never dreamed for a moment like this to come … but anyone who knows me knows I've had it written down since I learned acting awards were a thing," I say honestly, and chuckles spread through the audience. Does Judi Dench find me funny? I sure as hell hope so.

"You know, all my life this is what I wanted. Not winning awards, per se, but … soaking in the magic that is being in a room full of people who understand you. Who love this craft with every fiber of their being and have been made better because of it. There have been so many times where my dreams seemed out of reach," my throat constricts with emotion, but I push through and keep going. "Then all it took was to meet my people, and nothing seemed impossible anymore.

"Because of this, there are some thank yous in order. I'd like to thank my parents, whose unwavering support is the foundation on which I stand on to this day; my greatest friends, Oliver and Phoebe, who are also some of the most talented people I've ever met, and whom you've probably seen on your tv screens and on the West End plenty of times; to my incredible, incredible partner," I look over at where Theo is sitting. "For loving me fiercely. For lifting me up every step of the way. And for being my forever favorite co-star," I laugh softly, and I can't see him clearly from here, but I know he is too.

"Finally, allow me to thank myself, for pushing through the rejection, and the heartache … and for rising above it with a heart full of gratitude and unshakeable hope. Thank you." I raise my award with one hand, and place the other on my heart, then make my way backstage for pictures and press coverage. My heart is running a marathon and I'm barely holding it together, when a warm hand touches the small of my back.

"What did I tell you?" Theo beams, and I nearly drop my award to twist towards him and envelope him in the tightest and happiest of hugs.

"You're my star," he whispers.

I'm never letting go.

The ~~End~~ Beginning

ACKNOWLEDGEMENTS

So … that happened. I wrote a book. Ha!
I’ve done a lot of reflecting in the past year, and if there’s something I’ve learned, it’s to not let other people’s perception of me stop me from doing all the things I want to do. That’s a very summed-up version of how this story came to life, but let it be known that acting is and will always be my greatest love. It taught me so much about myself, it made me stronger (just ask my acting teachers how drastically my crying rates decreased from year one to year three), but also made me face and embrace my fragilities, and I will forever be grateful for having this dream planted in my heart. I hope that whether you have any interest for theatre or not, you could still find a small piece of yourselves somewhere in these pages, and that you know you are never alone. It’s okay to be determined, and ambitious, and angry, and sad, and struggle with your mental health, because you’re human and you deserve to be loved because of everything that you are and not despite it.

That being said, much life Dafne, I have some people I need to thank without which this book wouldn’t have been the same. My wonderful beta readers: Rachel, who was basically my editor as well, without asking for anything in return; you’ve helped me immensely and I’ll never be able to thank you enough.

Cassidy, thank you for the enthusiasm and support from the very beginning, and for inspiring me with your incredible playlist (which everyone will be able to listen to via my website).

Elena, for reading all kinds of drafts and not laughing *once* and always being ready to offer precious advice, as well as sending me all the good memes.

Nilany, for your kindness and insight and for posting AFILAT'S first ever official review; and Gia, for helping an American English girl with her British slang.

To the wonderful bookstagram community, who's always been so lovely; in particular, to the friends who have consistently supported this process and me, helped me achieve a successful cover reveal, and hyped me through my various author-y breakdowns. You know who you are and I appreciate you very much.

I should also thank my dad, who sneakily found out I was writing a novel and kept the secret until it was ready to go so that I could surprise my family. You're the goat. And you'll probably not know what this means.

Finally, thank you to anyone who got here and took a chance on Dafne and Theo and me. If I managed to brighten up the day of even a single one of you, then I'll know it was worth it.

L.V. Oaks in an actor and writer from Italy. When she's not recording self-tapes or re-enacting the dialogues in any book she's reading with much more drama than necessary, she can be found rewatching her comfort shows or petting her dogs.

Let's connect on Instagram: @thefolkofbooks
TikTok: @lvoaks